THE
GUEST
HOUSE

Robin Morgan-Bentley

ORION

An Orion paperback
First published in Great Britain in 2022 by Orion Fiction
an imprint of The Orion Publishing Group Ltd
Carmelite House, 50 Victoria Embankment
London EC4Y 0DZ

An Hachette UK Company

1 3 5 7 9 10 8 6 4 2

A CIP catalogue record for this book is
available from the British Library.

ISBN (Mass Market Paperback) 978 1 4091 9424 8
ISBN (eBook) 978 1 4091 9425 5
ISBN (Audio) 978 1 4091 9426 2

Typeset by Born Group
Printed in Great Britain by Clays Ltd, Elcograf S.p.A.

www.orionbooks.co.uk

For Booba & Grandma

Chapter 1

Victoria

Saturday, 6 March, 7.43 a.m.

I am woken by an electric surge in my lower back and grasp my swollen belly. I look down and see ghastly floral bed sheets. The pillow is so soft and thin that it may as well not be there. For months I've lain awake, imagining this new pain dormant in my body, threatening to emerge and take hold of me. Now it's here and I'm in someone else's bed.

The ache runs deep, pierces sharp and subsides quickly. Jamie is snoring next to me, louder than usual, like the call of a lighthouse, punctuated by the occasional snort or gasp. I think about waking him but decide not to raise an alarm yet. It may be nothing and my husband has a tendency to panic.

A strip of daylight flares at the opening between the curtains a couple of feet to my right. I sit up and stretch over to draw them apart. There are fields and fields of pale green, undulating hills for as far as I can see. Patches of grass are covered with sheaths of silvery white ice. There are no other houses in sight and the only sign of life is a small cluster of birds, swooping in perfect unison from one side of the pane to the other. The single, narrow, winding road cutting through the hills is silent, untouched perhaps since we drove down it last night – the final stretch on our epic seven-hour drive from London to the North Pennines.

There would be complete quiet in the guest house were it not for the groaning wind forcing its way through cracks in the stone walls and wood-panelled ceilings. Its moans, rising and falling, are interrupted every few seconds by a rattle or a squeal. The ebb and flow of wind is continuous, like white noise, and I try to focus on the sound, anchoring myself on its constancy to calm me.

I ease myself up, grimacing as I inch my feet out of the bed and onto the carpet, then use both hands on the bedside table to lift the rest of my body. My feet are so hot, swollen and sticky that when I reach the bathroom, the chill of the tiles is refreshing. I lower myself onto the toilet, close my eyes and cherish the relief. I stay seated for a while and read a note above the sink that 'the wet wipes we have provided are for the bin, not the toilet :)'. I use a couple, drop them between my legs and flush. I've always been tempted by small acts of rebellion.

The owners have made a cursory attempt to be fancy, the hand soap decanted into a dispenser with a terrazzo effect and a small tube of hand cream perched on the windowsill, but the bath itself is in need of a good scrub, with black mould around the edges. I sniff and mildew prickles the back of my throat, then I haul myself up, rinse my hands and waddle back across the cold tiles and into the bedroom.

Jamie stirs and blows me a kiss from the bed but keeps his eyes shut. As I stand, I clutch the bottom of my belly and push in with my fingers, one by one, testing for more pain.

Judging by the frost on the grass and the condensation on the windows, it must be freezing outside, but I feel like I can almost see steam pumping out of the radiators and the heat of my own body is overwhelming. I don't know what to do with my hands and a bead of sweat itches down the back of my head and onto my neck. I need some fresh air.

I hold on to the wall as I edge towards the large sash window by my side of the bed. Placing both hands in the middle, I use all of my might to push upwards, clenching my jaw and shaking as I push, but it's not budging. I'm starting to feel dizzy and as I pace around the room looking for a key, I can hear myself panting.

'Jamie, Jamie, wake up. Sorry, I wanted to let you sleep, but I'm dying here. We need to open a window.'

Jamie sits up with a start, his mouth hanging open, his eyes still sticky.

'What's wrong? Is it Shrimpy?'

Shrimpy is the pet name for our unborn son, because he looked like a prawn on the first scan. We've already picked a name for when he arrives, but Jamie is consumed by a superstition that it's bad luck to refer to him by that name until he's out of the womb, so we stick to 'the baby', 'Shrimpy' or 'the little guy' for now. I think it's all a bit puerile.

'No, I'm fine. The baby's fine. It's just boiling in here and the windows are all locked.'

Jamie rubs his eyes, stands up and heads round the bed towards the window, squeezing past me in just his boxer shorts. He tries to open it from the bottom.

'It's locked, Jamie. I just said that.'

'OK, no need to snap at me,' he snaps at me, while still trying to haul it up.

He gives up, bent over with his hands palms down on the faded white sill. He looks back at me and breathes out deeply.

'The owners said they'd be up early to make breakfast. I'll go downstairs and ask them for a key. I'll get you some water, too.'

Jamie picks up yesterday's T-shirt and jeans from the floor, flings them on, heads out of the room and closes the door behind him. I sit on the bed, listening to the clack of his feet on the stairs. I bite the nail on my right thumb, too low, and it stings. This is it, I know it. The nearest hospital must be miles away, tiny, and I don't have my notes with me. I touch my belly. Does it feel more tender than usual?

When Jamie bursts back into the room, he's out of breath.

'They must still be asleep. There's no one downstairs.'

I sigh and look past Jamie towards the bedroom door, which is ajar.

'I'm just going to go out through the front door and stand outside for a bit. Can you pass me some clothes? I can't bend down.'

Jamie hands me his red hoodie and my favourite tracksuit bottoms, just about the only ones that I can still heave onto my body right now, and I sit on the bed and strain to pull them up. He watches me and I wish he'd look away. I glance down at my own body and feel disgusted by it. It's not that I didn't expect my body to change, but

I never actually pictured what I'd look like in the flesh, without clothes on, so stark and bulging and marked.

When I look down, I feel detached from myself, like I'm looking at images of someone else's body. Jamie says that he's never felt as attracted to me as he does now, in this late stage of pregnancy. That as much as he'll cherish the arrival of our first child, he'll miss this body. But he doesn't have to live with it, inhabit it, squeeze it into clothes that are getting progressively tighter, experience the surprises of a body that's constantly changing, morphing into something increasingly unfamiliar. We haven't had sex for months because I feel so undesirable. He's given up trying.

I sit on the edge of the bed, slip my feet into trainers and Jamie helps me with the shoelaces. I stand and reach beneath the hoodie to wipe away a strip of sweat from under my belly.

'I'm not going anywhere. I just need some air.'

I head out of the room and venture carefully down the steep wooden stairs, which feel treacherous as I can't see my own feet. I take small steps, holding on to the banister, feeling my way down. The walls are covered in paintings and prints, ornaments and photo frames, so crowded that there are only glimpses of the navy wallpaper underneath. Someone has made a real effort to make the décor quirky: a portrait of a Jack Russell in a top hat and bow tie, a framed film poster celebrating the twenty-fifth anniversary of *Grease*, a black-and-white photograph of a baby with curly hair, grinning from ear to ear.

At the bottom of the stairs, I head for the front door and tug at the large gold handle, but it doesn't move. I pull and

I pull but it's locked and there doesn't seem to be a way to open it without a key. I can feel my pulse quickening, the sting of my eyes welling.

I stumble into the kitchen and try the back door, but that is also shut. I start opening every drawer and cupboard, desperate to find a key and a way out, and when Jamie comes up behind me and grabs my right shoulder, I let out a sharp gasp.

'What are you doing? Just relax. I'll go upstairs and knock on their door. Their room is the one just opposite ours.'

I try to push past him.

'Don't tell me to relax. All the bloody doors are locked. I need some fresh air.'

Jamie puts his arm out and blocks my way.

'Please, let's not argue here. They've obviously just locked up before going to bed. I'll go and find them. It's not a big deal.'

'Hello?' I hear him shout as he heads up the stairs.

'It's not even eight o'clock yet, Jamie. You can't just wake them up.'

He doesn't acknowledge me and shouts louder.

'Hello? Is anybody there?'

I can hear him trying doors, one by one, pressing the handles down and then knocking, his bangs and shouts gathering momentum as he finds each consecutive one to be locked.

'Hello?'

I walk to the kitchen sink and turn on the cold water, testing the temperature with my hand before leaning right down and lowering my head into the hard, cool jet. Relief.

But then the pain comes again and this time it's stronger – a tornado of white heat building in pressure from the base of my spine. I pull away from the tap, arch my back and place my hands on the sink.

When Jamie comes rushing in, his cry of concern merges with the sound of the water still crashing into the sink, distorted, blurred, distant. He rubs my back and at some indeterminate moment, the pain subsides.

Jamie asks the question, as if there's any doubt, as if he needs the confirmation.

'What's going on, Victoria? Is it . . . are you?'

I turn round, craning my neck, and as our eyes meet, I feel the sting of forming tears.

'Contractions,' I whisper between breaths. 'I'm in labour. Danny's coming.'

Chapter 2

Jamie

How do you choose between brands of peas? I'm crouched over a freezer in the supermarket and I'm at an impasse. Every small decision now seems both trivial and insurmountable. I see the wrinkled, pale, ringless hand of a stranger reach from under my shoulder and pick up the biggest packet, so I do the same. I place it in the trolley, reverse and head towards the checkout.

As I push, I imagine the trolley as a pushchair. Danny is in there, sleeping with his thumb in his mouth, gently rubbing the bridge of his nose with his forefinger. I imagine that Victoria is a few aisles down, feeling for a perfectly ripe melon or loading a second trolley with nappies and formula for the baby.

When I reach the tills, I join the nearest queue, waiting for my turn while the woman in front loads the conveyor belt with the weekly shop for her family: packet after packet of cereal, powder for making chocolate milk, more bags of crisps than you'd need to feed an army. She's moving

9

at incredible speed, like a conveyor belt herself, grabbing three items at once and flinging them down. I look to my right and see that the till next to me has a much shorter queue, but I'm in no rush to get home.

When it's my turn, I keep my head down and pack the few bits I've chosen into my shopping bag. The checkout assistant looks at me, says nothing and I take out my card to pay. I get the pin code wrong twice and then take the card out and scramble in my pocket for a twenty-pound note. I place the items in a bag and I can feel her watching me, but I'll take my time, thank you very much.

As I walk outside to find my car, the shine of the early spring sun blasts me straight in the eyes. Families are obviously making the most of the rise in temperature this weekend, arriving en masse to buy Scotch eggs and sausage rolls for the first afternoon of the year that they can spend in the park or the garden.

A blue Audi speeds past me and parks in the space next to my car. I hear the crunch of the handbrake through the open window. The driver's door opens and a man in a tight-fitting black T-shirt steps out, his arms covered in tattoos, his jeans riding low. The right rear passenger door opens and a little girl steps out. She's dressed up as a ballerina or fairy, in a pink tutu. She runs after her father, who is striding across the car park and into the supermarket.

When she catches up with him, he grabs her hand and they walk in together. I wonder what plans they have today. Is the man taking his daughter to a birthday party this afternoon? Or is she just wearing the tutu to the shops because that's what she felt like putting on today? I wonder what her name is. .

When I get back to the flat – a two-bed with a small garden on the hill between Tufnell Park and Highgate in North London – I go straight to the kitchen to unload the shopping. I place the crumpets in the bread bin, the meat in the fridge and the peas in the top drawer of the freezer. I fill the kettle with enough water for one cup and stare out of the window to the road ahead. A bus pulls up at the stop outside and a whole throng steps out. I turn back and pour myself a cup of decaf coffee and notice the time displayed in red digits on the oven: 9.22 a.m. It's going to be a long day full of nothing.

I try my best not to go into Danny's bedroom, but there's a force that draws me there, at certain points in the day. I can't stay away.

I walk in and run my fingers across the frames of his ivory dresser and the matching cot bed that was meant to last until he was four, and then the white noise machine that Victoria insisted was an essential. Propped on a shelf that I put up above the cot is the little blue rabbit that Victoria's mum knitted for him. I pick it up and slide my finger under the label on his ear that says 'made with love'. I was in charge of buying everything for the baby and relished the process. I'd spend hours in the middle of the night scrolling through forums, weighing up the pros and cons of one nappy cream over another, filling our shopping basket with 99 per cent water wipes, bath thermometers and black-and-white comforters.

The cot we picked is sturdy, with thick wooden bars and a drawer underneath because you can never have enough storage. There are no pillows, loose blankets, teddies or bumpers on the sides, because they can be hazardous. The mattress is new and still in its bright blue plastic casing. The wall behind it is light green – a nauseating hue in real life, greener in the sunlight than it looked online, but a better option than all the sky-blue-for-a-boy patterns that Victoria insisted would impose gender stereotypes upon our son. From the mobile over the crib dangles a hippo, a lion and a polar bear, and the bear in particular now seems sinister, its beady eyes following me round the room. And on the wall above the cot is the letter D – for Danny, yes, but now also for despair, for danger, for darkness.

Every time, after each scan of the nursery, I find myself on the verge of surrender. I pick up my phone, my hand shaking, my vision blurred, an impulse threatening to take over. My hand hovers over the nine. Just press it three times, Jamie. Take the risk. Tell them what happened in the guest house. But then I switch the phone off and bury it deep in the pocket of my jeans.

Just before midday, I drag myself off the sofa, having exhausted my tolerance for Saturday morning television, the ruddy-cheeked chefs trying to convince us that it's so easy to make ricotta strawberry French toast that anyone can do it for breakfast before the school run in the morning. I put on my trainers, hoping that a walk to the local park and back might distract me. I wait by the door to the flat, checking there's no one else lingering in the common spaces – I can't face banal interaction with neighbours – and emerge when I hear nothing for five seconds.

Before leaving the building, I flick through the stack of letters on the table by the main door. I've seen most of them for days now – bills and circulars addressed to the flat above. We never get anything particularly exciting, so when I see a large brown envelope with our names and address handwritten, I rip it open. Inside is a single sheet of paper, printed from a government website, and as I start to read, my throat dries and a rush of cold falls down both of my arms.

Sentencing Guidelines in the Crown Court
The below outlines the maximum sentence recommendation for common offences for the purposes of sections 224 and 225 of the Criminal Justice Act 2003.

Administering a substance with intent: ten years' custody
Cruelty to a child: ten years' custody
Domestic burglary: fourteen years' custody
Fraud: ten years' custody
Causing or allowing a child to die: life imprisonment
Unlawful act of manslaughter: life imprisonment
Unlawful burial of a body: life imprisonment

I look and feel inside the envelope for more, searching for a note, a name, a clue, an indication of where this has come from. But there's nothing other than this one sheet. Two of the crimes, and their sentences, have been highlighted in neon pink. Who sent this? Was there a witness? Who knows our secret?

I rush out of the building and catch my left foot on the frame of the door, stumbling as I slam the door behind me. I rip up the paper, once, twice, three times and, looking around me, stuff the shreds in my jacket pocket.

Chapter 3

Jamie

I've never seen anyone in so much pain. I crouch down with Victoria, holding her hand tight as she lies in the foetal position on the kitchen floor. I stroke her forehead, the sweat causing her auburn curls to form clumps.

The screaming subsides, her breathing regulates and we have a moment of respite. She belches, deep and guttural, and it makes me laugh. She turns her face up towards me, her mouth almost smiling for a moment, but her eyes are still shut.

'Sorry, that's disgusting,' she says, gurning. 'I feel like I smell. Do I smell?'

I kiss her on the forehead and lie.

'Not at all. Can't smell anything. You're doing really well.'

After all that we've been through to conceive – the appointments, the sperm deposits, the recurring disappointment of seeing just one clear line on a pregnancy test and not two – this feels like too late a hurdle to hit.

Victoria suggested a trip away and I agreed that we'd

15

benefit from a change of scenery, a last relaxing trip away for us, but I should have insisted on a weekend further from the due date and somewhere closer to home. I suggested the Cotswolds, but when Victoria gets an idea in her head, it's hard to change her mind. This part of the country means a lot to her, to us, but I had an inkling that something would go wrong and I ignored it. Sometimes I just sense it. A foreboding. A sniff of impending doom.

Victoria shocks me out of my trance.

'Jamie, don't panic. Go upstairs and get the car keys. We need to drive to a hospital.'

Her face is so pale that it's almost translucent.

'OK, I'm going. What else do you need? I told you we should have brought the hospital bag, just in case.'

I unbend my right knee and stumble slightly before getting to my feet.

'It's fine, Jamie. They'll have all the essentials at the hospital. Just grab a few clothes, my coat. Let's just get in the car and go. Be quick – the contractions are getting closer together already, I think.'

I rush across the hallway and Victoria calls after me.

'Just . . . be careful, OK? Take it easy. We've still got time. Don't end up hurting yourself – that's the last thing we need right now.'

I head up the stairs, trying to climb two at once. I want to move faster, I need to, and I feel a surge of anger rising inside me – frustration at myself for being too slow. As I reach the top, I feel a tightness in my left Achilles tendon and almost trip as I stub the big toe of my right foot in an attempt to hurry. I stop for a moment in the hallway between the bedrooms, already feeling the beginnings of a stitch. Where on earth are Barry and Fiona? Is there any chance they're still in their bedroom, asleep and oblivious to what's happening in the kitchen?

Their bedroom door is shut. I edge forwards and put an ear to the door. Nothing. I use my stronger right hand to knock gently. Nothing. I clench my fist a bit tighter and knock again, three times, and it stings a bit. Still nothing. I place my hand on the door handle. Pushing down, I wince as I realise that this is yet another locked door. They're definitely not in the house.

I go back into the bedroom where we slept and scramble around the floor next to my side of the bed. I find my wallet, an empty KitKat wrapper and my security pass from work, which I meant to leave at home. I must have emptied them from my pockets before bed. Where are my car keys?

I have a tendency to leave things in the wrong place, but I'm certain the keys were in my back trouser pocket last night, because I remember feeling the stab of the sharp car key as I sat down on the sofa in their living room. I check the pockets of the jeans I'm wearing and the coat I'd thrown on an armchair in the room and find only torn-up tissues, an old theatre ticket, empty sweet wrappers, receipts, a few coins, a five-pound note. But no keys. Where are they?

I scramble around on the floor again, looking for the shine of a Monopoly boot – the little trinket that I've used as a keyring since I was a child. As I sweep my hand across the floor, I feel nothing but the mild burn of carpet and a cramp in the back of my left knee. I long to feel something hard, to hit the cold edge of metal, to hear the jangle as the keys clang together, but nothing.

'Victoria! Victoria, are you OK?' I shout, and I hear a 'Yes, I'm fine,' in response from downstairs.

How long do we have? Please, please let the contractions stay far apart for now.

I look out of the window and see our car – the small silver Ford Fiesta. But the red van, presumably belonging to the owners, the one that I'd parked beside when we arrived yesterday evening, is no longer next to it. My mind is racing. Have the owners left the house and forgotten we're here? How long will it be until they come back? And where are our keys?

I leave the room, step back onto the landing and notice a glint of silver on the wooden floor, just in front of their bedroom door. I bend my knees, using the wall for balance, and pick it up. It's a small silver keyring chain with nothing attached to it. The loop is bent and spread open where it should be tight. I have one just like this. The ring is supposed to be connected to a miniature Monopoly boot and my keys. I've been meaning to get a new keyring. The boot always ends up loose in my pocket.

I crouch lower and feel my knee click. I run my hands on the wooden planks of the corridor floor, back and forth, feeling ridges and dips where the panels meet, and put my cheek to the floor, cold, so I can scan across and back, through floating specks of dust. And then I see it. About three inches away from the other wall, towards the stairs.

I crawl over and pick it up. It's the Monopoly boot, but my keys aren't there.

Chapter 4

Victoria

Monday, 5 April

'We have a *very* special guest today, boys and girls. The lovely Vicky is here to play some songs for us on the piano. Who's ready for a sing-along?'

It's Victoria. Not Vicky, not Vic. Victoria. And why call me 'lovely'? This perfect stranger has absolutely no idea if I'm lovely or not. For all she knows, I could be a vicious, misanthropic villain, plotting to sabotage this toddler group by screaming at the top of my lungs, grabbing the dummies out of each of the babies' mouths, stripping down to my underwear and gyrating provocatively round the piano stool. I am not, in fact, planning to do any of these things, but she doesn't know any better.

This is hardly the most glamorous gig, but the plus side of a job like this is that the repertoire is so easy that my fingers do their own thing and I barely have to concentrate. As I play the first chords of my self-penned, slightly jazzy version of 'The Animals Came in Two by Two', I go far away, into myself, and everything else disappears.

I think back to all those long nights in my halls at university practising for exams, battling with Shostakovich, Chopin and tendonitis in my right wrist. The utter humiliation of losing my train of thought midway through a recital and having to go back to the beginning. The pressure of performing Rachmaninoff in front of a panel of the world's best pianists – each of them watching every finger, waiting for me to bend one in slightly the wrong direction, brush a note with a pinkie that I didn't mean to, go too heavy on the reverb pedal, fall off my stool in the midst of passion. Would I have dared to dream of the dizzying heights of Bach4Babies in Marylebone, bashing my way through nursery rhymes surrounded by babies who are too young to recognise basic tunes, let alone appreciate the major sixths?

I can't help but keep tabs on my contemporaries from the Royal Academy, who post on social media about their latest bookings. The two girls I'm still in regular contact with have both had children and have long given up their aspirations of becoming the next Itzhak Perlman to go into teaching, opting for the more responsible route for a reliable stream of income. But there's a guy from the year above, Henry Thatcher (no relation to Maggie, apparently, although with an equally high-pitched voice), who seems to be doing really well. We're Facebook friends, even though we've only actually met once, at someone's twentieth, when he drunkenly spilled a glass of Merlot over my top and spent the whole evening buying me drinks to make up for it. At least he did until I had to turn him down as he lunged towards me in an attempt to stick his tongue down my throat. I might have had the upper hand that evening, but he's the one laughing now, as he's played at Carnegie Hall a couple of times and recently posted selfies of himself at Abbey Road Studios, playing the violin on a Lewis Capaldi track.

I look up over the edge of the piano at the cheap murals with their brash reds and sickly yellows, all the small coats lined up next to each other on their hooks, and I bite my bottom lip to stop myself from crying.

Even if this is not the most glamorous gig, I'm still taking it seriously. I'm wearing the classical pianist's uniform of modest, simple black top and skirt with plain pumps and though it's not the most challenging repertoire, I make sure my posture is right, that my fingering is perfect and that I perform with all the gusto I can muster. Life is long, I tell myself, and life will continue. I have to get through today, and then I'll tackle tomorrow and the day after that. And you never know who might be in the audience.

I allow myself to imagine that the mother or father of one of these babies could be a talent scout or an agent. Although the odds are against me, this little gig could be my big break – the start of something so major that it could take over my life and make me so busy that maybe, just maybe, I could live without every moment of every day being consumed by what I've done.

I've repeated all the verses twice and as I look round, I can see that I'm losing the crowd. Most of the toddlers literally have their backs to me now. Time to move on. My segue from 'The Animals Go in Two by Two' to 'The Wheels on the Bus' is seamless, even though the tempos of the two songs are quite distinct, but I fear this technical prowess goes unnoticed.

There's a very specific face that one has to put on when playing music to babies. The smile must be constant, of course, unwavering, and you have to sort of bob your head up and down in an exaggerated manner as you play. I haven't been able to pick my own repertoire, but if I had, I'd have given 'The Wheels on the Bus' a miss because I hate the stereotypes: 'The mummies on the bus go chatter, chatter, chatter, all day long,' because clearly they're not capable of very much else, while 'the daddies on the bus go ssh ssh ssh.' Is that the daddies telling the mummies to stop chattering? I don't like it.

I'm watching as all the mummies in this class are singing along with such enthusiasm and I wonder if they've really thought about what they're doing, about the values that they're instilling in their little ones by subscribing to such brazen chauvinism. One little baby, a bow clipped across her barely visible hair to signal, beyond reasonable doubt, that she's a girl, clearly objects to the song, because as we get to the last chorus, she blasts out a clump of white vomit, all over her mother's cream jumper. She's sitting right by me, so I keep going with my right hand, reach into my left sleeve for a tissue and pass it to her. She smiles and I force one back, but it stings.

I finish up with 'Twinkle Twinkle Little Star', a sure-fire crowd-pleaser, and then at the end I stand up, turn towards the audience and take a little bow. There's a flutter of applause and that always makes me feel good. And then very quickly, everyone goes off into their own world: one woman folding up a portable changing mat while trying to stop her son from crying, another getting frustrated as the zip gets stuck on her daughter's coat. In a cluster are three mums, clutching their babies on their shoulders, arranging a coffee date for tomorrow morning.

I pick up my tote bag from the floor, put on my coat and scuttle out, hoping to make it through the sea of faces without interruption. I can't engage with any of these people. I can't break down in public.

Just as I reach the exit, I feel a tap on my shoulder and freeze.

'Victoria! I thought it was you.'

I turn round and Lauren comes straight towards me, bringing me into a tight embrace. She's dressed casually, in a pink vest and grey tracksuit bottoms. I catch a whiff of her hair: it smells delicious, of raspberries and coconuts, and I bet she hasn't even washed it this morning.

'Lauren, hi! I didn't know you were here.'

In theory, Lauren is someone I should feel comfortable hugging. She's married to Andy, Jamie's best friend, and even if she and I aren't the most natural fit to be best buddies, we get along well enough and keep up the pretence, when necessary, that we enjoy spending time together. It doesn't help that there's always been a bit of rivalry between us, given that I used to date her husband, albeit briefly.

She continues the embrace, drawing her head back and looking straight at me, her thumbs massaging the tops of my arms. I can't make eye contact with her and I don't want her to touch me. I don't want anyone to touch me, because I feel dirty and ruined.

'Isla and I were right at the back; we arrived a bit late. Anyway, how are you doing? Did you get my message? I don't know what to say. I . . . I just can't believe that this has happened to you. After everything.'

She's got her head in a tilt, that universal signifier of sympathy, but I don't want that from her right now. If I'm going to talk about it with her, with anyone, I need to be prepared. I can't have this interaction sprung on me like this.

'Thanks, Lauren. It's . . . yeah . . . it's been hard. I don't really feel in a place to talk about it yet.'

Lauren darts back and places a hand to her mouth, as if she's said something out of place. She hasn't. I understand the impulse to ask. I'm just not ready.

'I'm sorry, doll. You know, I'm always here. We are always here, if you want to chat. I know you're not really a phone person, but if you and Jamie want to come round for dinner . . . Or if you want to pop round on your own, any time, for a girls' chat, my door's always open.'

I bite my bottom lip and catch a bit of dry skin. I'm not her doll and I don't want a girls' chat. We wouldn't even be friends if our husbands weren't obsessed with each other. And what does that mean, 'not a phone person'? I can be a phone person if I want to be.

'Thanks, Lauren. I really need to get back to the flat. I've got another gig tomorrow, a proper one, and I haven't even looked at the sheet music yet.'

That's a lie, but a small one compared to others that we've told over the past four weeks.

'Oh, that's great. Good to hear that you're able to dive back into work. Keeps your mind off things, I guess. Hang on a sec, Isla wants to say hello. Isla?!'

Isla, our god-daughter, who recently turned two, is just

behind Lauren, trying to grab a toy car from another little girl. She's looking so much more stable on her feet than when I last saw her.

'Isla, come and say hello to Auntie Victoria, will you?'

Her face lights up to see me and she comes bounding over, lifting her arms to be picked up. I lift her up and immediately feel a sharp pain in my groin.

'Hello, darling,' I say, swallowing hard.

I run my hand through her hair, dirty blonde and curly, and kiss her forehead. She's looking down at my tummy.

'Baby, baby!'

I put her down, too roughly, and Lauren ushers her over. When we went round to theirs a few months ago, Jamie thought it would be cute to teach her that there was a baby in my tummy. It's not her fault.

'Sorry, Vic. Really sorry. She's saying that to everyone at the moment.'

Lauren's staring at my right breast and I put a hand over my top to feel a wet patch. She can't look me in the eye, but she tries to talk it away by blaming Isla.

'Isla must be teething again. She's drooled all over you. Sorry, Vic.'

I rub the patch vigorously, willing the wetness to evaporate. We both know that's not drool. I scurry away without saying goodbye.

When I get back to the flat, I head straight into the kitchen and open the freezer. I pull my top up over my head, unclasp my bra and place a bag of ice on my left breast, a bag of frozen sweetcorn on my right. I drop my head down, soothed by the numbing. I look at the bra dangling down, a frumpy beige padded thing, and bring it to my nose. The sweet smell of the milk stain hits me at the back of the throat.

I'm in a little studio in Deptford, just south of the river. I inherited it from my dad and it's currently sitting empty between tenants. I lived here with Jamie when we first moved in together and I've come back for a few days of space, to try to make sense of the incomprehensible nightmare of the last few weeks. I place my bag down on the worktop and notice that the zip's open. I riffle through it, but nothing seems to be missing. I remove my phone and attach it to the charger that's plugged in next to the kettle. Then I unzip my skirt, letting it fall in a creased clump on the tiled floor, and walk over to the sink.

I take out a used mug, angle it very closely under the tap on top of all the dirty dishes and glasses, and fill it with water. I down it in one – it's lukewarm, but I don't care – fill it up again, down it again and gasp for breath. I look around. This kitchen is an absolute tip, but I don't have the energy to clear it up. I'd like to think that once upon a time I was quite house-proud, but I don't feel the same connection to this flat as I did a few years ago and I'm totally lacking in motivation to keep it clean.

I go to the fridge and peer inside. There's an open packet of salami, which I put to my nose, sniff and then throw in the bin.

I fill the mug again, step over yesterday's clothes, shuffle past the empty pizza box from Wednesday, and climb into bed, spilling a bit of water on the pillow next to me as I lie down. I look at my phone and the display is dim because the battery is so low. I have to squint to read it: seven missed calls and three voicemails. I take a swig of water and dial to listen to the voicemails.

Message 1, yesterday at 21:22 hours:

Hi, darling, it's Mum. I thought maybe we could meet for lunch next week, at Salieri's? I'm desperate to see you. I know you don't want to talk about what happened and I'm not going to force you. Just think it might do you some good to get out and about. Give me a ring when you have a second and let's get something in the diary, yes? Much love and all the best, Mum.

I know it's you, Mum. You don't need to sign off a voicemail like it's a letter. And of course she's suggested a restaurant that's just round the corner from her house. As long as it's convenient for her. I'll call back tomorrow.

Message 2, today at 13:02 hours:

Victoria, it's me. Jamie. I need to speak to you. We need to talk about the letter. Who do you think sent it? Maybe someone saw us. I'm freaking out here by myself. I need you. We need each other. I love you.

Message 3, today at 14:42 hours:

Oh, hello there. This is a message for Victoria Rawlinson. Emma here, calling from the midwifery team at Ivy Lane surgery. Just wanted to touch base to check in on how you and baby are doing because I've got a DNA, Did Not Attend, for your appointment on the 12th of March.

Hopefully it's good news and it means baby's made an appearance, but do give me a ring back when you can just so we can get all the records updated. We'll also need to schedule a couple of follow-up appointments, just to make sure both you and baby are doing OK. Give me a ring at the surgery. All right, then, bye for now.

I fling my phone on the floor and hear a crack as the case detaches itself. Jamie has been trying to talk to me about the letter since Saturday. And the midwife. That's another thing Jamie and I hadn't anticipated. My head feels heavy as it hits the pillow. The curtains are drawn and have been for the last few days. Though there's still sunlight shining through the edges, I know it won't take long for me to drift off. Sleep is such a solace for me now – an escape from the persistent voice in my head that reminds me, during every waking hour, of what happened to Danny. And of what I did. What I was made to do.

Chapter 5

Victoria

Saturday, 6 March, 8.18 a.m.

'Victoria, I've just found my Monopoly boot keyring on the floor by Barry and Fiona's bedroom. I'm sure I left the keys on the bedside table when we first got into the room. Do you think they took them? I've been knocking on their bedroom door, but they're either ignoring me or they've gone somewhere and locked us in.'

I haven't had a contraction for a few minutes and have levered myself up. I'm sat on a wooden chair beside the kitchen table. My vision is a bit blurred and there's a ringing in my ears. What is he talking about?

'Can you just chill out, please? The contractions are still really far apart. I'm fine. Remember at the antenatal class? They said don't bother going into hospital until you have three every ten minutes.'

'Yeah, but who knows how far we are from the nearest hospital? And how on earth are we going to get there without the car keys?'

Jamie's face has taken on a pale green hue and his breathing is getting heavier, shorter. His left knee is shaking and he's pacing round the kitchen, edging towards me and then retreating, trying all the windows in the kitchen, pushing and pulling, but none of them will budge.

'Jamie, I need you to calm down. The keys probably just slipped out of your pocket when you took your trousers off last night. Have you checked the room thoroughly? Under the bed?'

I can't count the number of times he says he's lost his keys or his wallet and then found them seconds later down the back of the sofa or behind the bed. I can't focus on this now. I'm counting breaths in and out from my nose, reaching ten and then starting again from one. I've had Braxton Hicks contractions for a few weeks, 'a rehearsal for the real deal', as the midwife put it. But this feels different – much deeper, more pronounced.

The prospect of giving birth for the first time has terrified me and I've spent all these months visualising it, thinking about positions and playlists and pain relief to try to take as much control as possible. Giving birth like this was never part of the plan. The pregnancy has been straightforward so far, but what happens if something goes wrong now? What if the baby is distressed and stops breathing as he comes out? What happens if I tear, as so many women do, and I bleed and bleed then lose consciousness, dying here and now, aged thirty-four, on the kitchen floor in a stranger's house?

'Have you got your phone, Jamie? Let's call for an ambulance, just in case.'

Jamie searches in the pockets of his pyjamas, looking hopeless, hot and lost.

'Jamie, why are you looking in your pockets? They're upstairs on charge. Do you want me to go and find them?'

I breathe out slowly through my mouth, push down on my thighs, stand and brush past him, and he follows me up the stairs.

'You should be taking it easy, Victoria. I can get the phones.'

I make my way to the table on the left-hand side of the bed while Jamie carries on to the right. I can see the white wire of my iPhone dangling across the table, but no phone. I get closer and look behind the table – strain to kneel and look under the bed, against the wall. Where the hell is my phone? And Jamie is doing the same on his side, holding an unconnected wire and rummaging around, increasingly panicked.

'They've taken our phones. They've gone off with our phones and our car keys.'

What?

'Don't be ridiculous, Jamie. What would they want with our phones?'

Jamie rushes past me, along the corridor and down the stairs. I follow him this time, afraid that he'll trip in his hurry, lose his step on his way down, go tumbling forwards.

'Be careful, J. Hold on to the banister.'

'There's a landline,' he calls back as he reaches the bottom of the stairs. 'We'll call 999 from the landline.'

I take it easy, because I know that another contraction must be imminent. I'm bracing myself for another wave of agony, another dive into the depths of this unfamiliar pain. I make my way slowly to the kitchen and find Jamie turning the dial on an old-fashioned red phone on the corner of the worktop. It's one of those antique corded ones that your grandma has – a hefty brick with a dial in the middle that makes a laborious, winding sound as you drag each number clockwise. He turns to look at me, his face totally devoid of colour now, his eyes wide, bright, petrified.

'It's dead. There's no dialling tone.'

'It's probably just not plugged in, Jamie,' I say as I head over to his side of the kitchen. 'No one uses landlines these days.'

I look down at the connection. The white wire to the wall has been cut. Jamie bends down to pick up a folded piece of white paper. He unfolds it and, as I feel the next wave of pressure burn from the base of my spine, we stand together, reading, while Jamie says it out loud.

You're in safe hands. Breathe in through your nose and out through your mouth.

Chapter 6

Jamie

Monday, 5 April

I know they're talking about me. I don't blame them – it's a great story. I'm in my office and they obviously don't realise that the walls aren't fully soundproofed. How dare they! I run this business – I founded it. Ultimately, I pay all of their salaries, fund their family holidays, allow them to pay their mortgages. I could fire them all on the spot. That would give them something to talk about.

'It's just so sad after everything they've been through. That poor wife of his – three rounds of IVF and now this. It's just so easy to take it all for granted, isn't it?'

Palvhi was my first hire at KnowScam. The first person I brought in to help with the financial modelling before we started looking for investors. Over the last few years, I've probably spent more time with her than I have with Victoria, poring over forecasts into the early hours of the morning, preparing for board presentations. I couldn't have got here without her, but she also has a lot to thank me for, really. And yet here she is, holding court at a large round table in our office.

She announced her pregnancy just a few weeks after we announced ours, but we must have been further along, because her baby still hasn't come and she's still at work. I've confided in her over the years, about all sorts of things. I can't help but feel betrayed.

'Yeah, well in the end they got pregnant naturally. They'd only recently got the news that the third cycle hadn't worked. Had been advised to give it a break for a while, let her body recover. And then it just happened.'

Lucy, the new head of technology, chips in. I was impressed by her when she interviewed, but she hasn't added any value yet, so it would be easy to get rid of her before the end of her probation period.

'That happens all the time, though. When the pressure comes off, when it's all a bit more relaxed. Something similar happened to my brother and his wife. Do we know if it was him or her who had the issues?'

Wow.

'Him. But don't tell anyone I told you that. Low sperm count. Poor morphology, as well, whatever that means. As far as I know, there's nothing wrong with her.'

I put my headphones on, put on my Hans Zimmer playlist and crank up the volume. I feel a burn in between my ribs, a dullness at the back of my throat, and I swallow hard to hold back the tears. I click between tabs on my computer and then open a Word document and start typing, to give a semblance of productivity. I know that no one will, no one can, ever read what I'm typing here, but by getting it down on screen, it's out of my body, exorcised, channelled somewhere tangible rather than filling my head. I write it and rewrite it to help work out if I could have foreseen, the night before, what was about to happen.

The drive up from London was almost comically disastrous. There was a nasty crash on the motorway section of the A1 – we passed the scene and it was cordoned off, ambulances and police cars signalling that it had all ended in the worst way – and then once we were off the motorway, the mist appeared. The narrow and winding roads in the North Pennines were so treacherous with black ice that I took them slower than I could have, afraid that a reckless turn might send us spinning, cause a crash and harm Victoria and Danny.

For the last section of the drive, it was dark, but the mist was so thick that putting the headlights on fully actually reduced visibility. I remember one road in particular because of its ominous name – Snake Pass – and I could only see a few feet in front of me, as other drivers, more familiar with the conditions and the contours of the road, sped past us. Both of our phones lost signal, so Victoria navigated using an old A–Z, putting on the inside car light and squinting to read the minuscule road names, spinning the map around in her hands, losing her patience when I occasionally leaned over to try to help. And then finally, just before 9 p.m., we turned left at a sign for Choristers' Lodge and drove over a cattle grid and down a rickety path leading to a house with a light on in the distance.

As we drove down the uneven path towards the guest house, I was tired, so drained by the intensity of navigating those roads that I barely registered my surroundings. Victoria had fallen asleep by the time we pulled up outside, her head gently resting against the window, her mouth slightly open so I could see the gap between her two front teeth. She had both hands on her bump. I parked next to a large red van and the crunch of the handbrake jolted her awake.

'Have we arrived? Was I asleep?'

I felt a tightening in my chest, a rush of adrenaline, love, which came out in a smile.

'Just for the last few minutes.'

Victoria leaned back and stretched both arms out, flicking down the sun visor and looking in the mirror.

'I'm knackered. What a journey. Thanks so much for driving, J. You must be exhausted.'

'Yeah, I can barely keep my eyes open. Also starving. We should have stopped somewhere for food.'

Victoria leaned over, gave me a kiss, and we both undid our seat belts. As I stood and stretched in the dark outside, a quick mist of mountain air tickled my upper arms, filling my nose and awaking a rush of endorphins in my forehead.

I watched as the front door to the guest house opened and we saw the owners for the first time. She was tall, wiry, like a sharpened pencil, her features severe, her nose straight, her mouth so tiny as to be virtually indistinguishable from the rest of the bottom half of her face. Next to her, he was short, perhaps once athletic but now showing his age, with a moustache that was so well carved that it looked like an elongated stamp, as if it might have been stuck on as part of a fancy dress costume.

We walked in the crisp blackness with our two small bags towards the front door and she spoke first.

'Hello there. You must Jamie and Victoria. I'm Fiona and this is my husband, Barry. Welcome to Choristers' Lodge.'

We were led into the guest house and greeted immediately with a subtle but tangible musk of damp. On the wall directly opposite the entranceway was a large crucifix, under which was a wall fitting inscribed with the words: *deo confidimus*. Fiona must have caught me looking.

'We're not religious, but it felt like a nice relic to leave in place. Everyone likes a bit of culture. You churchgoers?'

I shook my head.

'No, not at all, to be honest. But we were wondering about the name of the guest house on the way up, actually. What's the building's history?'

Fiona came round behind us and removed Victoria's coat, placing it over the banister. I took mine off and handed it to her.

'It was linked to the local Roman Catholic school. A boarding house for some of the boys and a rehearsal space for the choir. Why don't you come through to the living room while Barry takes your bags upstairs?'

She ushered us in front of her and out of the corner of my eye, I clocked Fiona noticing my limp.

'Oh, what have you done to your leg, Jamie?'

Here we go. If I were in a wheelchair and more obviously disabled, people wouldn't be so brazen as to ask so directly, so quickly. I think people often use it as an icebreaker with me, expecting an anecdote about an injury sustained while playing rugby or falling out of a nightclub.

'Oh, it's a long-term thing, actually. I always walk like this.'

I gave my standard answer and thankfully, Fiona didn't push it any further.

'You must have had a very long trip. Let me get you both a drink. Red or white for you, Jamie? Can of beer? And Victoria, how about some juice? We've got apple, orange. Oh, orange might be a bit too acidic for you, actually.'

She glanced down at Victoria's protruding belly and Victoria frowned. She hated the assumption, while she was pregnant, that she'd always rather stick with something soft.

'We'd love to pop out for something to eat,' I said. 'Anywhere you can recommend that's not too far?'

Barry laughed, shaking his head and spitting slightly through his broad Mancunian accent.

'Oh no, it's gone nine o'clock. We're not in London now! Fiona, why don't you make them a little sandwich or something?'

Fiona called through from the hallway, 'I've actually got some leftover chilli from the other night in the fridge, if you fancy that?'

I really didn't fancy it. I guess it's fair to say I'm pretty paranoid about food hygiene and the idea of my pregnant wife eating something that a stranger had made and left in the fridge for a couple of days made me want to stay hungry. But it was too awkward to refuse and we both nodded.

Fiona served us a bowl each at the kitchen table, and I remember it steaming and smelling like a sweet tomato soup rather than chilli. Victoria was playing with it, mixing it around the bowl before taking a tentative spoonful, her teeth clinging to the spoon, barely shielding a grimace. Barry came back into the room and took a seat next to Fiona, opposite us. On the wall behind them was a wooden noticeboard with names engraved in gold, each with a year next to it.

'Who are the people listed there?' I asked, pointing towards it.

Fiona turned back.

'Oh, another thing that we've kept up from when we bought the place. Those are the names of the choirmasters. I think they also stayed here, to keep an eye on the boys.'

Victoria and I looked at each other. She held her bump and I scratched my neck.

'Where's the school, then? Is it nearby?' I asked, intrigued to find out more.

Barry joined in. 'No, the school was demolished a long time ago. You won't find much around here these days. What made you choose this place? Because we're hardly in the middle of a beaten track for tourists, are we? I doubt you're here to visit the old mines.'

Fiona tapped Barry on the knee, tutted and shot him a little scowl.

'Victoria found it, actually.'

Victoria swallowed a last mouthful of chilli and then placed her napkin in the bowl, which was still half-full, and looked to Fiona.

'Well actually, this part of the world is a bit special for us,' Victoria started. 'My family is from around here and the first time Jamie and I went away together, we rented a little cottage not too far from here, just outside Stanhope.

'To be honest, I did actually try to book the same place again. But it was booked up this weekend, so I found you guys instead. Thought it looked quaint and I was intrigued by the history of the place. And you know, remote. We needed to get away.'

I smiled and said something, quickly, before there was too much time to dwell on that last bit.

'I love it round here. As soon as you get out of the car, you notice the difference. The air feels so much cleaner than in London.'

Fiona nodded. 'Oh yes, of course. Full of pollution where you are. Your lungs must be full of carbon monoxide.'

'*Real* Cumbria, this is,' continued Barry between mouthfuls of chilli. 'Not like the Lakes with all the tourists and jagged cliffs. Here, it's rolling hills. Serene one moment, bleak the next, and we like it that way.'

Fiona leaned forwards, her palms out in an apology.

'Nothing wrong with the Lakes, of course. Beautiful. That's a national park, but *this* is an area of outstanding beauty. Lots of lovely routes around here, for all abilities. Although it's so icy out there and what with . . . well, I suppose you've got to take it easy with little one on the way, haven't you? And what with his sore leg, as well.'

She was addressing Victoria, but I answered.

'It doesn't hurt, actually, but yeah, nothing too strenuous for either of us.'

People always assume that I'm in a constant state of agony, that my limp means I must be wincing every time my heel hits the floor. I changed the subject.

'What do you both do for work, then?'

'Well, we keep this place going. I think people like the intimacy of a guest house that feels like you're just visiting family for the weekend. You can use all the rooms downstairs and we like to eat all together if guests want to. We cook in front of you,' Fiona replied. 'That's all these days.

It keeps us busy. I'm a retired midwife and Barry used to be in the police.'

'Chief Superintendent when I retired, as a matter of fact.'

A knock on my office door. I minimise the document.

'Sorry to disturb, Jamie. Is now a good time? Just wanted to get your advice on that workshop for Citizens Advice.'

It's Candice – a brilliant, relatively new hire, who we brought in to deliver training for charities about fraud prevention. It doesn't bring in the cash, but this part of the business is so important to me – it's the heart and soul of what we do.

'Yeah, of course,' I reply, wheeling my chair back. 'Actually, can you just give me a sec? Want to finish this thing off. I'll come and find you.'

Candice closes the door and I reopen the document.

From the kitchen table, Victoria was looking through a door to the living room at the back of the house, towards a piano in the far corner. I guessed that she was straining to read the sheet music on the stand. It was a challenge she likes to set herself, playing the notes in her head. I kept the conversation going.

'How many guest rooms have you got here, then?' I asked, peering behind me towards the spiral staircase. 'Are there other people here this weekend?'

'Well, there are three guest rooms,' Fiona replied. 'But I'll be honest with you – business is hardly booming at the moment. You're the first booking we've had in a few weeks.'

Barry threw Fiona a disdainful look, but she continued.

'Frankly, at our age, it's all getting a bit much. We're thinking about putting it on the market, actually. Moving away, somewhere even more remote. I've always fancied somewhere really wild, like the Hebrides.'

I studied the contours of Fiona's hands and judged that she must be in her early sixties. Behind her was an old-fashioned coal fireplace and on the mantle was a collage of photos: a wedding photo, faded, with Barry a lot slimmer and Fiona sporting a fringe so aggressive it looked like it was going to whip you if you looked at it the wrong way. There was a photo of them both on what looked like a cruise liner – a cheesy pose on the deck with a calm sea in the background. And right in the middle was a picture of Barry with a baby boy on his shoulders. The child looked less than a year old, with dark curls and a grin on his face revealing two burgeoning teeth at the bottom.

'Have you always lived in the area?' I asked, moving backwards on my chair as subtly as possible to try to get some support from the thin wooden bars behind my back and the flat cushion I was sitting on.

'Oh no, dear. We both grew up in Manchester, and we stayed and worked round there after we got married, too. We only moved up after we lost our son, Harrison.'

And then there was a pause, because neither of us knew where to take the conversation next. We'd just met these people – that seemed like too big a thing just to throw in casually.

Fiona leaned in towards us, smiling.

'What about you two, then? I bet you both have very flashy London jobs.'

'Well, Victoria's a musician, actually,' I answered, rubbing Victoria's thigh.

Fiona lit up.

'What, professionally? How lovely! Which instrument? Wait – let me guess: flute? Clarinet?'

'Piano, mainly. I was just looking at yours over there.'

Fiona looked back in the direction of the piano.

'Oh yes. I used to play. Well, I still do. Never professionally, but I've always had a good ear for it. Apparently, we have an ancestor who was a concert pianist in Austria. Years ago. No idea if that's true or not.'

Victoria perked up a bit, smiling.

'Well, they do say musicality runs in the family.'

Fiona laughed.

'I suppose they do. You must be very good, then, if you can make a living out of it.'

Victoria went crimson, lowering her head slightly.

'Oh, I don't know about that.'

I stepped in.

'She's being modest. Victoria trained at the Royal Academy. She's played at Wigmore Hall. Got a standing ovation. The Duke and Duchess of Cambridge were there.'

'Ooh, we love Kate, don't we, Barry? Now there's an example of a good mother.'

The truth was that this had very much been a highlight in an otherwise unremarkable few years for Victoria, although I'd never say that to her face. The last gig she'd done was in a retirement home, playing Beethoven's Moonlight Sonata to a room of a hundred OAPs, many so senile as to not remember even their own names. I took the afternoon off work to support her and although we didn't discuss it, we both knew that the rapturous applause she'd received had been undiscerning and manic.

'And what about you then, Jamie? What line of business are you in?' Barry asked.

Does anyone under the age of forty use the term 'line of business'? It was as if he was expecting carpenter or electrician. Real men's work.

'I run a start-up. It's to do with . . . well, fraud prevention, really. It's called KnowScam. We help businesses, banks and things like that on their anti-fraud strategies.' I found myself tilting my head slightly and raising my intonation at the end, almost apologetically. 'And then we also help charities and individuals to learn how to prevent themselves from becoming victims of fraud.'

'Well, I say,' commented Fiona, folding her arms and smiling at her husband. 'We *are* going up in the world at Choristers' Lodge. A pianist and a tech entrepreneur – how *glamorous*! You do hear horrible stories, don't you? Old ladies having their whole bank accounts wiped by people from God knows where.'

Often, people change the subject when I tell them what I do. The words 'fraud prevention' aren't the most riveting. I was pleased that Fiona seemed engaged.

'Yeah, you know, I think as more and more people are getting comfortable with technology, doing online banking, there's more scope for it, unfortunately. It's actually by far the most common crime now, but people don't realise it until it's too late.'

Fiona laughed. 'Oh, we're actually quite good on the computer, even if we are old codgers. Or I am, anyway. I've had to learn, over the years, for work. Don't know how we'd run the guest house without email and that.'

Barry interjected. 'She's certainly trigger-happy when it comes to online shopping as well, I can you tell you that. Most days there's something or other that arrives.'

He directed this at me, shaking his head, like I represented the whole internet.

'Can you point me towards the bathroom?'

The awkwardness was subverted by Victoria, who stood, clutching her yellow tote bag.

Fiona stood, too.

'Oh, I'll come and show you where it is, dear. You have to go through to the back of the house, unfortunately. It's terribly uncivilised. You'll have to forgive us. Come – follow me.'

I felt a pang of panic as I found myself alone with Barry. I wouldn't describe myself as an introvert, but there was something about Barry that made me feel uncomfortable. I remember scanning the room looking for an object, a picture, something to comment on, a topic for conversation. On the windowsill there were about a dozen ornamental insects: a glass bee, a wooden spider, a beetle with crimson eyes, two shiny beads of light staring out over the room. Each of these trinkets was a different size, its own material and design, but curated to live together, a family of different species. To my left on the floor by where Fiona had been sitting was a wicker basket, filled with antique dolls – mostly female but with one little boy slumped over the edge of the basket, a fixed smile staring out towards me. Barry must have caught me looking.

'Fiona collects things. Antiques. All sorts of old tat. One or two things worth a bob or two, mind you. Or they would be if she ever let me sell them.'

He got up and walked to a glass cabinet in the corner of the room and opened the door, beckoning me to join him. On the middle shelf, above the usual glasses and decanters, was a large hunting knife, with a thick brown wooden handle and a silver blade, at least six inches long and curved up at the tip. I'm not the kind of man who is impressed by knives.

'Go on. You can take it out, have a feel,' he said.

I played along, holding it and pretending to inspect the handle, looking at my reflection in the blade.

'We've got a piano that dates back to the seventeenth century,' I offered. 'It's a family heirloom of Victoria's. We've also got this dresser in our bedroom. It's Baroque, apparently. She found it online.'

He didn't seem that impressed and then there was a moment of silence between us while I stood beside him, still holding the knife in front of me. He took a decanter from the cabinet and poured himself a glass of whiskey. He didn't offer any to me, but I'd have refused anyway. I didn't drink while Victoria was pregnant, partly through respect, in solidarity, but also because it felt like something tangible that I could do to feel connected to the pregnancy. Barry sipped the whiskey and I put the knife down on the table before gathering the bowls of chilli, stacking them, standing and making my way towards the sink. I was intercepted by Fiona.

'Oh, what are you doing with those, Jamie? You're our guests. Let me get those for you.'

'Thanks. It was delicious,' I lied. 'And I think as soon as Victoria's done, we'll head up to bed.'

As if on cue, Victoria emerged, shaking her hands dry as she headed across the kitchen towards us.

'Fresh towels on the bed for you both. And the pillows are new – we just got them in. Duck feather! I've put an extra one out for you, dear. I remember when I was pregnant, back in the Stone Ages, I liked to sleep with one between my legs. Helps with the backache.'

Fiona headed towards the sink, passing Victoria as she went and giving her bump a friendly rub. Victoria recoiled. She hated this, the unsolicited touch, the assumption that this part of her body, by protruding, was on offer for all to grasp a feel. Barry stood up and gave me a firm handshake. He looked at Victoria.

'Jamie said you're into antiques, like Fiona,' he said. 'An old piano and things like that. I bet you don't have any knives like this one.' He pointed to the table and Victoria looked at the knife and nodded.

'Wow, it's stunning,' she offered, her lips raised in a forced smile.

Fiona interjected. 'Well, breakfast is usually 8.30 a.m. on a Saturday and Sunday, 7.30 a.m. Monday to Friday, but we tend to get up early, so just come down and let us know if you fancy anything before.'

'Oh, that's very kind.' I said. 'We might still be asleep, to be honest.'

But Barry had already turned his back to us, heading up the wooden staircase.

I feel a knock on my desk.

Palvhi, my so-called friend, has walked over. I minimise the document, take my headphones off and force out a smile.

'Hi, Jamie. Off in your own world there. What are you working on?'

'Hey, Palvhi. Just . . . Oh, nothing exciting. How are you? You look great. Can't be long to go for you now.'

Palvhi is resting her hands on her bump and cocks her head, so far that it's virtually horizontal, and I want to stand up, take it in both hands and force it back into the default position. I don't want her pity.

'If there's anything I can do. Even if you just want a shoulder to cry on. I can't even begin to imagine what you're going through, Jamie. And your wife, so terrible.'

No, you can't, Palvhi, I think to myself. And imagine if I told you the real story.

I spend the rest of the afternoon at work searching for things I know I shouldn't. I take myself into a meeting room with my laptop, open an incognito browser and check the usual places: TripAdvisor, Booking.com, their pathetic little website and the government website listing the maximum sentences for our crimes. I search for Barry and Fiona on Google and Facebook, to see if anything new has come up. I browse the local newspaper websites, afraid as I click on each new page that there will be something new – a photo of them, of us, of Danny. A shocking headline, a big revelation. But there's nothing and I end up looking over the same things, again and again.

The TripAdvisor page still states 'permanently closed' and there are no new reviews. The other websites aren't taking bookings at Choristers' Lodge – it looks like there aren't any vacancies, that all the dates are booked up, but I know that there will be no new guests at the breakfast table. And there's the old news article that I keep reading – a constant reminder of who we're up against.

The Keswick Reminder
25 March 2008

Cumbria police chief gets top award at Buckingham Palace for leading hunt for little Emily's killer.

The police chief who oversaw the investigation into the disappearance of Emily Whittington has been awarded the prestigious Queen's Police Medal for Distinguished Service at Buckingham Palace.

Barry Johnson, fifty-two, Deputy Chief Constable of Cumbria Constabulary, was awarded the gong in the Queen's New Year Honours list. He is pictured below with HRH the Prince of Wales, who handed him the coveted medal in a ceremony at Buckingham Palace yesterday morning.

Chief Constable Linda Wachsmann paid tribute to her deputy, saying: 'I am hugely proud of the recognition that Barry has received for his work co-ordinating the investigation into Emily Whittington's disappearance in February last year. He displayed the highest degree of professionalism, leading a major operation under intense public scrutiny that led to the eventual discovery of Emily's body, and the arrest and subsequent conviction of her assailant.'

Emily Whittington, four, disappeared from a playground just outside Keswick on the 4th of February last year. Following a 48-hour search, her body was found in the attic of Tony Clyde, fifty-seven, from Newcastle. Clyde was subsequently found guilty of murder and sentenced to life imprisonment.

Deputy Chief Constable Johnson, who attended the royal ceremony with his wife, Fiona, also fifty-two, commented: 'I am hugely humbled by the recognition. The investigation into Emily's disappearance was a true team effort and I can say with certainty that we wouldn't have been able to resolve it so quickly without the tireless effort of the entire Cumbrian force.'

Scrolling down, I zoom in on the photo. Barry is short but muscular, so much so that Prince Charles, standing on a step in front of him, appears spindly. Barry smiles in a way that looks forced, insincere, and it looks like Prince Charles is saying something to him, his mouth slightly open and his eyebrows raised. What's he saying? Thank you for your service? Thank you for your work to find Emily's body? Little does he know, I think.

What we can be certain of is how much the stakes are heightened, given his status. If it had been anyone else, I can't help but think that this could have all turned out differently. If it was anyone else, could we have gone to the police? Could anyone else have planned this? Could anyone else have made us do what we did? I'm certain that if it had been anyone else, we'd still have Danny.

Chapter 7

Jamie

'I'm going to go and find help. Don't worry, Victoria, I'll sort this. You just . . . take it easy, OK? Breathe through the contractions.'

I'm on the floor with her, rubbing her back, but it's not enough. I need to do more. This is an emergency. How many contractions has she had? They're definitely coming quicker. I feel hot and cold at the same time – one minute clouded by angry voices berating me for agreeing to this trip, the next overcome with clarity and a resolve to fight. A shock of panic rises in my forehead then disappears, and with it an ache that oscillates between my stomach and groin, subsiding for one moment and then re-emerging sharply the next, up and forwards, back and down.

I stand and feel a pang of cramp in my hamstrings. My left foot, my weaker side, automatically goes to its tiptoes when I stand and now it's shaking, threatening to buckle. I can hear soft noises coming from my mouth, muffled tones. I ignore them. I need to find someone – anyone – who can

51

drive us to a hospital or call for help. It's going to happen. She's going to give birth. We need help.

I lean down and kiss Victoria on her cheek while clutching her hand.

'I'm going to find help. We're going to get an ambulance.'

She doesn't respond.

'Victoria? I'm going to leave you, OK? But I'll be back.'

She snaps.

'I can't do this on my own. See if you can find someone quickly, someone with a phone, but come back if . . . It's . . .'

And with another contraction, she howls – a deep, guttural yell that sounds too deep to have come from her.

I grab my coat and trainers from the room upstairs and run back down, through the kitchen and into the living room – my version of running, anyway, which is more of a determined trundle. I try every drawer and cupboard, desperate to find a key. There's an antique chest in the living room, but every drawer is locked. I pull so hard on the wide one at my feet that I lose my balance and stumble back, just catching myself before falling.

I walk to the other side of the room, sweeping my hands across the bookshelves, poking my fingers in between volumes of Tolstoy, as if in the middle of a fantasy film, where the right movement of the right book might magically open a secret passage, a way out. I see the large sash window looking out onto the driveway. Could I smash it and climb out? Other men would just go for it. They'd clench their fist, break the window with one punch, climb out and go and save their wife. But I've never broken any glass in my life.

I close my eyes, screw them tight and a surge of adrenaline gives me resolve. I clench my right fist and lunge forwards as fast as I can. Nothing. The glass feels cold against my knuckles, but it doesn't break. I look around the room for something that might make it smash and see a fire extinguisher tucked behind the door. Could I actually do that? I close my eyes, grit my teeth, lift the extinguisher and throw it at the window.

The noise of the glass shattering is apocalyptic, unbearable, and I put my stronger hand to my face to shield myself from the fallout. The glass shatters into a shower of pebbles, and I cower as I feel some land on my neck and down my T-shirt. I can hear Victoria shouting from the kitchen, but I'm on a mission now.

I lift the fire extinguisher again and use it to scrape away the fragments that are stuck to the edge of the windowsill. I put the extinguisher down and drag over a chair, hoisting myself up. I close my eyes, grind my teeth and clamber out, surprised by my own agility as I manage to lift my left leg over and then manoeuvre my right through, as well, sitting on the sill before edging myself down. I let out a yelp as I land on my left ankle, which is warm and tight as I walk on it. If I'm not careful, I'm going to tear my Achilles tendon and then I'll be totally out of action.

I shuffle forwards, blasting through the soreness in my ankle. I turn back as I edge further and further away from Choristers' Lodge and see a single light on, coming from the kitchen, where my wife is stranded, abandoned, on the verge of giving birth to the son who we've fought so hard for, who we've craved for so many years.

It's a bitter morning, the wind cutting me right across the face – an icy piercing in the temples that stings as I cross the gravel. I'm walking with my left heel right up, even more than I usually do, and feel like the world's most graceless ballerina.

Looking left and right, I squint into the distance, searching for a building, a shed, a car, something that might indicate human life. There are just fields and fields, hills up, hills down, stone walls, pebbled paths, a few small forests of conifer trees and, at the top of the furthest peak in the distance, a couple of wide patches of snow. A whip of wind hits me on both cheeks and I smell grass, wood and mud. I pull the lapels of my coat tight together to keep my chest warm. I was so exhausted when we arrived last night, and the roads and paths so poorly lit, that this is the first time I'm seeing just how isolated we really are. Not anywhere is there a single house, pub, parked car – not even a sheep to indicate that I might stumble upon a farm and therefore a farmer, and thus a phone, a means to call for help.

I limp up the uneven grassy path from the guest house, feeling my trainers stick and then release from the mud, and then carefully walk over the metal bars of a cattle grid underfoot. I decide to go left – we drove from this way and I'm sure I saw some houses on the road a few miles before we reached the guest house – sticking to the right-hand side of the road, so I can spot any cars coming towards me as I head downhill.

I exhale slowly and deeply, trying to quieten the chatter in my mind, quickening my pace, walking unevenly as I head down the hill. I watch my feet carefully, trying to focus on each step as I go. Usually if I were on a walk like this, with the ground uneven and unpredictable, I'd link arms with Victoria and that would give me some support should I tumble. And despite deep concentration, a real effort to watch my step, I'm barely a few hundred yards down the hill before I trip and stub my foot on a large pebble, toppling forwards and stomping around in an effort to regain balance. If I fall down and seriously injure myself, then what? What if I break my leg out here alone? I'll be out here, she'll be inside – it doesn't bear thinking about.

At the bottom of the hill, I stop for a moment, tighten my coat again and look down at my legs. With my jeans clinging tight to them in the wind, the discrepancy between the size of my left and right leg is noticeable. I can't help but feel, for an instant, self-conscious, let down by my body. I imagine bumping into someone I know, an old friend from university, one of those horrible investors, who would look me up and down in indignation and bemusement.

'You? Jamie? Hiking in the Pennines? There's something I never thought I'd see.'

My mind goes back to Victoria. What's she doing now? Is she screaming through another contraction? Is she praying for me to come back?

I take a deep breath and start the ascent up the next incline with a new resolve. I suppose it helps, in a way, that I'm unfit. The effort of the climb is enough to distract me, my heavy breathing now focused on pumping oxygen around my body to overcome the physical challenge rather than panic. Sweat trickles down both of my temples and I can feel a rawness on both sides of my groin as my thighs rub together.

When I reach the top of the next hill, I spot a cluster of buildings in the distance and this gives me the impetus to keep going. Both of my legs are tired now, the front of my left foot scraping across the road with every step. I think of Victoria, in this moment so in need of my support, and I allow myself to imagine being the hero for once.

I edge closer and closer to the buildings, but they look like they've been abandoned, old farm buildings no longer in use. I knock frantically on the door of each building, but the only response is the whistle of wind as it seeps through broken panels of wood. I return to the road and perch on the edge of a stone wall, my body dripping with sweat, my chest tight and my legs so tired now that they feel detached from the rest of my body.

I look at my wrist: just after 9.30 a.m. How long has Victoria been on her own now? It must be at least an hour, maybe more. How long has she been in labour? Maybe two hours . . . three? How much further can I go before I've gone too far?

I spot a set of green railings just above me, at the top of the next incline, and I push myself there and perch on them for a moment. My hips and my lower back are starting to ache, and I feel immediate relief as I rest my legs. The mist has cleared now and in the near distance I can see the guest house, the sun gleaming off the beige stone walls, our little silver car sitting quietly outside. I squint to see if I can spot the broken window of the living room and it occurs to me that Victoria must be feeling a chill through to the kitchen.

I'm about to get back on my feet and carry on walking, when I hear it – the hum of an engine – getting louder. I jump down and look right. It's a red van, coming up the hill towards me and in the direction of the guest house. I step into the road and flap and shout to get the attention of the driver. My voice echoes in the hills: 'Stop-stop-stop-stop!'

The van begins to slow as it approaches me. Its growl fills the peak of the hill as it veers to the right and I step back to allow it to stop. I can see Barry in the driver's seat window. He looks at me and smiles, his moustache creasing in on itself. But the wheels don't stop and the engine revs louder as he carries on, away from me, the smoke from the exhaust warming my hands before melting into the air.

I run after the van, screaming and waving, but either he didn't recognise me or he's choosing to leave me here, stranded. In the distance I see the guest house, the tawny hue of its concrete standing in stark, lonely contrast to the perfect blues and whites of the sky. The hill down towards the guest house is steep and I don't want to trip, so I stop and bend to gather my breath and rub my aching hips. I look down to the guest house and even though the van hasn't got back there yet, I now see that there are two lights on – one downstairs in the kitchen, where I left Victoria, and one from an upstairs bedroom.

I'm sure only the downstairs light was on before. Has Victoria gone up to the bedroom? Is she getting ready to push? Or is that Fiona? Has Fiona been there the whole time? What is going on in there? Why was Barry out driving? Why didn't he stop for me? I need to get back, and quickly. Victoria needs me.

Chapter 8

Victoria

Wednesday, 7 April

Mum is running late and while I wait for her to arrive, I flick through messages on my phone. It's only natural that people have tried to get in touch. Word spreads fast, particularly when something tragic happens, but I've managed to avoid contact with most people. Before all of this, I never went anywhere without a phone charger. It felt like a major component of my day, spotting charging points and an opportunity to give my phone a bit more juice. But I've deliberately been lax in charging it since we got back from Cumbria, knowing that if it remained switched off, I wouldn't have to see the messages and then feel bad about ignoring them.

But losing a baby, whatever the circumstances, isn't the kind of news you can keep from your mother. And, for all of her faults, and despite her usual emotional unavailability, she was very supportive during the pregnancy, if only with practical things like helping me with the shopping when Jamie was on a business trip and I was feeling too sick to get out of bed. I'm an only child and when we told her that I was finally pregnant, the look of sheer elation in her eyes at the prospect of becoming a grandmother was one that I'll never forget. Against all the odds, she taught herself how to knit watching YouTube videos, specifically so that she could make a little hat and scarf for Danny's arrival.

We had to tell my mother that Danny hadn't survived without her being able to see the lies. I'm sure a lot of women would call their mothers immediately after losing a baby, if they didn't already have them by their bedside. But it was very different circumstances for us, and Jamie and I had to have a consistent story, a narrative that people wouldn't question.

'What are we going to tell people?' I asked as we hit the motorway.

Jamie was driving and I was next to him, dosed up on paracetamol. We'd stopped at a supermarket to buy a hot-water bottle and I was sat there, pressing it against me, willing for it to be hotter and hotter so I wouldn't feel anything at all.

'Just as few details as possible,' he said, not taking his eye off the road. 'People won't expect a blow-by-blow account. You went into labour early while we were away for the weekend, it all happened quickly, we didn't get to a hospital in time. Danny didn't make it.'

The words stung. He didn't make it.

'Can you call my mum for me, Jamie?' I asked, placing my hand on his. 'I can't do it. I can't lie to her about this.'

He turned to me, looked behind him and then pulled up on the hard shoulder. Cars whizzed past as he put the hazard lights on and picked up his phone.

'Straight to voicemail,' he said. 'I'll leave a message.'

I put my fingers in my ears to muffle the words.

'Hi, Glynis, it's Jamie. I'm afraid we've got some horrific news. There's no easy way to tell you, so I'm just going to go for it. We lost the baby. I don't know if Victoria mentioned that we were going away for a few days, but yeah. We were in a guest house and she went into labour a bit early and we just couldn't get to a hospital in time.

'We're still coming to terms with everything and not really in a state to talk so much about it, but obviously wanted you to be the first to know. And physically, Victoria is doing just fine. We can be thankful for that. So yeah, um, call us back when you get this.'

She called back moments later and because Jamie was driving, I had to speak to her. I broke down. I didn't give anything away. We've spoken since, but I've kept the phone calls brief, managed, and she seems to have respected my desire to veer away from the issue. Our family has a knack for brushing things under the carpet and in this case, I'm grateful for that.

A meal with my mother is a struggle at the best of times. She's an actress, or rather a former actress, although she'd never admit that. Her biggest claim to fame dates back to her time as a reasonably successful child actor: she was cast as the first-ever female Pip in a BBC radio adaptation of *Great Expectations* and has been dining out on it ever since.

When I was a child, she used to get me to stand up in front of the guests at her dinner parties and recite a passage from the beginning of the book, reliving the whole experience vicariously through me. There would be some uncomfortable polite applause, led by Dad, who would then quietly apologise to me for the embarrassment and tuck me into bed. Now, she gets the odd job here and there – her most recent triumph being a non-speaking part in a life insurance advert for TV – and she spends every Saturday morning in the local village hall, teaching other people's children how to act.

We're meeting at an Italian restaurant near her house in Buckinghamshire. It's the first time we'll have seen each other in a few weeks. The last time was after my final midwife appointment, when she made a remark about how I wasn't showing much for being so far along. I'm dreading the intimacy. Our relationship has always functioned best at a distance: we speak occasionally on the phone and things are civil, sometimes even fun. But when we meet up in person, she continually oversteps the mark, making a comment about my hair, or a snide remark about my dress being too short. And then I snap at her, tell her to stop treating me like a teenager, and she cries. Then we have to make up and pretend everything is all right before we go our separate ways. It's hard to stay angry at Mum, though. She can't help who she's become, after everything she's been through. When we lost Dad, she was just forty-two.

She always manages to cause a commotion of some sort when entering a room, and I hear her from the other side of the room before I see her. Her voice is too posh – the result of years of trying to shed any trace of her regional roots – and sometimes it comes across as farcical, as if she's doing an impression of the person she wants to be.

'The name's Radcliffe. Glynis Radcliffe. I specifically booked a table by the window. You'll just have to ask that young couple to move. Or I can, if you'd prefer?'

In swans my mother. What she lacks in height she more than makes up for in volume. She's a slight woman, having not eaten carbs since she was about sixteen, but her face maintains a roundness that somewhat shields her advanced years. As always, she's got a full face of make-up on – bold eyes and bold lips – and so much product in her short dyed blonde hair that it's as stiff as a bird's nest.

She's got a thing about sitting by the window, based on the assumption that it keeps you front of mind for the staff, so you don't have to wait around to get their attention. I leave my things on the table and go to the maître d's rescue.

'Hi, Mum, no need to make a fuss. Come on, we've got a nice table at the back.'

And she gasps as she sees me, clearly noticing that quite a bit of the bump is still there. Placing one hand over her mouth, she pulls me towards her with the other while cradling her blue calfskin Valentino handbag close to her side with her elbow. We don't usually touch and the smell of her perfume coats the roof of my mouth in a sickly-sweet film. It's overwhelming, as if she's bathed in rose water to cover up her own carnal smells. She stands back and looks me up and down.

'Oh, darling, you look so tired and puffy.'

She grabs my arm as we walk across the restaurant, linking arms, like we're two girlfriends going for a spot of afternoon tea. I can feel her trembling and see her bottom lip quiver.

'Do you mind if I sit facing outwards, dear? I like to be able to see the room.'

'Yeah, I know, Mum, that's fine.'

She takes off her faux fur coat, glamorous but far too thick for the bright spring morning, and imperiously passes it to the maitre d', who drapes it over his arm. She's wearing a short floral dress, over the top for the occasion, and slightly too loose at her freckly bust. She glances around the room, as if looking to find someone she recognises.

'I was here just last week, actually. With Emily's mother. Do you still see Emily?'

Emily is an old friend from school. We haven't seen each other since the nineties.

'No, not really, Mum. We've lost touch.'

'Oh, that's a shame, isn't it? You should give her a call. Nice to have good people around you at moments like this.'

Here we go.

'I think I'll probably just order the caprese salad,' she says, glancing at the menu. 'Although I really should cut down on the cheese. I wish they'd come and take our order.'

'We've only just sat down, Mum. I'm going to have some pasta, I think.'

She goes to open her mouth but stops herself, looking me up and down.

'Well, I'm sure you'll get your figure back in no time.'

I bite my top lip.

'Darling, I'm absolutely devastated. Beside myself. What a terrible thing to have happened. And after you worked so hard to get pregnant in the first place.'

Her eyes are gleaming, her voice breaking like a prepubescent boy.

'Do you mind if we talk about something else? I'm just . . . not here, OK? I can't.'

Mum takes a handkerchief out of her purse, wiping her nose.

'Whatever you want, darling. I'm here for you.'

I needed that.

'How's Lionel?' I ask.

Lionel is the man she's been seeing for the last year. He's the latest in a string of lovers that she's taken since my dad died when I was a teenager. They never stick around for long. Lionel seems slightly more suitable than the last one, who was twenty years younger than her and training to be a cleric, which is absolutely not my mother's scene.

She rolls her eyes.

'Oh, he's OK. I'm just finding him a bit *boring*, if you know what I mean. And that's nothing to do with his diabetes – he can't help that, of course.'

A chirpy waiter comes over to take our order.

'Oh, hello, madam. Nice to see you again. This must be your sister – I can see the resemblance.'

Oh, stop it.

Mum beams. 'Well, you've just earned yourself a hefty tip. I'll have the caprese salad, please.'

'Dressing on the side?'

'Well, done, that's it.'

The waiter turns to me.

'And what about you, madam?'

'I'll have the penne arrabbiata, please, but without the—'

Mum interrupts. 'Are you sure you don't want the salad also, darling? It's delicious.'

'No, I'll have the pasta, please.'

The waiter scribbles it down and then places the pen in his mouth.

'Oh, don't do that, dear,' my mother scolds. 'You'll end up chipping a tooth.'

I take myself to the bathroom.

When the food arrives, we both dig in immediately. I haven't eaten since lunchtime yesterday and stuff the pasta down so quickly that the kick of the chilli goes right up my nose. Mum eats all of the tomato and cuts the cheese up into little pieces, taking the odd bite before putting her cutlery down and pushing the plate away.

'How are Jamie's parents doing? What's the weather like all the way down there at this time of year?'

Jamie's mum and dad moved to Cape Town just over a year ago to look after his nana, who has been diagnosed with colon cancer. They've always been a real presence in Jamie's life, and therefore in our marriage, and it's been a relief to have them at a distance.

'Yeah, they're doing well, I think. Nana Rawlinson is pretty stable now, as far as we know. It's just a case of keeping her comfortable.'

Mum's doing her best to look like she cares, an earnest little frown creasing her brow.

'Ah, bless her, the dear old thing. Well, I suppose she's had a good innings, hasn't she?'

Mum signals for the waiter to come over, an imperial pinch of the fingers.

'Yes, Madam? Perhaps you'd like to order dessert.'

The waiter waves a menu in her direction, but she brushes it away.

'We'll share the fruit salad, please. Two forks.'

I hate fruit salad. It's the juice at the bottom. Mum purses her lips, leans towards me and lowers her voice.

'Now, darling, we can't just pretend nothing has happened. I know you said you didn't want to talk about it, but I must admit, I've been feeling terribly down about everything myself and really want to be there for you as well. How are you getting on?'

That's the most exposing thing I think she's ever said to me and I feel a warmth in my belly.

'Thanks, Mum. I'm doing OK. Each day it gets a bit easier, you know?'

I can see her welling up, her eyes sparkling. I brace myself to tell the rehearsed story, the story we've concocted through internet research to recite if pressed.

'Did they say why . . . what might have caused it?'

'We didn't really go into it in detail, but they think it might have had something to do with the placenta separating itself from the baby.'

'Oh, gosh, how horrible. And when he was born . . . did they try to resuscitate? I mean, my friend Gloria's grandson was very ill when he was born. It was touch and go, but they took him into ICU and—'

'Mum, they did everything they could, I promise.'

She picks the napkin from her lap and covers her face with it, whimpering.

'Oh, and after everything that happened when you were

little. You've always been so *unlucky*, my darling. What about a funeral?'

'We did something small while we were up there. It was very dignified – the hospital dealt with it really well.'

'I suppose the hospital wasn't fully equipped, was it? Medically, I mean. Where did you say you were in the country, up north? Perhaps if you'd stayed in London and it had happened at UCH or the Royal Free, they'd have . . . Who was the doctor in charge? Was it a consultant?'

I need to get away from the table. I can feel the anger bubbling up to my temples, my eyes beginning to salt, and if I don't take myself away from her, I'm going to shout, I'm going to blurt it out.

'Sorry, Mum, I need to . . .'

I go back to the toilets and lock the door to a cubicle, pull down my maternity briefs and sit with my head between my legs, letting my tears flow freely now, rocking back and forth. A chain flushes next to me and I hear a light tapping on my door.

'Are you OK? Anything I can do to help?'

'I'm OK. I'm fine, thanks. Just . . . time of the month.'

I look down and see a small packet of tissues being slid under the cubicle door.

'Thanks, I really appreciate it.'

When I return to the table, Mum stands up as I approach. She's reapplied lipstick and is all red round the nose.

'Sometimes it helps to have a little cry, doesn't it? Let it all out.'

'Sorry, Mum,' I say, sitting and pulling the chair forwards under the table. 'I'm just tired at the moment, you know.'

'Why don't you think about doing some kind of service? A memorial service. We can do something at my house. It doesn't need to be too big or fancy. It might help to give closure. I'll pay.'

'Mum, you know we're private people. We're not going to do that.'

She rolls her eyes and continues.

'Did you get to hold the baby? Before he . . . before they took him away?'

She needs to stop.

'Yes, Mum. Look, I really don't—'

She puts a hand to her mouth.

'And did they . . . did you keep the wristband? When something similar happened to my hairdresser's grandson, the parents got a little frame with footprints and handprints. Didn't they offer that?'

I feel sick and a pang in my chest. What would happen if I just blurted out the truth? I don't know if I can control myself. She's my mother – how can I lie about something this big?

'No Mum, they didn't.'

She continues.

'How's Jamie doing? He must be finding it very hard, too. It's nothing to do with his disability, is it, what happened?'

And that's the final straw. She always gets it slightly wrong with Jamie and is so heavy-handed when talking about his cerebral palsy. When we first got together, she asked if he shouldn't be with someone more 'like himself' and whenever he came to her house, she'd mention how she found it remarkable that he seemed so intelligent 'despite everything'.

There's nothing hereditary about his condition and even if there were, it wouldn't be her place to speculate.

'Mum, I'm going,' I say, pushing myself up and out of my chair.

She's silent, with her elbows on the table and her hands covering her mouth. I carry on talking as I walk away from her.

'I'll pay the bill on the way out. Please, just . . . give me a bit of space.'

Chapter 9

Victoria

Saturday, 6 March, 9.31 a.m.

What was that noise? As each contraction stops and I emerge from inside myself, I remember that I'm alone in this house, and an invisible noose around my windpipe knots and yanks tight. I don't believe in ghosts, or in anything supernatural, but I do sense if a place has a bad vibe. It's as if there's a negative energy that lingers, that something horrific has happened here that's not been shaken off fully.

The contractions are still a few minutes apart and I'm willing them not to come faster. They've become more intense, twisting the sides of my belly and ripping deep trenches of agony inside me. I try to focus on counting my breaths but can't reach four without screaming.

I haven't been particularly anxious about the birth. In fact, in comparison to some of the other women at our antenatal class, I must have seemed nonchalant. One woman was so horrified when she saw the length of the needle used for an epidural that she placed a hand to her mouth and went running off to the toilets to be sick. Another referred to the day she'd go into labour as doomsday and kept asking the course leader what would qualify her for an elective caesarean. She looked so terrified about the whole thing that I wanted to give her a hug, tell her that everything was going to be OK, because her vacant husband didn't seem to be stepping up to the plate.

I can't pretend that it's not happening any more. Where the hell is Jamie? It must have been longer than an hour now. What's taking him so long? What happens if the baby comes all of a sudden and I'm here, alone, with no one to help me? I'll die here, I know it. I can't do this, I'm going to die.

A door slams and I jolt forwards. What was that? Has Jamie managed to pick a lock and make his way back in? I can hear footsteps overhead, a light, quick patter.

'Jamie? Is that you?' I shout with all of my strength into the empty kitchen. My voice trails off and I whisper, 'I need you. Please.'

But it's not Jamie. Through the kitchen door I see Fiona at the bottom of the stairs. She is dressed in some kind of medical uniform. I feel a chill down both arms. The blue of the dress has faded to a light grey, and while you can tell that it might have once fitted her, Fiona is now so emaciated, so long and thin, that the fabric falls off her at the arms.

'Hello, dear. I trust the contractions are coming along nicely. I heard you howling! I think you must be in established labour already but I will check to be sure.'

'Where have you been?' I shout. 'The baby's coming. I don't know what to do. I feel like I need to start pushing.'

'You're in safe hands with me, and try not to panic,' she says, turning to look back at me over her shoulder while dousing and wringing the towels.

'You can't be fully dilated already. And even if you are, this won't be the first time I've had to help deliver a baby in a hurry.'

Fiona walks into the living room and her hands rise to her face as she looks around.

'Heaven Almighty, what's happened here? There's glass everywhere. What *have* you done to the cabinet? We'll have to charge you for that, I'm afraid.'

I watch as Fiona pushes back past me in the kitchen, finds a black bag and a dustpan and brush. Out of the kitchen window above the sink I then see the red van parking alongside our car. Barry steps out, his khaki trousers and a black T-shirt flapping in the wind, and then walks to the front door. I hear it unlock and his steps as he walks inside.

'Please help me,' I yell after him, grabbing my belly as I feel the next contraction emerging. 'I need help, I need proper help. I can't do it like this – you need to drive me to a hospital.'

I breathe out fast and shut my eyes and clamp my teeth, tensing my cheeks as tight as I can to contain the fire scalding inside me. My body contorts and twists into itself. I feel like glass is slipping down me, tearing into both sides of my stomach. I can't breathe but hear myself howl so I must be alive. Somewhere around me I can sense Barry heading towards the front door, holding a black bag. The glass inside jingles. He does not stop to acknowledge me in any way. He takes a key out of his jacket and leaves again. Fiona turns to me.

'You can go and lie down upstairs, in our room. Everything is ready for you.'

The contraction begins to subside and I beg.

'Please – can you just drive me to a hospital?'

And then, all of a sudden, Fiona's face turns from ivory to crimson, her lips tight, her nose flared and chin protruding.

'You'll do as you're told, young lady. We'll be delivering the baby here, in the guest house. If you know what's right for you, you'll head up to the bedroom right now, lie on the bed, and wait for us to come up to you.'

I roll to my knees and push myself up, gripping the kitchen table for support. I walk across the hallway, willing the tears to stop streaming down my face, and lean on the banister with my forearms as I climb the stairs. I push into their bedroom and my body aches as I fall forward onto the bed, on all fours. I feel the scratch of old knit on my face, lift my body and see that towels and blankets have been laid out on top of the sheets. And then, on the bedside table, a glimmer from a pair of scissors and at the foot of the bed a large red bucket filled with soapy water and draped with flannels. I'm in a makeshift labour ward.

Chapter 10

Jamie

Saturday, 10 April

I'm woken by a phone notification. A text message from Victoria.

> Morning, J.
> Have had a terrible night again — I don't know how much longer
> I can go on with so little sleep. I know we said I'd come back
> at some point today, but I still don't feel up to it. Still feeling
> like I need my own space to get everything straight in my head.
> Please don't worry about the letter. I think we both know who
> sent it. I'll call you, OK? Hope work isn't too painful.
> Love you,
> x

I toss my phone on the wooden floor and hear it land. I hate it when she does this, when we regress to communication through text message like two teenagers in a petty tiff. Couldn't she have called me to talk this through? I dial her number, but it rings and rings. I dial again, wait until the voicemail starts and then hang up. Is she screening my calls? Why won't she talk to me? There's no point in just dodging everything – we need to work through it. We need to share the trauma and work out how we're going to move forwards and rebuild our life together.

It was only meant to be a few days apart. Victoria was the one to suggest it, saying that she needed a bit of space to think things through, to process what was happening, to get her head straight. And the truth is, we've been on two different cycles of grief. Perhaps it's easy to assume that the pain would be constant. But I've found that some days are harder than others, and often when I'm having a better day, Victoria is at her worst. I only took a couple of weeks off work, partly because there were a few meetings I knew I couldn't miss, but also because I decided that it was good to keep busy, to keep my mind occupied, rather than moping around the flat thinking about what had happened to us.

In the office, for a few hours at least, I could divert my attention to very specific tasks and take my mind off the horrific circumstances. But then I'd get home and find Victoria still in bed, surrounded by dirty plates and empty food packets, and I'd be straight back into the pits of despair. Victoria seemed to find it easier at the weekend, manically emerging from her daze and announcing that she wanted to go out, to walk around Hampstead Heath or go to see a film at the cinema. But she'd end up going on her own, because I couldn't face the possibility of bumping into other children, other families on a Saturday cheerfully going about their weekend routine. Or even worse, seeing someone we know, having to tell the lies and then nod along as they offer their condolences.

And so we've started spending less and less time together, drifting further and further away from each other. When Victoria mentioned that she needed some space and was going to stay in the studio for a bit, it seemed like a sensible suggestion. We've done this before, when we've got into a bit of a rut. It's good for us to spend time apart sometimes.

When the buzzer goes, I'm still in bed, in just boxer shorts. Is that Victoria? Has she changed her mind and come over? But why would she be ringing the buzzer? I go over to the intercom phone, my voice cracking, the first time I've used it today.

'Hello?'

'Delivery for Mr Rawlinson.'

I'm not expecting anything.

'OK, thanks. I'm coming down.'

I grab the first dressing gown on the back of the bedroom door and fling it on. I go out into the corridor that we share with the other flats in the house to open the door to the delivery man.

He looks a bit startled to see me and when I look down, I realise I'm wearing one of Victoria's dressing gowns – pale green and frilly at the edges. I fold my arms and force a smile.

'Got quite a few boxes for you, Mr Rawlinson. Someone's been on a spending spree.'

The delivery man steps aside to reveal a stack of boxes. What is all this stuff?

'Do you mind helping me to take the boxes into the flat?' I ask, struggling to look him in the eye. 'I've got a disability, so find it hard to carry stuff that's too heavy.'

I'm pointing to my leg, just in case he needs proof. Usually, Victoria would have joined me by now, to help me carry them in.

'Of course, mate. Happy to help.'

I take the top box, smaller than the others, and hold it in my right arm as I walk towards our front door. He follows me and as we're going inside, I notice the airmail sticker on the box, together with the company name, and feel a tightening at the base of my stomach. By the time we've walked the length of the flat and are inside the living room, I can feel my breath catching.

'I'll just go back and get the last couple for you,' he says, turning round quickly and galloping away.

I call after him.

'Actually, do you know what? I don't want them. I need to return all this stuff.'

He stops by the front door and turns to me.

'What do you mean? I'm just the delivery driver, mate.'

I need him to get rid of this stuff.

'I know, I'm sorry. It's just . . .' I say, walking towards him, my arms out and my palms facing out towards him. 'Can't you return to sender? Or just . . . take them to a dump? I don't care about the money, I just . . .'

He laughs and walks out of the open front door, picking up the last couple of boxes in the hallway.

'I'm sorry, my friend,' he shouts. 'I don't mind helping to get the boxes into your flat, but I'm not customer services.'

He walks back to me and dumps the boxes at my feet, offering a tense fake smile. I can hear him mumbling as he turns and leaves the flat.

'Take them to a dump . . .'

I shut the door behind him, walk back to the living room and open the smallest box first. It's a packet of five babygrows from a company called Magnetic Mummies. One of the things I worried about most, when preparing for Danny to arrive, was how fiddly some of the baby clothes might be. Just a few days before we went up to the Pennines, on a forum for parents with cerebral palsy, I saw a recommendation for an American shop that sells baby clothes that clip open and shut with magnets. I spent close to two hundred pounds and then to compensate for that, I selected the cheapest delivery option, knowing at the time that it would take weeks for it all to arrive.

I know I should just give them away or send them back over the Atlantic, but I don't. I open each individually wrapped one, smiling at the hippos and elephants, the strawberries and the apples, putting each one to my face and feeling the cotton on my cheeks.

With all the boxes opened, I take the clothes, in piles, into the nursery and stand by the changing table, folding each of them. It's not the easiest task for me. With the full use of only one hand, I struggle to do it neatly unless I concentrate, hard, folding as tightly as I can and then rolling them into baguettes. As I do this, I notice a photo of Victoria and me, fixed onto the wall opposite. The first photo of us together, on that sticky dance floor in Islington.

I suppose the story of how we met isn't the most conventional or the most romantic. It was actually through my best friend, Andy. Victoria and Andy were together first. They met online, had a few drunken dates. But it was never anything serious. She was just one in a string of conquests for Andy. He said he found her too intense. It was the eyes, he said.

When she came with him to my twenty-third birthday party, I couldn't believe how beautiful she was. Her eyes were like emeralds, slightly wider apart than most people, and her eyelids swelled as she listened to conversation. She was shorter than me, curvy with wavy auburn hair. And when we talked, her voice felt familiar, warm and homely.

Throughout the night, we kept catching each other's glance across the room and when we finally got to talk, I found myself doing impressions of each of the Spice Girls, one by one, and she was somehow finding them funny. Impressions are my default if I'm nervous and want to win someone over. In a way, it's linked to my disability. My parents say that, as a baby, I walked late but made up for it by talking unusually early. By two I was speaking very fluently in full sentences. I hear an accent or a particularly idiosyncratic turn of phrase, and it sticks. Mel B comes very naturally.

When Victoria left, the hug was a lingering one. She and Andy parted ways not long after that, but I still thought about her.

A year or so later, Andy and I were out at a nightclub and Victoria was there, too, on the dance floor in front of us. Andy had been going through a 'dry spell' and convinced me, his most faithful wingman, to join him on the pull. She was there with some friends, whispering to them, and then they all looked up at me at the same time. She must have seen me already. They were talking about me. I approached her with Andy's blessing.

'Oh, go for it, J,' he said, taking a swig of beer. 'I knew you liked her. She's a nice girl.'

I brushed aside my inhibitions and walked towards them. It didn't matter that I wasn't the greatest dancer. We tried to talk above the cheesy nineties pop music and she touched my side. And then I kissed her. It felt immediately comfortable, like it was always meant to be. Like everything over the last year had happened in the right sequence and for the right reasons to bring us together in this sweaty, vodka-fuelled fumble.

We became, almost instantly, inseparable. After swapping numbers on the way out of the club, we texted throughout the next day and then arranged to meet for dinner that evening. I'm five foot eight and have narrow shoulders, so I liked that I felt tall and big around her. With her waves and my tight dark curls, we seemed to match naturally.

We drank, lots, and I have no idea what we talked about, but I remember laughter. I walked behind her when we left the tapas bar so she wouldn't notice my limp and we got in a cab together to her flat. At the time, Victoria was living in a studio in Deptford that her dad's grandfather had bought decades previously and that had turned into a family heirloom, gradually accruing in value as prices in and around Central London became more and more astronomical.

That evening we went straight to bed, but we didn't have full sex. We kissed and explored each other's bodies. We hugged each other tightly and I brought her close, smelling her neck, breathing her in. It was the most sensual night of my life.

We went on another date two days later, to the cinema, and kissed in our seats in the back row like teenagers.

My phone buzzes again. I'm in the middle of folding a black-and-white baby vest, decorated with little panda faces, my left arm holding it in place while my right folds one arm in and then the next. What the hell am I doing? We can't keep all this stuff. Why am I standing here, folding clothes that will never be worn?

I want them to disappear. I can hear myself crying, my cheeks tight and wet.

I grab the folded vests and babygrows and chuck them in fists into a crumpled pile on the floor by my feet. I take my phone out of my pocket, but it's just a text message from UNICEF confirming my regular donation. Nothing from Victoria.

The photo on my home screen is of Victoria, glowing, looking at the reflection of her bump in the bedroom mirror. I stare at it, my eyes glistening as I consider the miracle of the human body, the unlikelihood of it all. Could we ever go through it again?

I try calling Victoria again and her phone rings seven times before the voicemail message kicks in.

'Hey, this is Victoria, I'm not here right now. Please leave me a message. Bye.'

I hate leaving voicemails. It feels old-fashioned and impersonal.

'Hey, sweetheart, it's me. Got your text. Please can you call me back so we can talk things through properly. I totally get where you're coming from, but I could really do with hearing your voice right now.

'We just got a huge delivery of clothes for Danny. Please ring me back. We can't just bury our heads in the sand. Andy and Lauren keep on calling, asking us round for dinner – apparently, you bumped into her in town and were a bit weird? They only mean well.

'I think we have to get back to some level of normality sooner or later. Don't want to raise suspicions. Ugh, I shouldn't be saying this on here. Sorry, I'm rambling. Just call me back, OK?'

Lying to Andy about what happened to Danny is one of the hardest things I've ever had to do. He's the first person I met at our little village primary school in Hertfordshire. We were assigned coat hooks next to each other and he helped me to get mine up on the first day when I was struggling because of my balance. He's one of the few people who really understands my disability, intuitively knowing when I need help getting down steep stairs and when to slow his walking so I can keep up.

I've sorted out jobs for him a couple of times – he worked for KnowScam for a few months, helping us with our first major advertising campaign, and then I hooked him up with a friend of mine who has a money exchange start-up and needed a marketing manager. It's a bit awkward, actually, because they let him go recently. I'm not sure he's quite cut out for the pace of tech.

I told Andy that we'd lost Danny before I'd even spoken to my parents. I lay awake in bed, the night after we got home, and I sent him a text message. I couldn't call him or anyone. By text message, I felt like I could be more in control – less at the whim of unpredictable questioning that might force me to crack. I've never been able to keep things from Andy – he knows me so well that he often realises things about me before I've even come to terms with them myself.

I told him that the baby had come three weeks early, that

Victoria had gone into labour while we were in the guest house and that we hadn't been able to get to the hospital in time. I told him that the baby was stillborn. That the moment he came out, we knew that he wasn't going to make it. I told him that Victoria bled – she bled so much that it was touch and go for her, too. And that while we're mourning the loss of Danny, I'm just unbelievably thankful that I didn't lose Victoria, as well.

Of course, he rang me as soon as he read the text and I burst into tears when I heard his voice. He told me that he was there for me, always, and that he knew there was nothing he could say to make it better.

I've been happy to speak on the phone to him and to have text conversations since then, but he's been trying to get us to see him and Lauren in person and I've been dodging his invitations. He sent me another one last night.

ANDY: Jamie, when are you guys coming round for dinner?
ME: We will soon, I promise.
ANDY: Is it our cooking?
ME: Ha! No, don't be silly.
ANDY: Look, mate. I think it'll do both you and Victoria some good to get out of the house for a bit. I know what you're like – you can get yourself in a rut when you're alone. We don't have to talk about it, you know. Whatever you want. We just want to be there for you, buddy. How about Friday night?

And I didn't reply to that one for a good few hours, because I was annoyed by the 'get yourself in a rut' comment. But then I know that Andy only means well and that he has a tendency to get it a bit wrong from time to time.

ME: Let me chat to Victoria. It'll be nice to see you both. Friday night works, I think. Will get back to you. x

Andy and Lauren met a few years after Victoria and I got together, but they got married before us. Victoria and I are godparents to their daughter, Isla. She's a gorgeous kid, with a real zest about her – a cheeky little look in her eye that tells you when she's about to empty a box of toys onto the floor or chuck an apple at you. She's obsessed with the word 'hot' but doesn't quite understand it, so she'll waddle around and pick up an ice lolly and say 'hot', or hit her head with a rattle and say 'hot'.

I love spending time with her and have missed all three of them over the last few weeks, but I know Victoria will freak out and clam up around them. If we arrive late enough on Friday, Isla will be in bed.

I text Victoria.

Hey, I've said yes to dinner at Andy and Lauren's on Friday night. Just us four. Let's put on a brave face. Hope that works for you. x

I throw my phone on the sofa in the living room, remove the dressing gown and boxer shorts, and get into the shower for the first time in days. It's time to take control of our situation. Move on with our lives and start adjusting to a new reality. There are plenty of marriages that crumble after the loss of a child, but our situation is different – more complex and precarious – and if we don't stick together, we'll have no chance of survival. There's no turning back now. Our secrets keep us bound together.

I spend most of the evening going in and out of the flat

with plastic bags full of vests and babygrows, tiny socks, little knitted cardigans, watching them on their final journey into the depths of the big grey bin on the driveway of our building. At another time, I'd be horrified at the waste. In another scenario, these clothes would be going to charity shops, for babies and parents not as fortunate as us. But tonight, I'm allowing myself to be selfish. There's something cathartic about this digression. It feels good.

As I head inside for the final time, my legs feel as though they're about to give way. I pick up a couple of letters for us that are sitting on the table in the shared hallway. I'm so dazed that I manage to tear the contents of the first one as I open the envelope. It's a circular from the local MP, appealing for support ahead of an upcoming election. The second one is big and brown, like last time. And I recognise the handwriting – the same thick navy curls – addressed to Victoria and me.

I open it, trembling. Inside is a leaflet for Choristers' Lodge. A pathetically thin, dated brochure with its name at the top in a big black font above pictures of the surrounding hills and the bedrooms. *That* bedroom.

I fling it to the floor, as if by just touching the leaflet, I'm somehow implicating myself further, and out drops a postcard. It's a postcard from Ullswater Lake in the Lake District, gleaming royal blue, surrounded by the ebbs and flows of the Cumbrian landscape. And on the reverse side, a message.

Look at the surface of the water, so serene. No one would know what's underneath. Keep your mouths shut, so it stays as one body, and not two.

Chapter 11

Jamie

I can barely walk as I approach the front door. I'm dragging my feet along the gravel and my trainers are completely scuffed, grey. Both of my calves so sore that they're almost numb, detached, my legs moving in spite of themselves. When I reach the front door, I bang with my fist, expecting no response, but Barry answers.

'Welcome back, Jamie. Come in.'

He's dressed in khaki camouflage trousers and has a wide smile on his face as if he hasn't a care in the world. I crane to look over his shoulder. Where's Victoria?

'What the hell is going on? Where's my wife? She's in labour! We need to get her medical help, now. Where's my phone?'

'Calm down, Jamie. Everything's in hand. Why don't you come in and have a glass of water? You look a mess.'

Barry puts his arm round my back to guide me back in and I flinch. Everything about him seems dangerous now, threatening: his stamp-like moustache is suddenly sinister, his outfit makes it look as if he's about to go out in the woods and shoot rabbits.

'Please don't. Just get your hands off me. Where's my wife?'

'Don't you get aggressive with me. We're trying to help you. Victoria is in safe hands, upstairs with Fiona. She's a midwife – she knows what she's doing. There's no time – the baby is coming now.'

'What are you talking about? She needs to be in a hospital. Please – drive us to a hospital.'

And then I hear her cry out, from upstairs. It takes me a moment to recognise it as Victoria, because the scream is so intense, so full and deep, and my instinct is to run to be by her side. I brush past Barry, taking one step at a time but as fast as I can, and then rush into the bedroom with a door ajar, just across the landing.

I cannot believe my eyes. For the duration of my journey into the misty countryside to find help, I'd pictured Victoria as I'd left her: sat in the kitchen, gently breathing, working through infrequent contractions, in pain but managing, getting through it while waiting for me to return. But here she is, on all fours on a bed, facing away from me, her arms clasped over the top of the headboard and around a large silver bouncy ball.

She's taken off most of her clothes and I can see the strap of her black bra, but she's not wearing underwear. She's bearing down and breathing into a wet flannel, dousing it with a purple bottle of essential oils and breathing it in again. The room smells of lavender, jasmine and blood. There's a laptop on a dressing table and it's playing hypnotising forest sounds, with birds chirping over the slow flow of a waterfall. I've seen Victoria's naked body thousands of times, but she's unrecognisable.

'Victoria. Victoria, darling.' I try to keep my voice soft and calm. 'We need to get you to a hospital.'

'Oh, there's no time for that, dear.'

I turn and coming out of the en-suite bathroom is Fiona. She's in a midwife's uniform and is tightening latex gloves on her wrists. As she approaches Victoria, panting, compromised, I lunge forwards and grab her by the arm. I'm angry, scared, but don't mean to be violent.

'Please, just . . . step away. Leave my wife alone. We need proper medical care, not something—'

Fiona flinches and gives me a glare that burns right through my eyes.

'Please don't grab me like that. There's no time to get all worked up. The nearest hospital with a maternity ward is an hour's drive away – Carlisle – we'll never get her there in time. Your wife is nine centimetres dilated. Do you know what that means? We need to get this baby safely delivered. You can trust me.'

'No-no-no! We need to . . . Surely it's better to . . . What if something happens and the baby needs to go into intensive care and . . . I mean, he's a few weeks early and . . . Victoria, what do you think?'

But Victoria is in the midst of another contraction, yelping, wincing, grimacing, sucking the flannel into her mouth and gripping the headrest so hard that her knuckles look blue. Fiona is holding a large plastic bowl in one hand and a thick white cloth is draped over her other arm. She brushes past me, lays the bowl down on the bedside table and unfolds the sheet, placing it gently on the floor by the side of the bed.

'Now, Victoria, darling, take my hand. That's it. We need to get you into a slightly better position. Baby's ready to say hello.'

'I can't do it, Jamie. I can't do it.'

She has her right palm to her forehead and her eyes closed. I want to do more to help. I want to share the pain. I rush forwards and take Victoria's left hand, kissing it gently.

'Do you need water?' I whisper to her, and she nods quietly.

'Jamie,' she says in between breaths. 'Thank God, Jamie, you're back.'

I go to the sink of the en suite, fill up a cup and she grabs it when I'm back, downing it in two gulps.

Victoria's contractions seem to be only seconds apart and she starts panicking.

'I can't do this!' she screams. 'I need to leave. We have to go home, Jamie. I can't. My body can't.'

I feel futile, helpless, disconnected, and all I can do is hold her hand and lie, promising her it will all be OK. That I'll make sure everything is OK.

Fiona guides Victoria down, so she's now kneeling on the floor with the top of her body collapsed onto the bed. I move so I'm beside her, standing awkwardly so she can reach out and keep hold of my hand.

'That's it, darling. You're doing really well. Go with your body. You're ready and you can do this. He's almost here.'

Fiona then turns back and looks me up and down.

'Sorry, love, we need some space this side,' she says. She points to the other side of the bed. 'Why don't you go downstairs and have a cup of tea with Barry?'

I raise a fist now and can feel my forehead pulsating.

'What the hell are you talking about? Why would I leave my wife here with you? Why have you got that uniform on? I'm not going anywhere.'

Fiona turns to me, pursing her lips and tightening her eyes.

'Don't you raise a fist at me. This is an emergency situation now. You need to get out of the way. Go and stand that side of the bed and we'll get the baby delivered.'

I'm flustered but I obey, and stub my foot as I scramble past Fiona, almost tripping on the edge of the bed. I reach the other side and then lie forwards across the bed and wipe Victoria's brow, gathering the sweaty strands of hair that are plastered on her forehead and brushing them back gently.

'How are you feeling, Victoria, darling?'

As soon as I've asked it, I know it's a stupid question. She's feeling worse than I could even imagine. I've made a specific effort to prepare myself for this moment, scouring through parenting forums to pick up the best tips on how best to support one's partner during labour. I found some of the advice so patronising that it verged on insulting. 'Be patient!' was a particular favourite, as if any man waiting for his partner to give birth was himself a petulant child, eager to get home and watch the football. Of the useful things I did pick up, though, was that women often found it helpful to be distracted from the pain, so I'm desperately trying to wrack my brain for anecdotes and jokes that might make her laugh.

'Hey, Victoria, remember at our wedding when my great-aunt Jane's left boob fell out of her top on the dance floor during "The Show Must Go On"?'

'Jamie, not now,' she whispers. 'Please, stop.'

This stings. I look round at Fiona, and she's laughing and shaking her head. I try again.

'Just breathe, Victoria. Everything's going to be OK. I can't believe how brave you're being.'

But that doesn't work either and causes her to lose it.

'Shut up!' she screams. 'Jamie, I need you to shut up.'

I take her right hand and stroke it, gently, determined to do something to help. The other person in this room is a stranger, but I feel like I'm the one Victoria would choose to kick out. I don't want to be an inconvenient accessory, a hanger-on.

When the next contraction comes, Victoria squeezes my hand so tight that I feel the bones crack and I bear it, enjoying the rush of pain, feeling that at least a modicum of the pain she's experiencing to bring our child into the world is being channelled through me.

Fiona, now in full midwife mode, offers her next instruction.

'OK, Victoria. When the next contraction comes, go with what your body is telling you to do. If you feel the need to push, push as hard as you can into your bottom. Hard as you can into your bottom.'

And the next yell is the most blood-curdling yet, the next step of pain, as if we've passed a threshold, and I can tell that it's getting very close now. I look over to Victoria and see now that there are tears streaming, fast, down her cheeks. I lean over and wipe them as they come with my left index finger, and my own eyes start to sting. I can feel my chest tighten and my stomach turn in anticipation of what's coming, a landmark occasion in life. Not exactly how or where or when we've planned, but still monumental.

I see Fiona, this stranger now in the most intimate of places, this woman kneeling down by my wife's crotch, her sleeves rolled up and her hands massaging Victoria's thighs. What would we have done if this woman hadn't happened to be a midwife? Fiona, who seemed last night to be so eccentric, and this morning so threatening, has appeared, in the right place and at the right time, to bring our child into the world.

I can tell that we're almost there, that the arrival of the baby is imminent, and so I lift up my T-shirt and throw it on the floor.

'What are you doing?' pants Victoria.

'Skin to skin,' I say. 'The baby needs skin to skin when he arrives. Helps with bonding.'

I catch a scathing look between Fiona and Victoria, and it punches me in the chest.

When the next contraction comes, Fiona and I chant in unison.

'Push, Victoria. Push.'

And we catch eyes, smirking at the coincidence. There's something tribal about this and I squeeze down hard on Victoria's hand as she pushes and groans and overcomes the pain.

'Now soft blows out,' Fiona says. 'Soft blow, soft blow. We're almost there. Keep going, keep going. Soft blow.

I can see his head! Keep going, keep going. Next push.'

And then we hear it, for the very first time. The gasp for breath, the cry. Danny, our son, out into the world and safe.

Chapter 12

Jamie

Tuesday, 13 April

The bereavement meetings take place in the hall of the church a three-minute walk up the hill from our flat every Tuesday and Friday evenings from six thirty to seven thirty. During the first meeting that I went to a week ago, I didn't feel like talking much. Everyone else there seemed to know each other and I felt like all eyes were on me. Like they were all desperate to hear my story, to find out why I'd joined the group, what had happened to Danny. And I knew that the intention was good, that the whole spirit of the organisation was to share stories as a way of processing them, but I couldn't chat to my closest friends and family about it all, let alone reveal it all to a group of strangers.

And so for the first session I mostly just sat and listened as others shared their stories, in the best ways they could. Some of them made me cry. There was Jane, a woman from Golders Green who lost a two-year-old to a particularly nasty form of meningitis and blamed herself for not spotting the symptoms earlier. Then there was Alison, who was forced to abort a child at thirty weeks owing to concerns about her own safety. Alison was convinced that even if she hadn't survived the labour, the child would have done, and felt guilty that she'd chosen her life over that of her unborn child. The man with her seemed to be there in a support function: accompanying his wife but never properly engaged, as if immune to the full shock of it all. As if a man couldn't possibly show the same emotion as a woman. He kept looking down and checking his phone in his pocket, somehow coming to the conclusion that nobody would be noticing as long as he didn't actually have it out in his lap. I noticed.

I tried to convince Victoria to come with me to the sessions, but she just wasn't having any of it. She'd had a bad experience in therapy when she was a teenager – someone who she was sent to see after her dad passed away. The therapist had apparently patronised her, talking to her as if she were a little girl of eight who didn't understand about life and death, asking her to make pictures of her late father as a way of 'painting the pain'.

She won't even talk to me properly, is ignoring my calls and told me to 'just shut up and stop talking' when I told her about the second letter. But it was a proper threat this time – that someone else could be killed. Maybe that's why I need this group. I need people to talk to, even if I can't tell them the truth.

Having introduced myself last week and spoken only a little bit about my background and what had brought me here, I promised myself on the way out that in the next session, I'd tell a fuller version of the story. I know that the more comfortable I become reciting the narrative, the more I practise telling the story as it is to be told, the less I'll feel the truth hanging over me, the less compelled I'll feel to shout about what really happened. I feel confident enough now that it's clear in my mind, that I've got everything straight enough, to tell the story convincingly, without any hesitation and without risking any suspicion.

And so when it comes round to my turn, I stand up, clear my throat and start talking. I hear a few whispers and can feel everyone shuffle themselves slightly in my direction. Here goes.

'Yeah, hi, everyone. Thanks for being so . . . well, yeah, so welcoming over the last two sessions. Sorry that I haven't . . . well, it's been hard for me to figure out exactly what to say and um, you know.'

I'm sweating and I bet everyone can see it. When I sweat, the tight curls above my ears stick to the sides of my forehead, turning inwards. I brush them back with my fingertips. Alison is smiling at me, encouraging me to open up, nodding slightly and licking her lips. Come on, Jamie: feed me your pain.

'I've always wanted to be a dad. It's something that was important to both me and my wife, Victoria, right from the very start. Not that I brought it up on our first date, but I do remember very early on testing the water with her, checking that children were in her plan, too, that it's something she envisaged for the future. And we were on the same page: we both wanted two, possibly three, but definitely not four, because that would just get out of hand.'

Light tittering in the audience.

'Anyway, I think when we were first together, we were young and naïve and expected it all to be very straightforward. I suppose if you've got no reason to believe otherwise, you just assume that you'll be able to fall pregnant pretty soon after you start trying, right? So, we weren't in any rush and we started trying when she hit thirty and I was thirty-one, about four years ago.

'And there was no panic initially. The first few months we just accepted that it was a numbers game, that it wasn't unusual for it to take a little while, and we enjoyed the process. But then it all started to get disappointing every time Victoria got her period, and things naturally became a bit more regimented. For a time we were making love three or four times a day even, on the right days as dictated by an app. It certainly took the passion out of it.'

Some smiles and earnest nods of the heads.

'So yes, we contacted the GP and went through the motions. I ate more nuts and wore looser boxer shorts. We both stopped drinking and tried to cut down on junk food. But these things always seemed too insignificant to me, not active enough to make a difference.

'We did our first round of IVF on the NHS and only one embryo was strong enough to implant. It didn't work. We had to delve deep into savings for the second round. Victoria wanted to give up after that, saying that perhaps it just wasn't meant to be, that maybe the universe didn't want us to be parents. But something in me told me that it would be third time lucky. I just had this instinct, this feeling that one more round and Victoria would fall pregnant.

'Thankfully, our parents could lend us some of the money

and we went through with it, with a different clinic this time. It didn't work. My sperm count is very low. But then the very next month – just as we'd given up – Victoria woke up one morning and said her breasts were feeling more tender than usual. I went out and bought a test and it was positive.

'It genuinely felt like a miracle. The doctors said there was only the tiniest chance of us getting pregnant naturally and we did it. Maybe the fertility drugs helped us, we don't know. We couldn't believe our luck.'

I'm going into too much detail, aren't I? But people seem engaged, interested, invested in our story now. I figure the more details I can include while telling the truth about the first part of our story, the better – to make the end, the lies, more convincing. I continue.

'And then the pregnancy was pretty smooth sailing. Victoria had some morning sickness, but nothing too extreme. You know, like nausea, rather than actually throwing anything up. I think she only vomited once, actually, but to be fair, I felt pretty queasy, too, so it could have just been some dodgy chicken.'

I'm being flippant about it now, but at the time, I totally freaked out. It was just a few days before our three-month scan. I felt annoyed at myself for having suggested an untested restaurant, a trendy new burger place, and as soon as we walked in, I had a feeling that the kitchen wouldn't be the cleanest. I tried to convince Victoria to order the veggie burger, just to be on the safe side, but chicken is what she craved throughout the pregnancy and she's never been one to be told what to do.

When she started feeling nauseous in the car on the way home from the restaurant, I pulled up at a bus stop and then held her hair back as she vomited on the red road markings. If she hadn't been so insistent that we drive straight home, I'd have taken her to A&E right there and then. I spent the next few days, leading up to the scan, convinced that Victoria was coming down with food poisoning and that the baby would be harmed. It was all fine in the end.

'As the weeks of the pregnancy went on and we moved from month to month, trimester to trimester, my anxiety levels gradually diminished, as I believed that the risk of something going wrong was getting smaller and smaller. We bought everything that we thought we needed: buggy, cot, changing table, a whole pile of babygrows to get us through those first few weeks. We were ready to go.

'And then, just a few weeks before the due date, we went on a bit of an impromptu trip. Obviously, by that stage it was too late to go on a plane anywhere, but Victoria found a gorgeous little B&B in the New Forest and we decided to go there for a few nights.'

Am I blinking too much?

'The guest house was run by a young gay couple, Fred and Jasper. They'd only recently bought the place, having sold their flat in Central London and decided to live a more peaceful rural existence running a small B&B in the countryside. I remember we arrived on the Saturday afternoon, and Fred and Jasper, Victoria and me and another couple who were just checking in sat on their terrace and drank some tea. Fred had made a lemon drizzle cake, which was a bit sharp for my liking, but it went down well enough after the drive down there.

'We then went up to our room and lay on the bed, watching an Australian reality programme about dating on Netflix, my hand gently caressing Victoria's bump. We went to sleep early and I waited until I could hear Victoria's breathing slow down before allowing myself to sleep. I think it was about 2 a.m. when I was woken by her screaming from the bathroom. She . . . I . . .'

I don't know where Fred and Jasper came from, or the cake, or the New Forest. I hate reality TV. I'm getting carried away. But having started with such confidence, suddenly I find myself unable to continue, as if someone has all of a sudden forced an apple in my mouth.

I stammer and stutter, cough a bit, try very hard to continue my sentence, but nothing's coming. And now I can feel tears streaming down my cheeks. I look around me to a sea of sympathetic eyes, all that bit wider than they were before, all willing for me to continue, to spit it out. But the truth is, they all know what's coming. For this particular group, the 'screams from the bathroom' can only lead to one thing.

I manage to muster some strength, skipping the gruesome bit of the story, heading straight to its inevitable denouement.

'They did everything they could in the ambulance, but it was clear that their priority was to stem the bleeding, to try to save Victoria's life. There didn't seem to be much discussion about Danny at all, about whether or not they could save him. It was a foregone conclusion that we'd lost him.'

My voice is cracking. I take my seat.

At the end of each session, they serve some refreshments and this week, it's white chocolate chip muffins and very heavily diluted orange squash. I didn't stay last week but feel compelled to this time, having just laid my soul bare, or near enough.

An older woman comes up to me, Christine, her hair wispy and blonde and her eyes wide and inviting. She's recently lost her husband, to pancreatic cancer, which I think is one of the most brutal ones.

'What a horrible ordeal you've been through. It's hard, isn't it? Because you don't feel like any words can convey the feelings. Language just isn't set up to express those things fully.'

And I like that. I feel so heard by Christine in this moment, so understood, that I want to grab her, hug her, be held by her as if she were my mother. Can I not tell her what has actually happened? It's not fair that I should know her truth and for her not to know mine.

Do I really deserve her sympathy? What's the risk in telling this woman, just this one person who has no link to anyone else?

It's on the tip of my tongue, so far forwards that it might just roll out. But I know that once I say it, it's gone. I can't take it back and I can't stop everything that will follow. The consequences of what we've done. I can't unsay these words that have been careering round in my head every moment of every day – three small words that I'm desperate to scream. I feel like a fraud as I gaze into the woman's eyes. Doesn't she understand?

Danny is alive.

Chapter 13

Jamie

Saturday, 6 March, 11.51 a.m.

'Is he OK? Is he healthy? Let me see my son.'

Victoria is panting still, desperate for a glimpse. I don't know if she doesn't hear or chooses to ignore, but Fiona continues regardless.

'Would you like to cut the cord, Jamie?'

Fiona is holding out the handle of a pair of scissors. My hands are shaking, but I take them and before I know it, I'm cutting Danny free from constraint, giving him one first leap of independence. The cord is surprisingly tough and rubbery, and I grimace and squeeze as hard as I can. I feel my face tensing out thick, fast tears and them sticking to my face. Fiona isn't a stranger any more. Her eyes are gleaming, brimming with delight. Her gaze is fixed on Danny. She's also welling up.

'Oh, I'm getting all emotional now,' she says, suddenly flustered. 'It's just a big moment, isn't it?'

And it really is.

Fiona takes little Danny, wiping the fluid off him with one

towel and then wrapping him in another. He has tiny wisps of hair and a little button nose. His eyes are squeezed shut. She lifts him, placing him over her left shoulder, gently tapping his back as she wanders past Victoria towards the bedroom door.

Victoria is lying on the bed now and I avert my eyes from the bloody sheets at her feet. I lean over and kiss her on the forehead, and then on the lips, and she starts crying, bubbles of saliva forming and popping as she speaks.

'I can't believe it, Jamie. He's here! He's really here.'

And that sets me off, too, and whatever has happened between us recently, all the arguments, all the hostility, are forgotten.

'I love you, Victoria. You did it. We're Mum and Dad.'

Victoria sits up with a gasp, straining her neck as she watches Fiona carry our son out of the room.

'Where are you going? Come back! I want to hold my baby,' Victoria calls.

'It's OK, my darling. I'm just going to get him cleaned up,' she calls back.

Barry is here now, clearing up the bedside table. I didn't even notice him come in. Was he here for the birth? Did he see Danny's head come out?

'You're not the first person to have a home birth, you know,' he calls from the en suite, where he's washing his hands.

'Just relax – try to take it easy and be thankful that you've got Fiona looking after you.'

I look over to Barry and he's got a dirty smirk on his face.

'Relax? We still need to get to a hospital. Victoria has lost blood and the baby needs checking over. We need to call an ambulance, to be safe.'

Barry looks at me and laughs, and then gathers a couple of sheets in both hands before heading out of the bedroom, crossing over with Fiona as she walks back in.

'The placenta now, Victoria. Let's get that out, shall we?'

She draws a small syringe out of the pouch of her uniform and approaches Victoria, who doesn't like needles at the best of times.

'What are you doing? What's in that syringe?' I interject, standing in between Fiona and my wife.

'It's standard procedure, Jamie. Syntocinon. Gets the placenta out nice and quickly. Just step out of the way, please. You're not needed for this bit.'

Victoria objects.

'I don't need that. I can do it naturally. Please – don't inject me with anything.'

She's lost all the colour in her face, pleading as Fiona prepares the syringe.

'Listen to me, Victoria. The placenta needs to come out. There's no time to drive to a hospital. It would take us at least an hour to get there and trust me, you don't want a retained placenta. I don't have to do the injection, but it'll be more painful for you if I don't. Jamie, why don't you hold your wife's hand? It'll just be a little prick and then it's done.'

'Where's my baby?' cries Victoria.

There are trails of dried tears on her cheeks and a bubble inflates from one of her nostrils.

'The baby's just fine. I've put him down in the nursery. Barry's watching over him. We need to focus on you now, Victoria. Are you ready, then? Just a little prick and then it'll be over.'

I get to my feet.

'I'll go to the baby. I should be holding him.'

But Victoria grabs my arm and looks me straight in the eye.

'Just stay a second. You know what I'm like with needles.'

Fiona comes forward and jabs the needle into Victoria's thigh. Victoria squeezes my hand, mine just as clammy as hers, and then looks up at me.

'Is that it? Is it done?'

Fiona chuckles.

'It's done. See? Didn't even feel it.'

She grabs Victoria's hand, while mine is still there. I feel her flick me away.

'OK, Victoria, I'm going to squeeze your hand now while you push again. Just gentle pushing and the placenta should come out pretty easily. That's it, darling, gentle pushing.'

Victoria exhales heavily and I watch as the placenta emerges from her body, deep red on one side and shiny, translucent on the other. There's a fine line between the beautiful and the grotesque. I watch as Fiona places the placenta in a towel, folds it up and puts it in a large plastic bag. I look back and see blood – drying on the towels on the floor but still wet on Victoria. I go all cold.

'Sorry, I . . . what's going on? How much blood has she lost? We need to get you to a hospital.'

Fiona responds, her tone short, like a teacher losing patience with a petulant child.

'Jamie, will you just stop worrying on about the hospital. It's all over now, everything's in hand. Victoria's done really, really well. I've worked as a midwife for forty years

– there's nothing they can do for her there that I can't. I promise she's fine. The best thing we can do for her now is give her some time and space to rest and recover.'

I go to protest again, but Victoria reassures me.

'I'm fine, Jamie, honestly. Just . . . where's Danny? I want to hold him. I can hear him crying.'

And, tuning in, I can hear him, too: short, high-pitched bleats from across the hallway – Danny's only way of communicating, of calling out for his parents. I kiss Victoria's salty forehead and step out of the bedroom into the hallway. As I approach the bedroom next to the one where we slept last night, the bleats get louder and I feel a rush of adrenaline – a resolve to power through the limitations of my body, an electric surge driving me towards my son.

I push on the brass door handle, pushing all the way down and up and down again. But it isn't budging. What's going on? I start banging the door with both palms and it stings.

'Let us in! What are you doing with our baby? Open the door right now!'

I feel a sweep of nausea again, an itch all the way up and down my body.

'Open the door!'

The more I shout, the more the baby screams. The last thing I want to do is startle him, but I need to get in there. I start kicking the door with my right foot, but it's causing me to lose my balance on my left and I have to steady myself by holding on to the wall.

'Jamie, what's going on? Why are you banging? Where's the baby?'

Victoria is behind me, dressed in a bloodstained T-shirt and some bottoms that I don't recognise. She's limping towards me, clearly in pain, and Fiona is behind her, supporting her back. I kick again, so hard this time that I make a dent in the wooden door. Then I hear Barry bellow, like a troll disturbed from his slumber.

'What's wrong with you, man?'

When the handle turns and the door opens outwards, I fall back, knocking into Victoria, and we clutch each other and watch Barry as he comes out, cradling our son in his left arm and feeding him with formula in a tiny bottle. Danny is dressed in a blue sleepsuit with little yellow dinosaurs at the sleeves, his tiny fingers clasped in a fist as he sucks.

Where did that sleepsuit come from? Why do they have milk? We didn't bring any.

I walk forwards, compelled to take him, to claim our son.

'He'll be fine with this formula for now,' Fiona says. 'But after that and a bit of sleep, I think we should try to give him some breastmilk, if Victoria's feeling up to it.'

Victoria explodes, a guttural bellow.

'Give me my baby! I want to hold my baby!'

She rushes past me and grabs Danny from Barry with one hand, keeping the bottle in his mouth with the other. Her hands are shaking so much that I'm worried she's going to drop him, so we hold him and feed him together. Victoria starts sobbing, the tears re-staining the lines on her cheeks. She has no free hand to wipe them away, so I do it for her, gently dabbing her face and kissing her on the forehead.

As Barry heads past us and down the stairs, Fiona picks up a faded floral dressing gown from inside a cabinet in the hallway and drapes it over Victoria.

'You can use the shower in the en suite if you like, Victoria. Jamie, you can hold the baby while she cleans herself up.'

Her smile to me is condescending. Why is she giving me permission to cradle my own child?

'And then why don't you all have a rest, the three of you? We'll move the cot to your room. And once you've had a chance to recharge your batteries, come on down and I'll get us all a cup of tea and a slice of cake. I think we've all earned it, don't you? And then we'll do the first proper feed, Victoria. Get some colostrum in him. I'll help you, don't worry.'

Alone in the room, I wrap Danny in a bed sheet, trying to remember the swaddling technique from the books, keeping his arms down and folding one way, then the other, then up behind him, making sure it holds him securely but isn't too tight to his neck. I cradle Danny while Victoria lowers herself, gently, onto the right-hand side of the bed.

'What the hell just happened, Victoria? Where did that uniform come from? She's supposed to be retired. And the drugs? The syringe? And . . .'

Victoria is so tired that she's struggling to keep her eyes open and her speech is slurred.

'I need to sleep now, Jamie. Just a few minutes. He'll need more milk soon. Wake me up in . . .'

Her head hits the pillow mid-sentence and, almost immediately, her breathing slows. I lie down next to her, with

Danny face down on my chest, rising and falling with my breaths. I look down in disbelief at his perfect head, the fine cover of dark hair. When he's totally settled, I move him onto the bed between us and shuffle down so we're face to face.

His eyes are shut, but his tiny nostrils flare slightly and his mouth twitches as he sleeps. The top of his lips is perfectly curved in a tiny heart. On his forehead there are small red marks, battle wounds from the birth. I kiss each one. All the trauma of the past few hours, the locked doors, the panic, the screaming, the missing possessions and misunderstandings fade into an oblivious, irrelevant past. For a moment, we're a family.

Chapter 14

Victoria

Friday, 16 April

'I still don't understand why you didn't just tell them no. I can't tell you how much I'm dreading this. I'll end up blurting something out. And what about Isla? I don't know if I can put on a brave face around her.'

Jamie is sitting on the chair by the front door of our flat, lacing his shoes. I've called in on the way to Andy and Lauren's, so we can head there together. He's put wax in his hair and the air around him is thick with the woody musk of his aftershave. Next to him, on a small antique side table, is the postcard from Ullswater Lake. I've told him I don't want to talk about it. But when he was in the shower, I picked it up and stared long enough to memorise the message, word for word, before putting it back.

Look at the surface of the water, so serene. No one would know what's underneath. Keep your mouths shut, so it stays as one body, and not two.

III

It's a reminder not to go to the police. Is the threat to kill one of us? Or Danny?

Jamie has finished putting on his shoes and grabs his navy collared coat from the floor next to him.

'Look, if we can't even see our best friends, how are we ever going to move on with our lives?' he asks while putting it on and trying to pat out the creases on the lapels. 'What are we going to do? Just stay indoors forever and avoid all other human interaction? This is a safe, first step back into the real world. And don't put this on Isla, Victoria. We can't let this affect our relationship with her.'

I walk towards Jamie, who is now standing by the door, ready to go. I stop at the mirror in the hallway, take my cherry-red lipstick out of my purse and apply it generously.

'You look stunning,' he says, standing and coming towards me. 'I love you.'

I force a smile but say nothing in return. I look down at my shoes and he grabs my hand. I don't pull away completely but resist letting his fingers become intertwined with mine. Jamie looks at me, his eyes wide and gleaming, still waiting for me to reciprocate.

'Come on. The sooner we arrive, the earlier we can leave,' I say, pulling away, and I open the door to the flat.

We get an Uber the short distance to Andy and Lauren's flat in East Finchley and Jamie kisses me as we stand at their front door, waiting for them to answer. His lips are chapped and they feel coarse against mine. I can sense the desperation coming off him in waves – the desperation to patch things up between us.

He wipes his lips to make sure they're not marked and I tense as the door opens.

'J! Victoria! Come in, come in. So good to see you both.'

Andy looks different. His thick dark hair has grown, mostly upwards, and is greyer, and his beard is unwieldy, covering his neck and the tops of his cheeks. He's wearing a floral shirt, fitted jeans and brown Chelsea boots that are too trendy for him. I've always found his slightly scatty appearance endearing, his belly peeking out from a shirt that's just a bit too tight, trousers that are slightly too baggy. It's unusual to see him make an effort.

When he bends forwards to greet me with a kiss on the cheek, I feel his beard against my cheeks and I flinch slightly. There's something about unplanned intimacy now, even this small, even with him, that feels like a violation.

'Oh, you smell nice, Victoria. New fragrance?'

I'm hardly in the mood to go perfume shopping at the moment.

'Just my natural aroma. You all right?'

But Andy is already mid-embrace with Jamie.

'I've missed you, buddy.'

And they proceed to go through the motions of their ridiculous greeting: shaking, clapping, patting, hugging, grunting, clapping again and ending with a nipple twist.

'Here, go through to the dining room – Lauren's just putting Isla down.'

That stings. It would be impossible to ask him to make absolutely no reference to Isla, but I didn't expect to be hit with it before even taking my coat off. Jamie deals with it a bit better.

'How is she? Is she still awake? I'd love to go and say hello.'

Andy looks towards the stairs and tilts his head slightly.

'Oh, do you mind if . . . It's just we don't like to get her too excited at bedtime. It's been a real struggle getting her to settle lately – since hitting the terrible twos and all that.'

Jamie laughs.

'Oh, of course, yeah. No worries. We'll come in the daytime next time.'

Andy turns to me and gives me a smile that's too broad and I feel like replying that there's nothing in the world I'd rather do less at this particular point in time than spend an afternoon with Isla – sweet, unaware, untarnished Isla. There's a moment of silence, a pause that's extended just long enough that we all might have noticed it.

'Come through to the dining room. Excuse the mess – we meant to clear up all of Isla's toys before you came, but it was tantrum central when she was eating her dinner this evening and everything ran over. Before we knew it, it was already half seven.

'But anyway, you know what it's like – the second you put them away, they're out again and you start to wonder if there's any point in putting stuff away in the first pla—. Sorry, I'm rambling. It's probably not . . . I didn't . . .'

'It's fine, Andy. Just relax, it's fine,' Jamie says.

'Can I get you drinks?'

Andy heads in the direction of the kitchen.

'Yeah, I'll have a can if you've got a cold one?'

'Always. And for you, Victoria? What do you fancy? Wine?'

I haven't drunk in months, since we found out we were pregnant. I'd better take it easy.

'That'd be lovely, if you have any.'

Andy scurries towards the kitchen and I lead the way through to the living room, Jamie following me. I have to clamber over miniature teacups, a plate of plastic vegetables and a dinosaur jigsaw puzzle with giant pieces to reach the sofas on the other side of the room. There's an alternative version of this journey, where I stamp on each toy with my three-inch heel, in which I pick up the dolly, strewn so carelessly, half-naked, across the living room floor and hurl it at the mirror above the fireplace.

I take a seat on the grey settee and Jamie sits next to me, too close. I shift slightly away from him and he comes up to my ear, his whisper passing right through me.

'Just . . . be normal, OK? You've got a face of thunder.'

And I look him straight in the eye and give him the broadest grin I can muster. I really go for it, showing every tooth, my eyelids fluttering, my cheeks bulging. He reaches for my hand and his is clammy, and we sit in silence, waiting for Andy to return.

'Sorry, Victoria, we're out of red and we didn't have any white in the fridge, so it might be a bit sort of tepid, but—'

'It's OK, Andy. I'm not fussy. Just glad to be able to drink again.'

And Andy laughs nervously, as if I've broken a taboo by making even an indirect reference to my pregnancy. I'm glad to see that he's come in with the whole bottle and that his pour is generous. He doesn't notice, but he pours too vigorously and some wine coats my finger. I wince as I take the first few gulps: it's obscenely sweet.

'Delicious. Thanks, Andy. Can I help in the kitchen at all? What's on the menu?'

'No, you're fine, honestly. Just take it easy. I've made cottage pie but with Quorn mince – hope that's OK. Lauren's sister is staying with us for a bit. She ran out of money on her travels so had to come home and couldn't face moving back in with the in-laws. She's vegan now, apparently.'

Of course Florence is vegan. She's quite a bit younger than Lauren and has been struggling to eke out an identity for herself for years now, yo-yoing from one fad to the next. When we first met her, she was still in high school, her hair a fluorescent green, and she was dating a computer engineer called Steve who was twice her age. When that ended, she got really into the Church and even talked about becoming a minister at one point. Then she went travelling, which is where she discovered her calling to save the environment. The last I heard, she was volunteering with orangutans in Costa Rica.

If I'd known that she was going to be here tonight, there's no way I'd have agreed to come. I feel annoyed at Jamie for not telling me she was going to be here – he knows how much she gets under my skin.

'Victoria, Jamie, so good to see you! You remember my sister, Flo?'

Lauren glides in wearing a black jumpsuit, her caramel brown hair tied up with a pencil, and she looks radiant. She's got one of those faces that doesn't need make-up – almost completely symmetrical, her forehead totally free from wrinkles, her eyes big, round and emerald, her cheekbones defined but softened with a mist of light freckles.

The rest of us look best when we're enhanced. She looks at her best with her hair back, face out, exposed.

I've found it hard over the years not to feel competitive with her, not to feel desperately unattractive in her shadow. She works at an all-boys secondary school, teaching geography, and I can only imagine the whispers that go on in the changing rooms about her. The quiet, secret fumblings of teenage boys under the covers at night dreaming about their older, married geography teacher with her curves and her lips and her perfume that lingers long after she's moved through the corridor.

Florence looks like a slightly masculine version of her sister. Their builds are similar but Florence's jaw is wider, there are no freckles and her hair has been cut and dyed in a severe sheer black bob. She's wearing a yellow vest that doesn't cover her stomach and clashes with her orange pleated trousers.

'Of course we remember,' Jamie offers. 'Nice to see you, Flo. How were your travels?'

'Yeah, incredible, thanks. Ended up spending most of the time in a rainforest in Costa Rica – literally one of the most biologically intense on the planet. And it's amazing how much you can bond with a primate. Obviously, everyone knows that they're evolutionarily not that distant from us but, like, I didn't expect to have such a personal connection with some of them. It's tragic, because they're super endangered now and losing them completely will cause such an imbalance. The environment is so precarious.'

I see she's caught that traveller intonation, her voice rising at the end of every sentence as if asking a question.

The bangles on her wrists clatter against each other as she talks. Lauren rubs her sister on the shoulder and gives her a kiss on the cheek.

'We're so proud of you, darling. While the rest of us have been in our little jobs, sending emails and marking essays, you've really been making an impact.'

She can't actually believe that larking around with a group of primates for a few weeks makes any kind of difference to the big picture, can she? It's awkward, but I play along.

'Right, yeah. I barely remember to recycle most of the time,' I admit. 'Lauren, could you pass me the wine?'

She reaches over to pass the bottle from a side table and Florence looks at Lauren, looks at the bottle and then turns directly to me, cocking her head.

'Should you be drinking?'

'What do you mean?' I reply, scowling.

'Oh, no judgement. I just thought . . . well, I suppose a glass or two is fine, but you're pregnant, aren't you?'

I feel like I've been punched in the gut. What? Doesn't she know? I feel sick. Why haven't they told her? I don't know where to look. I close my eyes, scrunching them tight, waiting for the moment to pass.

'Oh, gosh, I'm so sorry,' Lauren interjects, stepping forwards towards me as if physically trying to block me from her sister. 'Sorry, I thought I'd . . . Flo, will you come with me into the kitchen for a sec?'

Lauren grabs her sister by the arm and leads her back through the assault course of toys.

'No, it's OK – it's OK, Lauren. You don't need to tiptoe around us. I was pregnant, but we lost the baby, Florence.

A little boy. Danny. He's gone, but the bump's still there. Do you want to have a feel?'

Florence puts both hands to her mouth and I stand, leaning on the arm of the sofa to lever myself up.

'Let's just . . . I'm going to go to the bathroom and then let's . . . well, let's change the subject, shall we?'

Dinner is served on a round glass table that's too small and covered in a pale pink cloth, which is supposed to hide, presumably, the large crack across its whole diameter. The consistency of the Quorn makes me feel a bit queasy, so I shovel it around the plate like a pile of cement, hoping that if I grind it hard enough into the bland tomato sauce it's swimming in, it'll look like I've eaten some of it. It smells of onions.

Florence is being even chattier than usual, as if to make up for her blunder by filling the heavy air with empty words, but every time she opens her mouth, I have to bite my bottom lip and swallow hard, for fear of crying or shouting or saying something I'll regret.

'The thing is with Greta – and don't get me wrong, it's great what she's achieved and she's really impressive for her age – but what she actually says isn't that insightful.'

I catch Lauren's eye across the table, and she gives me a smirk and raises her eyebrows. She gestures towards the wine. I nod and she pours me another glass.

'Anyone could drum up support on Twitter and give a few rousing speeches if they put their minds to it. The fact that she keeps getting nominated for the Nobel is an absolute joke.'

I take a big glug of wine and turn towards Andy, but he and Jamie are deep in conversation about a teacher from school – 'Yeah, apparently Mr Hayes and Miss Martinez

were in a relationship – who would have thought?!' – and
I roll my eyes at the thought that they're still entertained
by playground gossip that's two decades out of date. I turn
back to Florence.

'So, Flo, what's next on your bucket list? Volunteering
in an orphanage or something?'

That came out as more facetious than I intended. I wonder
if it's occurred to her to get a job at any point, but keep
this to myself.

'I'd *never* volunteer in an orphanage. Those places are just
human trafficking operations – most of the kids aren't even
orphans. No, I'm going to stay here for a bit, save some
money and then hopefully I'm going to go to Kenya to
do some conservation work. I've got a friend out there – I
could really make an impact.'

'Oh, how do you plan on getting there, Florence? Are
you going to cycle?'

Here we go, the wine's talking.

'What do you mean?'

I lean forwards on the table, cupping my wine glass.

'No, I'm just wondering, because it's all very well doing
all these things, but if you're really serious about these issues,
isn't there an argument that the benefit to the environment
of any work you actually did out there would be totally
outweighed by your own carbon footprint?'

Jamie places a hand on my thigh under the table and I
move the chair away from him. Lauren stands up.

'I think it's time for dessert, don't you? I've got a lemon
panna cotta in the fridge. Florence, will you come and give
me a hand?'

'I'll come, too.'

Andy takes my plate and stacks it on top of Jamie's before heading into the kitchen. They're long out of earshot, but Jamie still whispers to me, his teeth clenched.

'Victoria, what's going on? Shall we go home? You can't snap at Lauren's sister like that – she hasn't done anything to you.'

'Sorry, it came out wrong. I just find her so . . . and I've probably had one too many glasses of wine. It's fine. I'll be good. Sorry.'

'Anyone fancy a bit of port?' Andy shouts from the kitchen.

Even though I can't stand the taste of port, and it tends to give me heartburn, I need the anaesthetic.

The panna cotta is served in little shot glasses and the room would be silent if it weren't for the clanging of the little silver teaspoons against the side of the glasses. There's still a wreckage of dolls, fake vegetables, brightly coloured rattles and blankets on the floor on the other side of the room. No one has bothered to clear them away. I can't resist another little dig at Florence.

'Doesn't panna cotta usually contain gelatine, Flo? Or are you not vegan when it comes to dessert?'

Andy smirks, Jamie squirms and Lauren looks up from the baby monitor app that she's been checking on her phone throughout the meal. Florence is so shocked that she drops her shot glass on the table. It cracks and tips, cream oozing onto the tablecloth.

'Look, Victoria, I'm sorry about your baby, but don't take it out on me,' Florence says.

Lauren shoots up, both hands over her mouth.

'Florence! How can you be so cruel? Apologise to Victoria, and to Jamie. Now, please!'

'Oh, sit down, Lauren, you're not in the classroom now,' I hear myself snap, my face hot with the blood rushing to my cheeks. 'Don't you think she can fight her own battles at her age? You always have to play the peacekeeper, don't you?'

Jamie is avoiding eye contact with everyone by gathering plates, creating a precarious stack that's not going to be helping anyone, with shot glasses in between the plates. He attempts to clear the cream from Florence's spilt dessert but actually just smudges it deeper into the fabric of the tablecloth.

'Victoria, come on, let's go home. Sorry about this, guys – we're going to jump in a cab. Victoria, I'll get your coat.'

I stay seated.

'Oh, shut up, Jamie. Don't patronise me. Maybe I should tell everyone about our living arrangements at the moment.'

Jamie's face flushes. Florence is picking up the little pieces of glass in front of her, smirking, and I can see Lauren watching her closely, wanting to take over.

Andy approaches me, clearly with trepidation, as if I'm an animal about to bite his hand off. He touches me on the shoulder.

'Victoria, just calm down,' he whispers. 'I know, I know, Flo is a massive pain and we can't begin to understand what you've been through. I think maybe it's best if you cool off outside.'

I flinch, dart back. Now, I stand.

'Oh, you don't know the half of it, Andy. You think you know everything – everything about Jamie, your old best friend, all our little secrets, don't you? You've got no idea. And do you know what I think about your port? I hate it. It's disgusting. You're not posh, you're not clever – you shouldn't be drinking bloody port.'

I turn to Lauren, who is just standing there, clutching an empty wine bottle, her mouth wide open.

'I guess we both know what he's compensating for, don't we?'

Andy turns to Jamie, shaking his head.

'Jamie, I think you need to take your wife home now.'

I pick up my glass and go to throw the port in Andy's face. He flings his arms in front of him, but at the last moment I throw it all over my own face, feeling the warm, sticky liquid against my skin, slowly trickling down, smelling the sickly syrup as it stains me. I watch as it drips down onto my dress, down, down, creating a puddle of maroon on their cream wool carpet. I drop the glass to the floor. Everyone's looking at me, mouths wide open, and I'm on fire.

'Yeah, that's it, everyone. Look at me!' I start flinging my arms around as everyone stares, slack-jawed. 'Look at the crazy woman who's lost her baby and lost her mind!'

I dart out of the dining room and leave the house. I've left my coat on their banister and I can feel the chill of the wind on my bare shoulders. I pick up some speed, striding down the road towards the tube station. I feel my legs moving, left, right, but it's like they belong to someone else. My ears are buzzing, my stomach churning, but the breeze on my forehead cools me down as I stride away. I don't even know where I'm going, but I need to move, as quickly as I can, away from that dinner table.

'Victoria, wait! Wait!'

I can hear Jamie calling after me and feel bad that I'm making him run. I know that he finds it hard to keep his balance in the dark. I was hoping he'd get the message that I needed some alone time, that he'd take himself back to the flat on his own. I slow down and hear his wheezing as he approaches.

'What the hell was that? I'm worried about you. I'm calling for a cab. Aren't you cold? Take your coat.'

He drapes my jacket round me and I pull him towards me, sobbing into the opening at the top of his shirt.

'I can't . . . I just can't function like this, Jamie. I can't take the burden any more.'

By the time the cab arrives, I've calmed down a bit and there's a bottle of water in the side compartment of the passenger seat of the taxi, which I down in one. I address the driver, aware of my slurring words.

'There will be two stops, driver. First—'

Jamie interrupts. 'What are you talking about? No no – just one stop, please. The address I put into the app.' And he turns to me. 'There's no way I'm leaving you to sleep alone in this state. I can sleep on the sofa if it bothers you that much. We can't let this ruin our marriage, Victoria.'

'Oh, come off it, Jamie. You and I both know that we've been in trouble for years.'

Jamie places a finger to my lips to hush me – he hates it when I talk openly in public. He's one of those people who cringes when he hears someone having a loud phone call on the train and clearly feels self-conscious that the taxi driver might be listening in on our conversation.

'Oh, for God's sake, Jamie. The driver doesn't give a shit.'

And it's true – he's on the phone himself, headphone in one ear, chatting away, immersed in his own family dilemmas.

'What can I do, Victoria? What can we do?' Jamie says, turning his face towards mine and reaching for my hand. 'Let's find a therapist, someone we can talk things through with. I know you're not a massive fan of—'

I pull my hand away. 'Are you joking? How on earth is that going to work? We can't sit there and lie to a therapist about what happened.'

I feel sick and place my head in his lap in an attempt to stop everything from spinning.

'Don't you think this is impossible for me, too?' he asks. 'Every moment of every day I'm thinking about Danny and what happened, whether we made the right decision. But I'm putting on a brave face and getting on with it. That's what we agreed. We're in the same boat, Victoria, you and me.'

I lift my head and use my left hand to push on the cold leather seat and haul myself back up. I look him in the eye.

'But that's the issue. We're not, are we?'

'What do you mean?' he asks, but he knows.

'We're not in the same boat. Do you think there might be a reason why I might be finding it more difficult than you, Jamie? If we go to the police, we'll get arrested and I'm the one who will . . . Danny is gone either way. I'm the one who did it. I'm the one who—'

Jamie places a hand over my mouth and I squirm, struggle and shout. The cab driver looks round.

'Everything OK back there?'

Jamie releases his hand and I sit up straight.

'We're fine. Everything's fine.'

The driver turns back, replaces his earpiece and carries on talking on his phone.

Jamie whispers in my ear.

'Don't you dare, dare say it. We're nearly home.'

We reach the flat. I open the car door, stumble a few steps forward and vomit onto the pavement. Jamie crouches down with me, pulling my hair back and caressing my back.

'Just get it all out of your system. When we get in, I'll put some toast on for you.'

'We're not sleeping together, you know. That's not happening. Just because I—'

'Victoria, with all due respect, I think I'd pass, anyway. I'm sleeping on the sofa. You need a good night's sleep.'

'Can you help me up?' I ask, reaching out for him as a night bus passes in front of us and its engine fills our ears.

Jamie heaves me up with his dominant arm and I slouch up against him. Another husband would take me over his shoulder all the way, carry me through to the bedroom like they do on TV. I know that Jamie can't do this, but I appreciate the effort as we limp together up the path from the road to the front door.

The flat is spinning. I find the bedroom and collapse on the bed, on top of the covers.

'Get undressed and under the quilt. I'll go and get you some toast and water. What do you want on the toast?'

And suddenly, I need him. I pull him close towards me, clutching the curls on the top of his head, and finally let the tears flow freely. I'm crying, wailing, my nose running and bubbles of saliva forming at my mouth. My voice is muffled and slurred as I bury my head in the lining of his coat, and he rocks me slowly, back and forth, while I wail.

'We can never be with Danny, Jamie. Never. And it's all my fault. I can't believe I did it. I can't believe I killed someone.'

Chapter 15

Victoria

Saturday, 6 March, 2.22 p.m.

Each cry from Danny tears through my skin like a knife in the side. Sharp and brief, hot and tender, the hits are relentless, one to the next to the next. My head is banging, my mouth parched, and my breasts so heavy and tender that I feel like I'm being dragged down by two lead weights. When I open my eyes, it takes me a second to adjust to my surroundings. Jamie is asleep beside me, still clothed, on top of the covers, and there's a throbbing pain in my groin. Where's Danny?

I shake Jamie awake.

'Jamie! The baby. Where's Danny?'

He sits up with a start, squinting, looking around in the semi-dark, the lights off but daylight edging through the curtains.

'Oh, God, what the hell is going on now?' Jamie asks, rubbing his eyes. 'Where have they taken him?'

Jamie leaps up faster than I've ever seen him move and bursts out of the bedroom door. I go to follow him, but as

I rise, I'm in agony. I move, step by step, out of the room and towards the stairs.

I lose all control of my legs, shaking my way down to a squat on the stairway, my face and hair plastered with salt. I watch from above as Jamie turns into the kitchen, where Barry blocks his entry. I let out a yelp as I see Fiona sitting at the kitchen table holding Danny, rocking him gently in an attempt to pacify him. But his mewls are getting louder, faster, more intense, and her shushing seems futile. What the hell is she doing with my baby? What did they do? Come into our room while we were sleeping and take him from between us?

Barry comes up from behind us and grabs Jamie on the shoulder.

'Step back, Jamie. Don't come anywhere near our baby.'

There's a pause for a moment.

'Your baby?' Jamie screams. 'Move, now!'

Barry blocks him and Jamie punches him in the face. The blow is significant, because I hear the thump and Barry arches back, clutching his eye and groaning. I feel I'm seeing a new Jamie – this act of violence may well be the first ever initiated by my husband, who is usually meek, restricted by his physical limitations. But the struggle that follows is frightening, because I know that he hasn't got a chance. I call out to him.

'Jamie! Stop!'

It's a brief blur, a kaleidoscope of twisted arms, heads under shoulders, arched backs. Barry is too strong, wide-shouldered and built like a fridge. I want to reach out to defend Jamie or at least pull him away from the struggle, but I'm paralysed. My body has been through too much, my limbs pinned down to the stairs. I lean over the banister and exchange a glance with Barry, his eyes bulging and moist, his lips tightly pursed. What is happening? I see a flash of silver as Jamie is handcuffed by Barry. He's dragged across the kitchen floor kicking like an infant.

'Victoria, get Danny! Get him away from them!' Jamie shouts.

From somewhere in the depths of me, I muster the strength to move, shuffling down the stairs on my bottom, step by step. I hoist myself up with the banister when I reach the hallway, turn and limp through to the kitchen. I approach Danny with my arms out, desperate to grab him but feeling incapable of it, too weak. If I take him, will my arms give way? Will I drop him, here, on the tiled floor, and watch as his delicate head splits open? I approach Fiona and Danny at the kitchen table.

'Please, Fiona. Please let me hold my baby.'

Fiona, still in her midwife's uniform, pulls out the chair next to her, standing slowly with Danny, placing a hand over my back.

'Of course. There's no need to get violent.' She turns to Barry and glowers. 'No one is stopping you from holding him. Here.'

I sit down and she places Danny in my arms. My nerves subside, the shaking steadies and I hold him, wrapped in a little cotton blanket, a hat so big for his little head that it goes down as far as his eyebrows, and for a moment everything else disappears. I'm unable to soothe him, scared that I'm going to rock him too vigorously, but his screams are beautiful – vital signs of life – and here we are, mother and son, in our own cocoon, for an instant untouchable.

Throughout the pregnancy, I was convinced that I wouldn't feel anything – that he'd arrive and I'd look down at him and just see a baby. But seeing his little eyelids, so fine and delicate, I feel an urge to protect him that's more powerful than any emotion I've ever felt before.

On the other side of the kitchen, Jamie is on the floor with his arms up towards Barry, who is stood over him, arms folded, lip curled. Jamie's wrists are handcuffed together. Barry takes the cuff off Jamie's left hand and attaches it to a short metal leg under the oven, stretching Jamie's right arm back with him. Barry switches the oven on to 200°C.

Oh my God. What is he doing?

Jamie tries to yank on the handcuffs to free himself, but the oven doesn't shift. He's writhing around, his breathing becoming increasingly laboured. He looks up to Barry, his mouth open as if to say something, to beg, but nothing comes out. Barry crouches down and squares up to him, their noses so close that they're almost touching.

I want to scream, but I'm frozen. I try to focus on holding Danny, on slowing my breathing for him, for me.

'We've some things we need to talk about, Jamie. I'm happy to uncuff you, but not if you're going to get aggressive,' Barry says. 'Stay still, try to calm down and I'll take them off, I promise. Please don't make this turn nasty.'

Nasty? Aren't we already there? I look to Jamie and he shouts, spitting his words.

'There's nothing to talk about other than the fact that my wife has just given birth to our baby and they both need urgent medical care. I don't know what this is, what you're planning, who you think you are, but we need to . . . we need to . . .'

Jamie reaches up to turn the oven off, but Barry turns up the heat, laughing.

'We can do this all day if you like.'

Jamie is hyperventilating now, his face completely flushed. He shuts his eyes and groans, trying to lift himself, to break free. Barry bellows – a sudden, shocking bark that blows Jamie back against the floor.

'Stay where you are, I told you!'

This command, the harshness of its tone and the sudden volume shift, seems to give Danny a second wind, his screams intensifying, piercing, higher than before, more urgent. And this, in turn, seems to trigger something within me and I feel a swell of cramp in my chest – an excruciating, tightening deep within me – and the air is sucked from my throat, from my lungs. Every muscle and bone inside me is torn and in flames. Intense pressure builds in me and I want to push it out, down and out of me, but there's only Fiona here. No doctors. No proper medication. What if the pressure doesn't stop? It'll rip me in two. It'll never stop. I can't do this. I give up. I'll die, I think. I'll die in this guest house.

'Help me! I need pain relief! Help me!' I shout from my chair at the kitchen table.

'Fiona, do fetch her something, will you? We don't want her in pain,' Barry snaps.

Fiona scurries over to the cupboard under the sink, taking out a red packet and bringing it over to me along with a bottle of water.

'There you go, dear. I was surprised you didn't ask for any pain relief during the actual labour. Not many women manage that. But of course the afterpains can feel worse sometimes. Have some paracetamol. Here – tip your head back.'

I comply, desperate for the drugs, and she passes a glass of water to my mouth. I swallow and feel immediate relief, just knowing that there are chemicals inside me, working towards making me feel better. Only now – hearing Fiona refer to the labour in the past tense like this, as something I've done – does it really hit me that it's over. The hardest part is over. Sweat cools my forehead in fine, sharp waves and I can feel the roots of each hair on my scalp tingle.

Fiona takes the seat next to me and with her index fingers, starts stroking Danny on the chin.

'Bless him. He'll be getting hungry again just about now. We gave him a bottle-feed earlier, but only a little bit. Are you hungry, my sweetheart?'

Fiona reaches round the front of me and pulls up my T-shirt.

'No need to be shy, dear. That's it, one breast at a time.'

I catch a glimpse of Barry staring and I feel worthless, like a cow being assessed by its farmer. Fiona softly cups my left boob and it feels tender as she guides it towards Danny's lips. I feel like an observer, like I'm watching this happen to someone else. I shut my eyes, like when watching a horror film on television during a scene that's a bit too much to bear. Only when I feel the tickle am I jolted into the moment – a tickle that turns into a pinch as my son clasps on for the first time.

He wriggles away for a second and I see that my milk is golden yellow and almost as thick as yoghurt. Danny finds my nipple again and takes it, his head tilted back and his eyes closed. I'd felt so daunted by the prospect of breastfeeding. I'd decided that I didn't want to do it. But of course I have to do it now. My body is all he needs.

Barry turns off the oven and speaks to Jamie, whose face is now flushed. He's sprawled on the floor, as far away from the heat as possible, with his arm still attached.

'I'll uncuff you, if you stay calm.'

Jamie uses his free hand to wipe sweat into the curls stuck to his forehead and balances on his lower right arm. He's facing me, trying to catch my eyes.

Barry takes a seat next to Fiona and I can feel him looking at me, as well. Staring at my breasts.

'Is it working? Is the milk flowing?' Jamie asks.

I nod and smile, looking down at Danny. It stings and the milk is thicker than I'd imagined, but yes, it's flowing.

Fiona turns to Jamie.

'The colostrum is so important – that's the special type of breast milk that the biological mother produces for the first few days. Full of so many nutrients.'

Jamie bites back.

'Don't patronise me – I know what colostrum is. What the hell is going on here? And what do you mean "biological mother"?'

Fiona shifts her chair so she's closer to me, leans down towards my breast and gives Danny a gentle kiss on his forehead. When I was giving birth, I relied on her entirely, soothed by her encouragement, clinging to the sound and tone of each syllable. I gave my life and my son's life to her. Now, I want to grab her head and smash it on my knee.

She glazes over, staring with intensity at something. I follow the line of her gaze and spot a photo next to the spice rack. Was it there before? I can't remember. It's the photo of a baby, no more than six months old, sitting in front of a barrier of cushions and grasping a brown teddy bear. He's beaming at the camera, at us.

'Twenty-seven years it'll be next month,' Fiona says, her voice soft, almost a whisper. 'Almost twenty-seven years to the day since I was in the same place as you, Victoria. Isn't it a wonderful feeling, knowing that you've just given birth to a whole new life? Doesn't it make it all feel worthwhile: the cramps, the sickness, the anxiety?'

I can't shift my eyes from the photo of the little boy, his large hazel eyes, his smile. I see myself playing piano for him, making him laugh, holding him on my lap as he bashes the keys. I imagine doing the same with Danny.

Danny has stopped feeding, so I move him to the other breast and keep looking at the baby in the picture. Fiona continues, rocking very gently on her chair.

'That's Harrison in the picture,' she says, watching me now. 'After he died, all those years ago, there's been such a hole in our lives. We had the best part of a year together – eleven wonderful months. And then it was all snatched away.'

Fiona places a hand on my leg, looking me in the eyes, keeping her voice light and slow.

'It happened at my sister's house. A big, posh house with marble staircases. The ironic thing is that they were to get carpets laid down the very next day. It happened on a Sunday evening and the carpet man was due on the Monday morning.

'Of course, tumbling down a whole staircase, he'd have been injured in any case. Maybe broken an arm. But landing on a hard floor? He didn't stand a chance. Can you picture it, Victoria?'

I wince and will myself not to see it. Fiona's hand feels like a brick on my thigh. Fiona is sobbing now and digs into the pocket of her uniform, bringing out a tissue that's so torn it's barely there. Barry reaches over and strokes his wife's hand, the faded gold of his wedding band clinking against hers as she opens her mouth again, a string of saliva extending between her lips.

She gathers herself and starts speaking again.

'For the first few years after Harrison's passing, we didn't even try for another baby. We felt that to replace him would be to betray him and that we didn't deserve to bring another child into the world. I'd mope around the house, seeing Harrison in every nook and cranny, imagining what he might be doing if he were still with us: running in the hallway, playing on the swings in the garden, doing his homework at the kitchen table. And Barry found it hard too, didn't you, Barry? That's when you really got stuck into your work. We were barely speaking for months.'

Barry takes his hand away and looks down as if affronted, embarrassed to have been brought into this. Fiona shakes her head slightly and then turns to me.

'But there's this instinct, isn't there, Victoria? A need that transcends everything else that we women have within us, to be maternal.

'After a few years we started trying again. We did everything right, didn't we, Barry? Everything was tracked, regulated. We ate the right food, gave up alcohol. Barry even cut down on his smoking. But it just wasn't happening.

'The truth is that at my age, even then it would have taken a miracle for us to have conceived naturally. I'd turned forty and had struggled for many years before that. We'd missed the boat.'

If I'm going to get us out of here, I need to let her see that I understand. I need to indulge her. Keeping Danny close to me with my right arm, I reach out towards her with my left and open my palm. It's shaking wildly, noticeably.

'Fiona, it must be so hard to come to terms with everything you've been through. I am truly so sorry. I hope you know that – I mean it honestly. Jamie and I also had trouble conceiving and, well, we both spent a lot of time adjusting to the possibility that we may never have children. But now, now we just need to think first about Danny, about getting him home.'

Fiona reaches to steady my hand, but Barry interjects. His delivery is quiet and clipped.

'You'll be leaving when we say. On our terms.'

Jamie tries to free himself, yanking the handcuffs, trying to pull away from the oven. He's almost in tears, his voice breaking like a teenager.

'What is this? Look at my wife! She needs a hospital. We need to get her and Danny to hospital now. We need an ambulance. Please, I'm begging you . . . Please, we'll pay . . . Whatever it takes . . . just—'

'Oh, bless you, Jamie,' says Fiona, still looking at me and taking my free left hand in both of hers.

'You have yourself a very valiant, sensitive husband here, Victoria. Don't worry, though, everyone will be just fine. I've delivered enough babies in my time and I can tell you that everyone here is perfectly fit and healthy. All Victoria needs is a long soak in the bath and a bit of rest.'

She smiles and delicately thumbs my knuckles in circles.

'You're very welcome to use our facilities, dear, once we've got the rest of this all sorted. Oh, now look – all that shouting and our baby Harrison is crying again.'

Jamie is shouting again as well, trying to shuffle to his knees.

'What do you mean, Harrison? What do you mean, sorted?'

Barry pounces, grabbing his arm and pushing him fully to the ground. I hear the smack as Jamie's face hits the floor and then Barry's bellow that makes my shoulders shake.

'Pull yourself together, man. Stop making a fool of yourself.'

Barry releases Jamie and he sits up, keeping his back against the oven, the right side of his face a deep red. He brings his knees to his chest and leans forwards, like he's winded. His eyes are wild, distant. I can see him trying to regulate his breathing, but it gets faster. He uses the back of his left hand to rub deep into his forehead and mumbles about Danny and me needing a doctor. I need to get to him, to calm him, to look him in the eyes and breathe with him.

'What the hell is wrong with you?' Barry shouts in his face. 'You're pathetic, look at you. Man up.'

I know that if he could have hit any nerve, if Barry could have chosen any turn of phrase to make Jamie descend more into panic, it would have been something along those lines. The thing that's always made Jamie most anxious, most likely to faint, like he does sometimes, is the prospect of others sensing his vulnerability, seeing him as less of a man.

Spotting the signs that he's on the way there, that he feels weak and out of control, I will him to breathe, slowly. I try to catch his eye, so he can focus on me and get out of his head. But Jamie is really sweating now, not just a few drops trickling down but visible patches of liquid, around his eyes, making him blink manically. His skin is turning, draining, and he's looking all around him. But it's happening now, I can see it – his eyes lose focus, his face drops down and he slumps to the floor.

I don't flap or scream or try to run over, because I'm too focused on Danny, who has started wailing again. I rock him back and forth, back and forth, gently kissing the top of his head. I calmly call out 'Jamie. Jamie, wake up. Jamie,' and raise my cheeks high as I say the final vowel sound to try to stop tears forming in my eyes.

Fiona has got up and runs to Jamie, kneeling down next to him, giving him light slaps over the face, squeezing his jaw. When he comes to, he lets out a snort and lurches up, wiping the sweat off his hairline and pushing himself up.

'The number of men I've seen lose it in the delivery room over the years,' she says, now tipping a plastic cup of apple juice into Jamie's mouth and smiling towards her husband. 'But I've never seen one faint hours later!'

Fiona chuckles to herself, walking towards the kitchen sink to fill up a glass of water.

'Let's not drag this out any longer than necessary. Barry, are you going to tell them? I think this has gone on long enough.'

Barry walks towards his wife and she stands. He places an arm around her shoulder and she an arm around his waist. He looks to Jamie, on the floor clutching the empty plastic cup, and then directly into my eyes.

'When you leave us, Jamie and Victoria, you'll leave Harrison with us. We've waited long enough — it's our time to be parents again. You're welcome to stay for a few days, recuperate, get everything together. But whether it's this evening or tomorrow or the day after that, when you leave us, our son will stay here.'

Chapter 16

Jamie

'Hey, this is Victoria. Please leave a message after the tone.'

There's no point in leaving another message – she's obviously not picking them up. She's always been terrible with her phone. Slow to answer texts, the silent one in group chats with friends, often failing to participate at all. But we haven't spoken for four days, since the morning after we went round to Andy and Lauren's.

I haven't been able to sleep. Every night, as I try to relax, different scenarios rear their heads, one by one, presenting themselves consecutively – not as possibilities but as urgent realities. Victoria has gone to the police. Victoria has gone back to the guest house. Victoria has capitulated altogether, taking fifty Valium and lying down on the bed in the studio in Deptford, waiting for it all to disappear.

It's after 5 p.m. and I get off the sofa and force myself into the shower, my first of the day. The thin jets tickle and cool the anxiety at the front of my head and I can think more clearly. Victoria would never do anything to harm herself. She just thinks she needs space, from me and anything that reminds her of Danny.

But the longer we spend time apart, the more I worry that the gulf between us will get deeper and wider. And then what will it lead to? Full-blown long-term separation? Divorce? She's threatened that in the past and it's always felt idle, a throwaway comment in the heat of an argument. But we've never sunk this low.

My thick curls are wet and coated in shampoo and I slick them back, tight to my head. With Victoria, I'm always expected to wait. To be told what to do next. I can't wait any longer. I've spent all morning stewing, confused, angry, but that's not going to solve anything. I need to go to the studio and speak to her, in person.

I rinse the final suds off my arms and chest and switch off the shower. I dress quickly in fresh jeans and a plain navy T-shirt, fling on my raincoat and leave the house into the pouring rain.

After twenty minutes on the Northern Line, I change to the overground at London Bridge. It's a nightmare manoeuvring myself between all the tourists at the station, all wrapped up in their mackintoshes, swinging their shopping bags back and forth, squeezing between each other, overtaking me in their urgency to reach their trains.

I've got a banging headache, so I make what I hoped would be a quick stop at a pharmacy to pick up some painkillers. There's a long queue at the main checkout and I've got no patience for those self-service ones, so I walk over to the prescription counter to pay because I see that's a bit quieter.

In front of me in the line is a young mum cradling a baby. She's after some gel to put on her son's gums to soothe his teething and I can't help but think about Danny. I imagine him grimacing and squirming, his own fledgling teeth struggling through his tender gums. When? In six months from now? A year?

The flat is in a dark grey block overlooking a primary school playground on a little side street and as I approach number 14, I feel a pang of nerves. The label on the buzzer still reads Radcliffe/Rawlinson from when we lived there together, her surname and mine in one breath. I press the buzzer, wait, press again and then press a third time. She can't be out. Where would she be, on this rainy Wednesday evening?

I step back into the road and look up to the third floor to see if a window is open or if I can see any sign of life. Nothing. A car hoots and I jump back in shock. The driver winds down the window, shouting abuse at me for standing in the middle of the road.

Ivy, who lives on the ground floor of the same building, cranks open the window to her flat and greets me.

'Oh, hello, Jamie. What are you doing, standing there in the rain? You'll catch your death – you look terrible.'

Ever the charmer, Ivy is single, perhaps widowed, perhaps never married, and counts on a tubby ginger cat called Stanley for company.

'Hello, Ivy,' I say, flattening down my sodden hair. 'Yeah, the weather is horrible, isn't it? Hope you're keeping warm.'

'Don't you worry about me, my love. You just need to be careful not to trip up in this weather, what with your disability and that. How is your leg these days?'

It's always older people who comment on my disability, perhaps because they perceive a commonality between their physical limitations and mine. But my disability, manageable though it is, isn't temporary, or particularly changeable. No matter how often I explain this, some people can never accept that my limp remains the same.

'Ah, all good, thanks, Ivy. Same as always.'

Ivy sticks her head out of the window, peering up through the rain to our flat, which is directly above hers.

'Are you looking for your wife? She got into a car about an hour ago. All glammed up, she was.'

The rain is hard. It tinkles on the chrome bars of balconies and I struggle to hear her clearly. I look up and take a step towards her.

'Any idea where she was headed?'

Ivy smirks and shakes her head.

'How am I supposed to know? How come she's living here at the moment, anyway? You had a falling-out, have you?'

I adjust the zip on my coat and take my phone out of my pocket.

'No, it's nothing like that. It's . . . it's complicated.'

I check my email accounts, on the off chance that Victoria has sent me something – although I can't remember the last time she sent me an email. I've only got one unread email in our shared Gmail that we use for bills. It's from Uber – a receipt for a journey that finished an hour ago, from this address to La Bodega in Soho. Victoria's gone to La Bodega.

When she first moved to London, it was her regular. The waiters and barmen all knew her name and would give her and her friends starters and cocktails on the house. Then they'd stumble over the road to Emporium – a horrible club that plays nineties pop songs on a loop – before stuffing down a dirty kebab and sharing a taxi home.

Occasionally, she and I would pop in there for a glass of wine before going to the theatre, or for a bite to eat afterwards. I feel a swell of relief to know that she's gone somewhere familiar, somewhere that doesn't involve her having a new life that excludes me. It also means that I know where to find her.

'Mobile phones are the problem, I'm telling you. Your generation – you just spend all the time on your phones and your computers instead of *talking*, really communicating. You know what I mean?'

I think it's a bit more than that in our case, but I don't want to indulge her.

'Sorry, Ivy, I need to go,' I say, raising my hands above my head in a futile attempt at creating shelter. 'I've . . . something's come up. It's been nice to see you. Maybe we can catch up again soon.'

Walking down the street, the rain still pelting down onto my hood, I stop at the newsagents on the corner to buy a pack of cigarettes – my first in years – and head towards New Cross overground station and on to Soho.

La Bodega isn't a massive bar and even though it's midweek, the weather isn't great so it's busy inside. I walk in and manoeuvre my way through the crowds, weaving between tables, doing my best not to trip on shopping bags and dripping umbrellas. Victoria is usually pretty easy to spot in a crowd: her auburn wavy hair often standing a couple of inches above her head. Her voice really carries as well, so usually I can hear her before I see her. But she's not here.

I look everywhere. I'm so thorough that people have started to notice me, wondering what I'm doing, whispering about me. In a last-ditch attempt to find her, I position myself by the ladies' bathroom and, when she's failed to come out after a few minutes, I approach someone else on her way in – a woman in her early twenties with short cropped black hair and thick-framed round glasses. She looks taken aback to have been ambushed.

'Excuse me. Sorry, I know this is a bit weird, but I'm looking for my wife. Can you just tell me if she's in there? She's got reddish hair, curly. Just . . . can you tell me if there's anyone like that in the bathroom right now?'

I get a dirty look and no reply, which is probably fair enough.

A table clears towards the back of the bar and I take a seat. While I'm in town, I might as well stop and have a glass of wine. What's my other option? Head straight back to the empty house, crack open the gin and sit on the sofa watching Netflix on my own?

I could call in at Andy's, but he'll more than likely be out somewhere with Lauren, at a dinner party with her friends from university or pretending to enjoy a foreign-language film with subtitles at an art-house cinema. He's said to call him whenever I feel down, whenever I feel like company, but I don't want to be a burden on him.

A waitress comes over and I order a bottle of the house red.

'How many glasses?' she asks, and the insinuation of loneliness gets my back up.

Why couldn't I be choosing to be here on my own?

'Two, please,' I respond.

And I take it slowly, sipping, watching as the minutes pass and the bar gets busier and then thins out. I've always been a people-watcher, and Victoria and I play a game where we have to guess people's names based on their appearance. I see a trio of women in their mid-twenties come in and neck three cocktails each within the space of thirty minutes before stumbling out and heading into the night. Debbie, Tanya and Carly, I guess.

Then there's an older gay couple, both blond – Matt and Steve – who order tapas and beers and laugh their way through a quick meal. There's also a family of five: mum, dad and three teenage boys – Rachel, James, Charlie, Jack and Reggie – the youngest of whom is clutching a programme from *The Lion King* and refusing to eat the meal that's been ordered for him.

After each glass of wine, I go outside and have a cigarette in the smoking area. I watch as people much younger than me arrive at the club over the road, many of them already tanked-up and being scrutinised by the bouncers before being let in.

I become increasingly conscious of people watching me, wondering why I'm here alone, so I pick up my phone to avoid eye contact. I got a text message from my dad last night that I still haven't replied to and I reread it, thinking about an appropriate response.

Your mum and I are going to get a flight home. We can't imagine what you and Victoria must be going through. I won't book until you give us the go-ahead, but please, it's what we want to do. Don't worry about Nana – we can get a carer in to look after her for a few days. Xx

Mum and Dad moved to Cape Town last year, largely to be close to Nana Rawlinson, who has colon cancer. It needn't neces-sarily be terminal, apparently, but she's refusing chemotherapy and other traditional forms of treatment and is determined to see out the rest of her life in her own home, surrounded by her beloved dogs. The problem is that recently, she's become so weak, in spite of all of her herbal remedies, that she needs someone to help her get around and do the most basic tasks, so it's fallen on my parents to fly over and take care of her.

My parents were born to care for people. For years, I've been their primary patient. I had a very rocky start to life. I was born a month premature and lost oxygen during the delivery. The doctors suspected that I might have cerebral palsy as a result – affecting mobility on one side of my body – but it wasn't officially confirmed until I was eighteen months old.

Both of my parents dedicated a huge amount of their time to my care: taking me to physiotherapy three times a week, arranging appointments with consultant after consultant, buying me orthopaedic shoes and walking aids to build up my strength in my left side. I have so much to thank them for. It's largely down to them and their determination when I was a child that my symptoms are now relatively mild and that I can easily live independently.

Their dedication also means they can be overbearing at times, still somewhat unconvinced of my independence, even though I've managed to start and run a very successful business without their help. And I can't have them fly over now for this. Nana needs them more than me and apart from anything else, how can I lie to them, after everything that they've done for me?

I draft a response and hit Send before I overthink it.

Hey, Dad,
Sorry for the delayed response. Please don't fly over – there's nothing you can do and Nana needs you there. I'd be upset if you came now. Victoria and I are getting through it. I've been going to this local bereavement meetup thing and it's helping. Are you still planning on being back in the UK for Christmas?
Xx

I end up spending hours at the bar, getting through the whole of the bottle of wine. I only leave at 11 p.m. because there's a group of very loud older women by my table: Martine, Simone, Karen and Esther – their actual names, I've been eavesdropping – and I can't hear myself think. It's stopped raining now and I stand in the smoking area for one last cigarette.

Over the road outside the club, there's a group of guys in their early twenties, each carrying a bottle of beer, huddled around a woman in a red dress that's far too tight for her. She's facing away from me, but the veins on her bare legs suggest that she's older than them. She's drunk, very drunk, and barefoot, and the boys are leering at her.

One of the boys, taller than the others, chiselled but still very baby-faced, lunges forwards, grabs the woman at the back of the head and pulls her towards him. She arches back and pushes him away, but he persists.

His friends cheer, chanting 'Milf, Milf, Milf,' and the woman leans her whole body back, stumbling backwards.

I feel an instinct to step in. I cross the road, conscious that I am, myself, stumbling, and start shouting.

'Hey, guys, guys. Back off.'

The shouting stops, the laughing subsides and the boys turn to me. One of them steps forwards, walking with a gait that he presumably assumes is threatening but to me makes him look like a penguin.

'All right, mate, chill out. Just a bit of harmless fun. Who are you – her dad?'

The woman turns round and I gasp, momentarily losing feeling in my legs. Her hair is straight and a different colour, much darker. Her lips are black from red wine and her make-up is smeared. She's slightly puffier in the face and sadder in her eyes.

'I'm her husband, actually. Get off her or I'll call the police.'

I grab Victoria's hand and she accepts it, in silence, and we rush away, around the corner, taking shelter in an alcove between two restaurants. I ask for her phone and use it to order an Uber. There's a large surcharge, but I don't care.

We get in and I try to speak to her, but she begs me not to. She doesn't even ask how I knew where she'd be. We both cry, as quietly as we can manage, all the way back to our flat.

Chapter 17

Jamie

Victoria's gaze is fixed on me, her mouth half-open. My vision is blurry, eyes stinging, and there's a low buzz in my ears. I take a deep exhale, screw my eyes shut and open again, and the numbness in my feet dissolves to pins and needles. I'm sitting on the floor and my right wrist aches, but it's no longer in cuffs.

Barry sits calmly opposite and above me, at the kitchen table, and places his hand on Fiona's arm. Fiona is focused on Danny, lying in Victoria's arms, his eyes shut, his tiny hands curled up into fists. Drunk on milk, new to the world, untainted, he has no idea how much danger he's in.

There has to be a way out of this. I have to calm them and myself down. Try to negotiate with them. Help them see it from our perspective.

'I can't even begin to imagine how hard it must have been for you. For you both,' I say, trying to steady my voice. My mind is buzzing and every part of my body feels defeated, but I force myself to keep speaking. 'Losing a child like that and now this. Seeing all this happen for us, so suddenly and in the kitchen of your house. But doing this to us – to Danny – won't make you happy or fulfilled.

'What did you think would happen after this? You'd just go out into the world and tell everyone you suddenly have a baby? Would you be able to live with the guilt of stealing a baby from his parents? And what about us? Why would we ever leave here without our son? You'd have to kill us first.'

Victoria is holding Danny tight to her chest, sobbing. Her wails are muted but persistent.

'No one is going to die,' Barry says, his voice not even slightly wavering, 'unless you choose for that to happen. Here's what you're going to do.'

Barry draws his chair back and stands. He starts pacing around the room, his eyes down. The only noises in the kitchen are the rhythmic clacks of his heels on the wooden floor and Victoria's cries.

'You're going to clean yourselves up and when you're ready, pack your bags and leave. You're going to hand Harrison back to us. We're going to keep our son.'

He stops pacing behind Fiona and places his hands on her shoulders, gently massaging her. I try to stand, feeling a tightness in both hamstrings.

'What do you mean, Harrison?' I say, rising on my tiptoes, leaning against the wall. 'His name is Danny. We'd just go straight to the police. As soon as we left, we'd go to the police.'

Fiona looks up at Barry, her brows furled. Barry leans in towards me.

'Of course you're going to want to call the police. But if you do, it's not going to end well for you.'

I raise my voice.

'What do you mean? What do you fucking mean?'

Fiona tuts, shaking her head. Danny starts crying, a series of muted, short, sharp blasts. Victoria rocks him gently and he's quickly soothed. Barry continues.

'Of course you're going to want to call the police. But I'd really recommend that you don't,' he says, keeping his calm and looking from me to Victoria and back again, like a teacher addressing his pupils and remembering to share the eye contact.

'If we get wind that you've raised an alarm to the police, if we hear sirens, if we see a police car or anyone we suspect to be the police approaching our home, we'll have no choice but to kill our beautiful baby. Beautiful, beautiful Harrison, who you can feel breathing in your arms. How could you make us do that?

'Do you know how long Fiona has longed to be a mother again? If, when you leave, we even suspect you're trying to report us, we'll be left with no choice but to kill the baby and frame you.

'Your DNA is all over the house, of course. We have the knife ready – Jamie, you handled it when you arrived, remember? And, Victoria, it also has some of your blood on it now. You'll lose your son and spend the rest of your lives in jail. It'll be your word against ours and I'm afraid they'll believe us, not you.'

I feel a stitch in my chest.

'I don't believe it,' I say, my forehead cold. 'You'd never kill a baby – no one could. And if he's alive, they're hardly going to believe that the baby belongs to her. She's old enough to be his grandmother.'

I point to Fiona and she grimaces, looking up at her husband.

Victoria lifts her head, still gripping Danny as he sleeps silently and rocking her body from side to side. Victoria throws me a wild glance and shouts.

'What utter nonsense. Why would they believe you over us?'

Barry continues.

'Until two years ago, I was in charge of Cumbria Police. I'm a hero here. I was given the Queen's Police Medal at Buckingham Palace for distinguished service. In any scenario, it'll be your word against ours. I'm confident that all of those officers – ones I have trained, nurtured, given pay rises and promotions to, whose misdemeanours I have quietly ignored – will find it hard not to believe me.'

He smirks but doesn't raise his voice. 'You can call the police if you want. Go ahead. There's no doubt whatsoever in my mind that you'll be dismissed, sooner or later. You'll be sent to jail. You'll be known, forever, as child killers. We'll all lose. Or you can find a way to live with the gift you've given us and move on. You're both still young enough to have a family of your own.'

I feel a surge of heat between my ribs.

'A family of our own? What is *wrong* with you?'

I grab the chair in front of me and push it to the floor. It lands with a thud and wakes Danny, who immediately starts crying.

'We won't do it. We won't leave here without our son.'

Victoria is holding Danny close to her breast and is shouting now, too, spitting her words at Fiona.

'What about what you've done? The drugs you've admin-
istered? The uniform you've stolen? We'll tell them. They'll
be able to test my body.'

Fiona raises her eyebrows.

'What good is that going to do, my dear? I'm a registered
midwife. The uniform isn't stolen – I've had it for thirty
years. Do you know how many home births I've attended
over the years? How many babies I've delivered in people's
homes at the drop of a hat? It's perfectly normal that I
should have all the gear.'

At this, Fiona stands and heads to the kitchen worktop,
where she picks up the kettle, fills it with water, flicks
the button and watches while it boils. It starts to mist the
window above it, which is already dense on the outside
with fog. She speaks, face still to the window.

'Of course, if there was any doubt about your guilt,
there's always the Facebook posts.'

What is she talking about?

Barry stands from the table, retrieving mugs from the
cupboard above the sink.

'People are so careless with what they share online. It's
an absolute goldmine for evidence.'

I look at Victoria and she can't look me in the eye.

'I don't have Facebook,' I protest.

Barry reaches into the left pocket of his khakis, produces
a clump of folded paper and flings it across the table towards
me. I can feel my heart pounding as I unfold the paper and
see a series of screenshots from Victoria's Facebook timeline.

'You'd think,' he says, looking at me, 'what with your
line of work, that she'd have the sense to have better privacy

settings on. She's hardly going to win Expectant Mother of the Year, is she?'

I look up and Victoria has her eyes shut. I'm shaking as I look through her status updates.

September 12th: Whoever called it morning sickness was having a laugh. It's morning, afternoon, evening, during the night sickness – this kid deserves a hiding already!

November 13th: Last few months of freedom before the screaming baby comes and wrecks our lives – who fancies a pint (of wine?)!

December 10th: Babysitting for @LaurenRayner and the damn kid won't go to sleep. And so many poo-filled nappies. Is it too late to change my mind?! ;) ;)

Barry's eyes are lit up, plump with excitement, and I feel sick. How could she write things like this? How did I not know about them?

'This stuff can be so persuasive,' Barry says. 'A jury can get lost in all the legal and forensic detail, but something like this really stands out. They can really relate if they hear about texts and social media posts from a mother who doesn't want a child. And the press would have a field day, too. Imagine the headlines! Little Danny's parents charged with his murder. Little Danny's mother joked that he "deserved a hiding". Is it too late to change our minds? Little Jamie's parent's sick Facebook posts.'

I look at Victoria and her eyes are now wide open, moist.

'I'm sorry, J. I didn't mean it. I was just being silly.'

That was just Victoria being flippant. It's her sense of humour. But a jury wouldn't have that context.

Barry comes over to me, his face right against mine, and spits his words.

'So you see, if it's your word against ours, you don't stand a chance.'

I hobble over to Victoria and place my hands on her shoulders.

'We won't surrender. There's absolutely no way we're leaving here without Danny.'

Barry takes a deep exhale, his tone warmer now.

'This is what you're going to do. You're going to tell anyone who asks, anyone who notices, that you've had a very unfortunate end to your pregnancy. Fiona has all the paperwork we need from the hospital to have the birth registered in Cumbria. Stillbirths happen far more often than you'd think, isn't that right, Fiona?'

Fiona turns at the window.

'Oh yes, dear. The number of stillbirths I've seen over the years. It happens for a whole multitude of reasons: problems with the placenta, high blood pressure disorders, an infection that happens in utero. Terribly sad, of course. But then most mothers do go on to have other children and at your age, you'll be just fine.'

Her last words are drowned out by the crescendo of the whistling kettle and she reaches up to take a teapot out of one of the cupboards. With Fiona's back turned, Victoria seizes the opportunity and edges her chair away from the table. Danny is turned with his face nestled between her right arm and her side and she uses all the strength she can muster with her left arm to hoist herself up from the table.

Danny is still calm, thankfully, but Fiona spins round and grabs him from Victoria, yanking him from under his arms, making his neck lurch, and then clutching him close to her body and shushing. Barry is right next to me, holding me tight in a lock. I strain and look at Danny. He's so tiny, so delicate. I feel a primal urge to lash out, to save him, but I can't move.

For a second Danny is still, but then he wails, the screams mounting and mounting, becoming unbearable. Victoria surrenders and falls to her knees, sobbing on the kitchen floor. Barry is so close that I can feel his breath and I spit right into his face. He's barely fazed and lets the spit linger in spots on his forehead and cheeks.

'You don't want to try anything like that. Do you know what the minimum sentence is for assault of a police officer?' Fiona says, rocking Danny and putting her finger in his mouth.

'Look, Jamie,' adds Barry, 'this needn't be so complicated. We've got more life experience than you two. Harrison isn't going to come to any harm. Unless you force the matter.'

Victoria, still on the floor, has more colour in her face now, a renewed resolve.

'His name is Danny, not Harrison,' she screams.

Barry releases me but stands between Fiona and me. Between Danny and me.

'Please, go ahead. Leave and call the police,' Barry says. 'I'm not stopping you. Jamie, calm down. We explained your options, so what you do next is up to you. Either Harrison lives or Danny dies. I hope you don't decide to have Danny killed.'

The 'k' of the word 'killed' pierces through me like a screwdriver through the eye.

Barry continues, 'Do you know what happens to men like you in prison, Jamie? Victoria, do you know what happens to mothers convicted of murdering their children?'

Fiona turns round from the kitchen counter.

'There's no need to talk in such extreme terms now, Barry. It's not going to come to that.'

I feel another swoop of panic, but this time I breathe through it, grasp hold of the excess energy and channel it into anger. I can feel the blood rushing through my arms, a renewed strength. I clench my fist and run towards Barry. He manages to grab me again and I'm screaming, not any words in particular but howls. And Victoria is crying, too, bewildered. And seeing her in such desperation just makes me feel angrier, more desperate, so I do something that I haven't done since I was a child and start thumping myself in the forehead.

My vision is blurred. I look ahead of me and all I see is the outline of the others, silhouettes hovering in front of me, moving back and forth.

The red of her hair, in waves, a few feet in front of me.

And then Fiona striding towards me, Danny still in one arm and something else in the other.

And then her face, up close.

And then a sting in my arm.

And then darkness.

Chapter 18

Victoria

Thursday, 22 April

I was a mess last night. I haven't drunk that much since university, when it was totally acceptable to slurp an indeterminable blue liquid from a bucket with a plastic cup, chugging down glass after glass before throwing up in communal toilets. When it comes to last night, everything goes a bit patchy after about 6 p.m. and now here I am, the morning after, still in my underwear from yesterday, back in my marital bed with a throat so dry that it hurts me to swallow.

I roll over and see the smudge of an 'E' on my wrist. Emporium. What? I've got a vague memory of being picked up by Jamie outside the club, of being escorted back here, of being led up the stairs into the flat. What the hell was I doing at Emporium?

I can hear Jamie pottering around on the other side of the flat, an orchestra of plates jangling against each other, the boiler groaning as he runs hot water, the faint murmur of talk radio seeping through the wall between us. I feel ashamed, embarrassed about my behaviour, even though I can't remember what I did or didn't do. I have an urge to get up, gather my clothes and scurry out of the flat without him noticing, as if this were some kind of sordid one-night stand.

For a moment, I entertain the idea of running out of the flat, because I know he won't be able to catch me, but I quickly chide myself for being so cruel. I feel unwelcome in my own bed and it's a strange feeling. While we've only been apart a couple of weeks, I don't feel comfortable in this place, because everything I see reminds me of our tragedy, of the awful burden that we've had to endure, of how every possible decision I can make can only lead me further from Danny.

Jamie walks into the bedroom, his dressing gown loosely tied, carrying two cups of tea. I go to help him, as I know that with his limp it's a struggle to carry hot drinks without spilling them.

'Oh, J, you're a star. Thanks so much. Morning.'

'Morning. Bloody hell, you were off your face last night, Victoria. You need to take care of yourself – you could have ended up in a ditch. I know you hate it when I lecture you, but can you imagine how gut-wrenching it was for me to see you like that? What were you doing at Emporium? We're married – it's like you've forgotten that we're married.'

That stings. I take a glug of tea, which Jamie has brewed perfectly to my taste: strong and with just the smallest drip of milk. It stings as it goes down, a burn between my ribs.

'I don't remember a lot, if I'm being honest, Jamie. I went for a drink at La Bodega and then must have wandered over to the club. I wasn't being too awful when you found me, was I? How did you know where I was? Did I text you?'

This feels like such a regression, a step back to a time when I'd wake up the morning after a night out riddled with guilt, plagued with anxiety about having made a fool of myself, of having offended someone by mouthing off. My worries then were so meaningless. I remember chatting to some boys now and they were *very* young – I wouldn't have, I couldn't have . . .

Jamie's brow is furrowed and I feel like I'm being mothered.

'Were you out on your own? Don't worry, you didn't really do anything incriminating. Your Uber receipts go to our shared email account, so I saw you were out and wanted to make sure you were OK. Thankfully, even in your most drunken state, you're so predictable that I knew you wouldn't have gone far from there. You fell asleep in the Uber, snoring like an elephant – that's about as embarrassing as it got.'

Jamie strokes my hair, fluffs the pillow from under my head and grabs the red dress that's scrunched up next to me. I suspect that he's lying to protect me.

'We'd better get this to the dry cleaners. Why don't you have a shower and then let's go out for breakfast?'

And for a moment, I'm tempted, because it's just so wonderful to be looked after like this. There's a comfort in spending time with Jamie that I can't get elsewhere.

But I can't face the prospect of sitting down opposite him, having breakfast and talking about Danny. About the threats in the post. Because that's where the conversation will go.

Every moment I spend with him is a reminder of what's happened. It's exactly why we need to spend time apart.

I roll over on the bed and swing my legs off the edge to stand.

'I probably shouldn't,' I say, facing away from him. 'I've got a gig tomorrow and I haven't even looked at the music yet. I'll have a shower, though, if you don't mind, and then . . . well, I just want to get back, Jamie.'

I actually do have a gig tomorrow, but it's only a wedding reception and I know full well that I could mess up the entire repertoire and no one would notice or care. And Jamie knows that I've never been particularly conscientious when it comes to prepping for jobs like that. He looks crestfallen, a smile and a nod belying devastation, and I don't mean it to be such a harsh rejection, but I just can't face talking about it.

'We need to talk about Danny at some point, you know, Victoria,' he says from across the bed. 'We can't just pretend it's not happening. This isn't something we can brush under the carpet – it won't go away.

'Your mum keeps calling me, saying she wants to support us, that you're not answering your phone, not letting her in. I can't keep speaking to her for you. We keep getting these letters. You say we know who it's from, but what if we're wrong? What if someone saw us? You're not letting me in. We need to talk about this.'

I turn. 'What is there to talk about, Jamie? What exactly do you want to talk about?'

I'm about to lose it again. I can feel the pressure welling up from my chin, through my cheeks, threatening to burst out in tears, but I need to keep myself together.

'In the cab on the way home from Andy and Lauren's, we were saying that maybe we should just go to the police. I thought maybe we were getting somewhere.'

And bang – I've lost it.

'What are you talking about, Jamie? How many times do we have to go over the same things? What do you think the police are going to do? Going to the police is exactly what could get Danny killed. And then with our baby dead, what do you think the police will do? Tell us that it's all fine, that we're totally devoid of all guilt because we've come clean, because we've been honest?

'You'd probably be fine, actually, wouldn't you? Danny would be dead and I'd be the one locked up in Holloway Prison, eating porridge with Myra Hindley.'

'You don't know that, Victoria!' he shouts. 'I've been looking into it. You could plead self-defence and then . . . Oh, you're so infuriating! We can't go on like this. I don't understand why we can't just communicate about this properly. We need to – for Danny.'

He leaves the room and I hear him grabbing his coat and stumbling out of the flat. A few seconds after shutting the door, he opens it again and comes back in the bedroom. He looks ridiculous, with his thick cream dressing gown visible under his smart navy coat. He throws a letter at me.

'You've got some post. And seeing as you're determined to be flippant, Holloway Prison is closed and Myra Hindley died years ago.'

He leaves, this time properly, slamming the door behind him with such force that the bones of the flat shake. I slip out of bed, down the corridor and into the bathroom. All of my stuff is still in the shower: the volumising shampoo I use for my hair, which Jamie is afraid to use for fear that his curls will go even thicker, an old shower cap that I use when I haven't got time to wash my hair, a disposable razor that I almost step on as I climb in.

The water pressure here is so much better than in the studio and I spend a good ten minutes washing myself, letting the water trickle into my mouth, scrubbing last night out of me as best I can. All the towels on the radiator smell damp, so I grab one of his dressing gowns off the back of the door and head back towards the bedroom to find a tracksuit to put on.

I try to stay focused as I walk back down the corridor, to resist the temptation to go into the nursery, but the door is open and I find myself in there. I do a little sweep of the room, touching each of the boxes stacked inside the cot – things that Jamie insisted on buying way too early in preparation for Danny's arrival: dummies, nappies, boxes of Calpol, a diffuser for colds, a steriliser for bottles that will never be used, packets of wipes.

I lean on the cot's rim and reach over to the dangling mobile at the far end, turn the switch and watch as the hippo, lion and a polar bear do their little dance, spinning round and round to the tune of a nursery rhyme. Jamie insisted that we buy a cot that had a drawer at the bottom and when I open it, it's empty but for a little pair of booties, red, just so tiny – Danny's first pair of shoes, so small that I can barely fit two fingers in. I lower myself to the floor, place my head between my legs and let myself go.

On my way out of the flat, I crouch to the floor and pick up the letter that Jamie had thrown at me on his way out.

Dear Mrs Rawlinson,
I am writing in regard to a missed appointment at the Ivy
Lane surgery. You were last seen by myself at the surgery on
26 February, when you were thirty-six weeks pregnant, and
no concerns were raised. However, you were due to come back
for an appointment on 12 March and I have you down as
'Did Not Attend'.
  I have tried to contact you on the mobile phone number
provided on a few occasions but have been unable to get
through. It may be that you have already had your baby, but
please do get in touch with us so we can arrange the necessary
postnatal appointments. You can reach me at the surgery or
on email (contact details above).
  Kind regards,
  Emma McNalty
  Community Midwife
  Ivy Lane Surgery

I screw the piece of paper into a ball and throw it to the ground.

Chapter 19

Jamie

There's a metallic taste in my mouth, like I've taken a bite out of a paracetamol. My eyes are heavy, the lids pinned down, and as I open them, I see the blurred outline of a ceiling fan above me. I'm fully clothed, on top of the covers, and Victoria isn't beside me. Below me, I hear the muffled bleats of a baby crying.

My baby.

Our baby.

I sit up and look around me.

I'm in a bed. How did I get here?

I rub my wrists and feel an ache at the top of my left arm. Images flash before me, the kitchen floor, skin, fists and blood. I go to lever myself out of bed and every muscle is aching, my hips sore and my left leg throbbing. I head out onto the landing and shuffle down the stairs, grabbing hold of the banister, taking one step at a time.

As I approach the bottom, I can hear voices coming from the kitchen – two women in calm conversation – and one of them is Victoria. I walk across the hallway through the threshold into the kitchen and see my wife sitting at the table, Danny at her breast, Fiona opposite her.

'That's it, gently does it. Tummy to Mummy, nose to nipple. Sometimes it helps just to tickle the chin and then . . . yes, that's it. Oh no, his mouth isn't wide enough. Let's just try—'

'I can't do it. I can't do this. I thought I could, but I can't.'

'Try not to get frustrated, dear. You did wonderfully the first time. It'll come. I remember with our Harrison, it was a good week before I'd got the hang of it. That's it – guide the nipple towards him and . . . oh, Jamie! Good evening.'

I open my mouth to respond, but nothing comes out. I don't know where to look, because this scene seems too ordinary, as if this were just a hospital and Victoria had given birth in a safe medical environment. Why is she so calm, so willing?

'Don't worry if it feels like it's just a few drops sometimes. It'll get easier.'

'Shouldn't we be topping up with formula? I mean, how do we know he's getting enough?' Victoria asks, trusting Fiona, obeying.

'His stomach is so tiny at the moment, Victoria,' Fiona answers, looking earnestly into her eyes. 'He doesn't need much. Let's monitor it over the next day or so and see how we go. Jamie, why don't you come and sit down?'

I can't stop looking at Victoria, staring at her, longing for her to explain what's going on, even if just with an expression. Why is she so calm? What am I missing here?

'What do you fancy for dinner, Jamie? Good that you had a proper rest.'

I don't remember going to sleep, or even going upstairs. The last recollection I have is of a struggle, a desperate attempt to set myself free. I look down at my wrists and see that they're red and as I press my fingers against them, they're sore, crushed by the handcuffs.

'I'm not having dinner. We're leaving. We're going to the police.'

And Victoria looks up, shaking her head.

'Jamie, sweetheart, it's no use. We just need to . . . Look, we need to do what's best for the baby, given the circumstances.'

Her voice sounds wrong, insincere.

'What? What do you mean, "the baby"?' I ask, lowering my voice towards her, looking closely at her blank expression and searching for my wife in her eyes. 'Are you suggesting that we should . . . that these people . . . ?'

What is going on here? What kind of hold have they got over Victoria? I stare at her, my eyes watering, longing for her to elaborate, hoping for a sudden movement, for decisive action, but she's looking right through me, terror in her eyes. Fiona steps in.

'Come on now, Jamie, it's time to give in. I'm sorry it has to be this way, but if we can come to an agreement, if we can keep it all amicable, then I'm sure there are ways you can still be involved in Harrison's life. Now, I wonder where Barry has got to. He's usually the one on dinner duty.'

Fiona rises from the table and heads into the hallway.

'Barry? Barry! Can you get some food on, please? The kids are starving.'

The window of opportunity is fleeting, but Victoria grabs the chance while Fiona's out of sight and mouths some reassurance at me, in a barely audible whisper.

'Don't worry. I've got an idea. Play along. I'll explain later.'

I suddenly feel exhilarated, replenished, a rush of adrenaline flowing through me with the relief that Victoria hasn't capitulated, that there might be a way out of this nightmare. I trust her implicitly. When Fiona re-enters the room, I smile, too quickly, and she offers me a smile back. Barry comes down the stairs and joins us in the kitchen.

'Nice to see things are a bit more civilised. Have we all come to our senses?' he asks, staring at me and leaning down to brush dust off his khaki trousers.

I taste mud in the air. I have to bite my top lip to prevent me from lashing out. Fiona goes to one of the cupboards, taking out a couple of saucepans.

'Victoria's been an absolute star, haven't you? How does beans on toast and fish fingers sound? I'm afraid we haven't got much in.'

The idea of putting anything in my mouth right now repulses me, but I have to trust that Victoria is on to something and play along. I'm going to struggle with enthusiasm, though.

'Whatever's easiest for you.'

'I would offer some of our red wine,' Fiona says, chuckling to herself. 'But better not as Victoria is breastfeeding.'

I force a smile.

And so we sit round the table, while fish fingers cook in the oven that I was chained to a few hours ago, as if this is the most ordinary thing in the world, as if this morning never happened.

Danny is now lying in front of Victoria on the kitchen table in a Moses basket that must belong to them. He sleeps, oblivious.

'Tomorrow is going to be a nicer day, by all accounts,' says Barry, gesturing towards the windows. 'I may go for a ramble.'

'Oh yes, that's a good idea, Barry,' responds Fiona chirpily. 'Maybe we can even take the baby out in the pram. Victoria and Jamie, you'll have to stay here, of course. We don't want to risk anyone we know driving up this way from town and getting confused.'

Victoria looks up.

'We don't have a pram. I mean – we have one back in London, but—'

'Oh, don't worry, dear. We've still got Harrison's old pram. It's in the cellar. We don't need one of those fancy new ones – it's all a marketing ploy.'

It's too much. Do they honestly think that they'll get away with this? How can they even dream that questions won't be asked, if they suddenly parade a newborn baby around their nearest town, at their age? I'm desperate to be alone with Victoria. What kind of plan has she got?

All of a sudden, Danny starts crying and we all turn towards him. Victoria rises to comfort him and nobody objects. She rocks him gently, as if she's done this a hundred times before, and he's soothed.

'I was thinking,' says Victoria, her eyes still fixed on Danny as she lowers him back into the basket, 'that it might be best if we stick around here for a while, so that I can breastfeed.'

'That won't be necessary,' interjects Barry. 'I'm one of four boys. None of us were breastfed. We all turned out fine.'

Fiona nods in agreement.

'It's very thoughtful of you, Victoria, and generous, but it's probably for the best if you keep your distance before too long.'

Victoria persists.

'It's just that I think we all want what's best for the baby, don't we? And it's supposed to be ideal to breastfeed for at least the first six months, isn't it? I could pump and, um, courier some milk up here.'

What is Victoria plotting? I look at her, trying to catch a glimpse of her plan in her expression.

'As I said, it's a very generous offer, Victoria,' says Fiona, 'but we all know that it isn't going to be viable. He'll be just fine on formula, but it can't hurt for the next few days for him to get the rest of the colostrum.'

And I say my bit, to play along.

'How long can we stay, then? How long does the colostrum last?'

Fiona turns to me with a condescending smile.

'There's no need to rush you. But three or four days should be more than enough. As long as Victoria's feeling all fit and up to the journey.'

Barry serves the food and we eat in silence. Victoria barely touches her plate. Every few moments she levers herself up and looks to the Moses basket, where Danny is sleeping soundly. I've been staring at him, trying to make sure he seems OK. The rise and fall of his chest as he breathes is just about visible when I concentrate.

'I think I'm going to go and lie down for a bit,' Victoria says, rising, after a few minutes.

She raises her eyebrows in my direction and I stand, too. 'And me.'

Victoria reaches into the Moses basket, but Barry stops her, stretching his arm across her.

'He'll be fine here,' he says.

Victoria stops, flinches and then agrees, so I don't object, either.

Barry follows us up the stairs and we're both as hesitant as each other as we ascend. I watch Victoria from behind and her gait is different, her legs wider apart than usual. She's clearly in pain. We're barely in the room when we hear the crunch of a lock – a reminder that however amicable our false exchanges were downstairs, we're still imprisoned. I think about Danny, willing for him to be fine, for this separation not to be harming him.

'What the hell's going on, Victoria? Sending them breast milk?' I whisper as we walk to the bed.

'Shh, keep your voice down. I'll explain in a minute.'

We both lie on the bed, above the floral covers, side by side, holding our breath as we hear Barry return downstairs. I hear his voice – a muffled comment to Fiona as he walks back into the kitchen. I strain to hear the words, but it's all too quiet. I place a hand on Victoria's belly, still swollen, and she flinches.

'Ooh, it's tender,' she says, placing her hand on mine.

'We need to get our phones back off them,' I suggest. 'We just need to call the police. I don't buy their threats.'

Victoria squeezes my hand and I feel her nails digging into my palm.

'No, we can't risk that. I don't think they'd actually do it, but you heard what he said about harming Danny if they catch wind.'

I stand and start pacing around the room, stopping at the window and looking out onto the driveway.

'What about that van? If we can get their keys, somehow, and get into their van . . .'

'Yes, that's what I've been thinking, too. We need to get hold of their keys,' Victoria says.

She's exhausted, lying on her side, her cheek to the bed and her eyes only half-open. She turns her body towards me by the window.

'I think we just need to play along for a bit, make them feel comfortable, like we're being compliant.'

'And then what?'

'Surely there's a chance they'll let their guard down, slip up at some point. It'll be her, I reckon. Let me bond with her. I can break her.' Victoria's eyes are now shut, but she carries on whispering. 'We're not leaving here without Danny. They'll have to kill me first.'

Chapter 20

Victoria

Thursday, 22 April

Dear Emma,

Thank you for your letter and sorry that I've missed your calls.
It's been a really hard few weeks and I've not really known how
to deal with it all. I'm hoping you can help me but ask that you
keep the contents of this email completely private.

I went into labour just over six weeks ago, while on a minibreak
with my husband in Cumbria. I gave birth to a little boy, Danny,
and thankfully, even though he was premature, everything went
well with the birth and he's healthy.

Danny was born in a guest house, with the help of the older
couple who run it. They lost their own child years ago. We were
blackmailed into giving away our baby.

My husband and I have been torn apart and cannot cope
knowing that our son isn't with us. I've done something terrible
and we don't know where to turn, because we've been told that
if we go to the police . . .

Seeing it written down on my phone takes it all to the

next level. I can't send this. The midwife is not a friend, or someone I can trust. Gentle, yes, and caring in a professional capacity, but I'm fooling myself to believe that I can tell her something as big as this, in confidence, and not have her act upon it. What is the duty of care for a midwife? And in any case, what could she possibly do to resolve the situation?

I've tried running through the scenarios in my head – the different ways that this could turn out – but as I write the email and see it there in black and white, I know that every route would lead to the police sooner or later and worse, the risk of Danny's death. I need to speak to her and make her believe that everything is finished. That Danny is already dead. We can't have her sniffing around. I need to reassure her enough, tick the boxes to make her disappear.

I turn on my bed, from my front onto my back, delete the draft email and dial her number. As the phone rings – once, twice, three times – I hold my breath for voicemail, because if it's voicemail I can just say my piece and be done with it.

'Hello? Emma speaking.'

I hang up. I can't do this.

She's ringing me back. I pick up.

'Hello, this is Emma McNalty. Who is this, please?'

'Hi, sorry, don't know what happened there. I . . . it's Victoria Rawlinson. I-I got your letter?'

I sit up and my free hand covers my mouth while I listen.

'Ah, yes, Mrs Rawlinson. Thanks so much for calling. Sorry if I've been chasing. It's just that when you didn't come for the appointment, and then I called the hospital and they had no records of you giving birth, I . . . Anyway, how are you?'

I move my hand to my chin.

'Not so good, really.'

'Do you feel comfortable talking about it on the phone, or . . .'

'No, it's fine, I just . . . well, we lost the baby, unfortunately.'

There's a pause. I shuffle on the bed. Which way is this going to go?

'Mrs Rawlinson, I'm so sorry to hear that. Did you . . . when did it happen?'

'Just over six weeks ago. My husband and I were on a trip to a guest house in Cumbria. It all happened very suddenly, while we were there. It was very remote.'

'Did you go to a hospital? Were you seen by a medical professional?'

'Yes, a midwife.'

'So you went to a hospital?'

Pause. I try to breathe slowly to settle my rising anger.

'Yes, we went to the local hospital. They were excellent. It's all quite a blur, to be honest, but everything was dealt with there.'

What am I saying? I've committed to it now – this is the version that I'm telling.

'That's good to hear. Which hospital was it?'

Shit.

'I can't remember the name, actually – it was just a little local hospital, quite remote, near to where the guest house was. It was lucky that we were able to get there quickly.'

My hand is back in front of my mouth and I chew my finger, biting down and then releasing, while she speaks.

'Ah, OK. Sometimes in these smaller hospitals the care can be excellent. Do you think you could look up the name of the hospital? It's just I need to make sure all the paperwork is in order.'

'Yeah, sure, that's fine,' I answer, trying to sound chirpy. 'I need to ask my husband – as you can imagine, I was pretty out of it at the time. Don't even remember getting there. Is it OK if I get back to you with it?'

'Of course, I understand. How are you doing with it all? Do you fancy popping into the surgery for an appointment? There's all different types of support we can offer at Ivy Lane.'

'To be honest, I'm finding it pretty hard to get out and about at the moment. I just . . . I don't know if I can face coming to the surgery.'

'Let's do a home visit, then,' she suggests, and I bite down again on my finger. 'I'd like to have a few checks done – make sure your womb has contracted and stuff like that. I'm sure everything's fine – it sounds like you're doing OK physically. I can organise it with the community midwife team or I'm happy to come myself, if you'd rather that? I've actually got a slot on Saturday morning, at 9 a.m.?'

'Thanks, yeah. That works. This Saturday coming?'

'Yes, the twenty-fourth. I'll see you then, Victoria. And if there's anything before then, you've got my number at the surgery, OK, sweetheart?'

'Thanks. Yeah, see you then.'

I don't want 'sweetheart' from her. I didn't expect that to be the outcome of the phone call. Are all midwives this diligent? You'd assume that the admin of it all would be a shambles. That I was nothing but a number – one of thousands of women in London going through the late stages of pregnancy at the same time. How many women have fallen off the radar without wanting to? How many women are in a vulnerable position, sitting at home in abusive relationships, waiting for a phone call, for someone to offer to come round and check up on them?

I open the calendar app on my phone and add an event.

Date: Saturday, 24 April
Time: 9 a.m.
Description: Tell midwife?

Chapter 21

Victoria

Sunday, 7 March, 2.06 a.m.

'Wake up, Victoria,' Fiona whispers.

I keep my eyes closed but I can feel her breath – I know that her face is right up against mine. I open my eyes and from the slither of light coming in from the hallway, I see her standing right over me, almost unrecognisable, with her head covered with what looks like a pink shower cap, her tiny frame held together by a thin dressing gown. She's cradling Danny, rocking him gently as he lets out a gentle moan.

'What time is it?' I ask, in a whisper.

'It's just gone 2 a.m. The baby needs to eat, poor thing. Come on, let's go downstairs into the kitchen.'

I look over at Jamie and see that he's stirring. He sits up, rubbing his eyes.

'What's going on?'

'It's fine, Jamie,' I reply. 'Go back to sleep. I'll be downstairs. I-I need to feed Danny.'

I give him a look intended to reassure him, to remind him of our conversation before we went to sleep. Going along with this, for now, is a vital part of the plan.

'Well, if you need me, I . . .'

Fiona interrupts.

'I think we'll probably be OK, my dear. It's an intimate moment between us women and the baby. You go back to sleep now, there's a good lad.'

I get up and slip on the loose tracksuit bottoms and T-shirt that are on the floor. I will him to turn over and go back to sleep. He watches as we leave the bedroom and Fiona shuts the door behind her.

'Barry's asleep as well. We'd better keep our voices down – he can get very cranky if he's woken up in the middle of the night. Here – you can hold Harrison while we go downstairs, if you like.'

She hands Danny to me and it's ridiculous that I should feel grateful, like this concession feels like such an act of generosity. His eyes are open, little blue slits in the dark, and as we take each other in, the feeling is electric. I used to roll my eyes when women said they felt an immediate connection with their child, but here he is now and I feel it. His crying intensifies into real bleats and I'm desperate to soothe him.

'Why is he crying? Am I holding him wrong?'

Fiona turns back, shaking her head.

'Don't worry, dear. He's just hungry. He can sense your milk.'

As she walks downstairs and I follow, I imagine pushing her. I picture myself lunging forwards and placing a hand firmly on her bony back, applying just a little force and then watching her go. All it would take is a little shove and she'd fly, tumbling down the wooden stairs one by one. She's so slight and frail, she'd at least break a rib or two. Then they'd have to call an ambulance and we'd tell them everything and all would be resolved. I could just say I slipped. But what if she wasn't badly hurt? What if Barry took revenge instead of calling for help?

At the bottom of the stairs, Fiona turns right into the kitchen, switches on the kitchen light and then heads towards the sink. I've managed to calm Danny by putting my little finger in his mouth and am surprised by the strength of his suck.

'Do you want a glass of water? You must make sure you're properly hydrated, dear.'

'I'm OK, actually. It's a bit chilly in here though, isn't it?' I say as I sit at the kitchen table. 'Do you mind turning the heating on?'

She turns away from me, opening a cupboard above the sink to adjust the boiler. With her back turned, I look around the room for something to grab, a weapon to clutch. For self-defence, or to attack? There's a block of knives by the hob – could I get to one without her stopping me? And then what would I do with the knife? She turns back and I force a smile.

'The weather's so unpredictable at this time of year, isn't it?' I say. 'It was quite warm earlier, but I'm freezing now.'

'Yes, well, I suppose in your swanky London flat the walls are a bit sturdier. Here, it's impossible to keep a draught out.'

Danny starts to wail again, his eyes screwed shut and his mouth quivering. It breaks my heart. Fiona rushes over, grabbing him from me and cradling him, rocking him and making a gentle shushing sound.

'Thank you for letting us know you're hungry, my sweetheart. Auntie Victoria's going to feed you now.'

'Auntie Victoria?'

'How does that sound to you? I thought that could be a nice way for you to stay involved. You know? Still feel part of it,' she says while lowering my own son towards me.

I feel sick at the suggestion, patronised, manipulated. I can't answer that – I can't even pretend that this would be sufficient – but I force myself not to protest.

'So, shall we start with your left breast? I think that one was a bit easier earlier, wasn't it?'

She starts lifting my shirt from the bottom and I pull away slightly.

'I can do it.'

My boobs are tingly and when I touch the left one, it's so tender that the idea of Danny latching on is terrifying. I try to position him in the right place, but he's turning his face away – he doesn't want me. He's crying more now, really squealing, and I use a hand to turn his face towards me. He puts his lips out and pinches so tight that I wince. It feels like my nipple is being pricked with burning needles: it's warm, it stings, it burns.

'Ooh, that's quite the grimace you've got on there, Victoria,' Fiona remarks, now sitting beside me. 'It shouldn't hurt that much.'

Her words spark a rage that shuttles right through me, helter-skelter, unearthing violent urges that feel foreign but exhilarating. This woman, this pensioner, is so frail, so pathetic in stature, that if I could find it within myself to hit her head, in the right place, maybe she'd fall to the ground and we could make our escape.

I close my eyes and bite my top lip, and within a few seconds the pain lessens, the flow gets easier, Danny's sucking settling into a rhythm, and for just a few seconds, I block everything else out. For a moment, again, I'm Danny's mother, like any other mother, feeding my son. But then I open my eyes and Fiona is there.

'There you are. See, it's not that hard.'

After a few minutes, the flow of milk stops, Danny loses his grip and he starts yelping – short, sharp animalistic bleats. I'm failing him.

'Why don't you try the other breast now?' suggests Fiona. 'Give the left breast a bit of a breather. We can always go back to it later if he hasn't had enough.'

And we go through the same thing with my right boob: an initial struggle to latch on, followed by the hot stab of his lips as he takes the first few drops. I'm surprised again that the purse of his lips is so firm, given how new he is to the world, and I stroke his head as he settles in, his eyes closed as he takes confident gulps.

'He's a good boy, isn't he? Clearly got a good appetite.'

'It runs in the family,' I say with an eyebrow raised.

'I think it might be a good idea, after he's had a bit on that breast,' says Fiona, 'for you to try to express some milk. I'd like to get some in the freezer over the next few days to make the most of the colostrum.'

Play along.

'Sure, that's fine. They do feel a bit heavy and sore, to be honest.'

'Oh yes, that's normal. Expressing will alleviate some of the pressure,' Fiona says.

She stands up and takes her dressing gown off, draping it on the chair she'd been sitting on. Underneath she's wearing a floral trouser and shirt pyjama set. It looks satin. She approaches the cupboard above the sink, opens it and takes out an empty baby bottle connected to a transparent nipple shield and baby blue pumping lever. She slides it across the table and I can see that it's old, the measurement markings worn, the shield scuffed. Did she use this same pump when she had her son?

'I don't expect you to fill the whole thing – you'll probably only manage a bit – but do what you can.'

We look at each other for a moment.

'I'm afraid I don't know how to use a manual one.'

'Oh yes, of course, dear. You do it by hand. Or if you like, I've got an electric pump upstairs – almost new – that could make it a bit easier. Why don't you carry on feeding the little one while I go and get it?'

Is she going to leave me on my own down here with him?

'Sounds good. Could you do me a favour and also grab a jumper from our bedroom? I think there's one just on the floor by my side of the bed.'

'Of course. I'm quite warm myself, but then I always am.'

Can she not see me sweating? I can feel a specific bead, dripping down the back of my head and onto my neck. I couldn't be any warmer, but asking for a jumper is the first thing I think of – a distraction to give me a bit more time down here, just Danny and me.

'Let me just give the little guy a kiss.' Fiona bends down and kisses him on the forehead, burying her nose in his fine dark hair. 'There's nothing that beats that smell, is there?'

And off she swoops, my heart pounding as I hear the shuffle of her slippers across the wooden floors and up the stairs, one by one, leaving me with Danny. I turn back and with her no longer in sight, I stand up, rising while holding Danny in place so he keeps feeding.

I slide the chair back slightly with my foot and it makes an excruciating creak. It's the first time I've moved around alone while carrying him and I'm petrified of dropping him. He's so small, so helpless, that if he were to slip from my grip, he'd fall straight onto the hard floor. But then I don't want to grip him too hard, either. What if I apply too much force on his neck and end up suffocating him?

I start making my way round the kitchen, using my one free hand to ease open drawers and cupboards, looking for anything that might spark an idea. Floral plates and bowls, rusted saucepans and chipped mugs, all ordered with precision. A drawer full of paper, old bills and medical letters, car insurance documents, old photographs and handwritten notes. The next drawer is full of little antique trinkets: a small gold bell, a red thimble, a hand mirror with bevelled glass and a brass handle.

I hear a door shut upstairs and look back, expecting her to appear at any moment to find me rummaging around the kitchen. What would she do if she caught me with a hand in one of her kitchen drawers?

I edge back towards the table, dart back into my chair, ready for her return. I'm sweating, out of breath, and need to regain my composure before she comes down. Her dressing gown . . . She's left her dressing gown dangling on the back of her chair and I see a flash of silver.

I hold Danny tighter to my body and reach forwards. Keys in an inside pocket. I finger the keys, the glorious cold, metallic edges. It's a whole bunch, different shapes and sizes and shades of rust, but one much bigger than the others: covered in rubber, a car key.

I can hear her moving around upstairs, each creak threatening her imminent return. I need to act quickly. I leave the keys in the pocket and scurry round to the kitchen worktop. I take a knife from the block, the second biggest, with a green handle, and slide it under the back of my T-shirt, tucking its blade up into the waist of my tracksuit bottoms. I can hear her footsteps now and feel a cold rush of adrenaline running down through my legs, shaking them, as I clamber back to my seat, holding Danny tight to my breast and watching as he sucks.

I can feel the cold blade against my back and am paralysed, terrified that if I make a movement that's too sudden, the knife will slip and clatter to the floor. Or, worse still, what if the knife slices me in the back?

I peer round the door and can see her silhouette on the wall as she comes down the stairs. I start singing to him, more to soothe myself than him, willing myself to catch my breath and regain my composure.

'You are my sunshine, my only sunshine. You make me happy, when skies are grey . . .'

'Oh, isn't that just picture-perfect, dear? I used to sing that song to Harrison all the time. It was one of his favourites. My mum used to sing it to me, apparently.'

Fiona has my jumper draped around one arm and is clutching an electric breast pump in the other. She's looking around the room, as if she's noticed that something is different.

Did I leave a drawer open? Has she noticed the missing knife?

'Oh, you look quite hot and bothered, my dear,' she says. 'Are you feeling unwell?'

'Oh, no, I'm . . . What do you mean? I'm fine, just . . . you know. Yeah, I guess I've just had a bit of a hot flush.' I force out a smile and reach out for the breast pump.

'I'll leave the jumper here, then,' she says, laying it on the table. 'There if you need it.'

She takes the dressing gown off the chair, putting her hand in the pocket to feel for the keys.

'Why don't you hand Harrison to me, then, while you pump? Do you want me to show you how to do it?'

My hands are shaking as I take Danny off my breast and lift him up in her direction. Danny cries, short bleats, but she's looking at my hands.

'No, it's OK. I went to antenatal classes, so I know how to—'

'Are you quite all right? You've gone all pale.'

'I'm fine, I'm fine. Just a bit . . . you know . . . Sorry, I—'

'I understand,' she says, grabbing Danny under the arms and kissing him on the forehead, placing her little finger in his mouth. 'It's a lot to take in. What you're doing for us, it really is the ultimate gift.'

I slump back and she starts singing. She has a clear, sweet voice and for a moment I allow myself to get lost in the lullaby.

'You'll never know, dear, how much I love you. Please don't take my sunshine away.'

And then we sit in silence. She cradles my son as I empty viscous yellow liquid from my breast into a bottle. My mind is racing, a plan forming. I can picture it coming together, everything happening at the right time and in the right sequence for us to make our escape.

'Victoria? Victoria?'

She's looking to get my attention, but I've tuned out – I'm somewhere else.

'You really are off in a world of your own,' Fiona says after a few minutes, jolting me back into the moment.

'Am I? Sorry, I—'

'No need to apologise, dear. You've managed quite a bit there. More than I expected. Shall we call it a night?'

I remove the pump and let my T-shirt fall down.

'I want to make sure you've got all the milk you need.'

'That's really very generous of you, Victoria,' she says, taking the equipment and bottle from me and putting them on the table beside us. 'You're a good person. We'll carry on with this tomorrow, then – our little night-time get-together, just for us girls – and baby Harrison, of course.'

I usher her in front of me and wait until her back is turned before standing. I rise slowly, willing the knife to stay in place. I follow her as she carefully climbs the staircase, cradling Danny, who is fast asleep in her arms.

I tighten my tracksuit bottoms with the string, as tight as they'll go, and walk with my back straight, feeling the blade, now warm, touch and release from the base of my spine with every step up.

Should I just do it now?

Pin her down and grab the keys from her pocket?

When we reach the top, she looks at me and adjusts the hair at the front of my face, which is plastered down with sweat. She's much taller than me and I close my eyes as she leans down and kisses me on the forehead, to avoid a visible wince, and she whispers to me with a smile.

'See you in the morning, then. Say goodnight to Auntie Victoria, Harrison.'

I don't reply but turn away, open the bedroom door and retreat.

Jamie is sat up in the bed.

'Where's Danny?'

I can't stand still. I'm breathing heavily, heaving, moving from the window to the door and back to the window again, closing my eyes, pursing my lips, willing the adrenaline to subside.

'I've got it, Jamie. I've worked out how we're going to get out of here.'

Jamie exhales, rubs his eyes and screws up his face.

'What do you mean? Why are you pacing like that? Calm down.'

He tries to keep his voice low, but it's urgent, like a soft bark.

I carry on pacing, shaking my head, taking deep breaths in and out.

'We'll get out of here. I'll do anything. Even if I have to . . . even if . . .'

I finger the knife at my back and make a quick decision to keep it hidden, even from him. Jamie whispers, quick, soft and angry.

'Victoria, get into bed. You need to rest. Please, let's talk in the morning. They're probably listening in at the door.

We mustn't do, or say, anything rash.'

I climb into the bed and he tries to cuddle up to me, but I know that if we spoon, if he touches my back, he'll find the knife.

'Please, Jamie. I need space. I'm aching all over.'

He kisses me on the lips and whispers to me.

'Let's chat in the morning. Try to get some sleep.'

I wait until I can hear his snoring before rolling my body, inch by inch, to the left, towards him, wincing with pain in my abdomen from the birth, and then remove the knife from under me with my right hand. I breathe out, place it under my pillow, roll back and finally sleep.

Chapter 22

Jamie

Saturday, 24 April

I jump when the buzzer goes. I'm not expecting any visitors.

I'm still in bed, on my phone answering work emails. I haven't been in the office for a while and have delegated most of the important stuff to Palvhi. She didn't ask too many questions, thankfully. I put my phone down on the mattress and get up, slide into my dressing gown, walk to the intercom and pick up the receiver.

'Hello?'

'Yeah, who is this, please?' I answer.

'Hi, this is Emma. I've come up from the GP surgery. I'm here to see Mrs Rawlinson.'

The voice is familiar – a Derbyshire accent, slow and calm. Why is she here?

'I'm afraid Victoria isn't in at the moment. What's this about?'

'Is it OK if I come in?'

I fling on a T-shirt and shorts and walk to the door barefoot. Why has she just turned up here? I feel sick.

I open the door to let her in. Seeing a woman in a midwife's uniform sends a shiver right through me.

'Hi, Mr Rawlinson. It's nice to see you again. Now unless I've got the time wrong, your wife and I have an appointment now,' she says, smiling and pressing a shoulder bag close to her hip.

'Did you . . . ? Sorry, no . . . She's not here at the moment.'

Emma takes her phone out of the pocket of her uniform and frowns at it.

'It is the twenty-fourth, isn't it? Yeah, we've got a home visit scheduled in. Do you know when she'll be back?'

'When was that scheduled?' I ask. 'I'm afraid the baby died. She doesn't need to be seen by a midwife.'

Emma takes a step forwards, still smiling, and I step back, grabbing the door and making to close it.

'I spoke to Mrs Rawlinson on the phone. I know the circumstances and I'm terribly sorry to hear what happened,' she says.

What is Victoria doing? Is there a chance that she's confessed to a midwife? I need to know what she's told this woman.

'Why is an appointment necessary when there's no baby?' I ask, tightening my dressing gown, feeling self-conscious about my thinner left leg being on show.

Emma's smile wanes and she purses her lips.

'Mr Rawlinson, I understand that you might be feeling angry, but I do need to check on your wife. It's part of my responsibility to ensure that she's coping, that she's recuperating physically. Perhaps I should contact her directly and reschedule?'

'Well, she's only popped out to the shops,' I lie. 'Why don't you come in? She should be back soon.'

Emma nods and follows me into the back of the flat, through the corridor. I rush ahead, clearing underwear off the sofa and turning off the computer monitor. I'm suddenly conscious that the flat smells like last night's dinner, a lingering whiff of fried fish. I leave her on a sofa in the living room, go back to the bedroom and grab my phone to text Victoria.

Come to the flat, now. Get a taxi. Midwife is here. What have you told her?

'Sorry, it's a bit of a mess,' I say when I'm with the midwife again. 'Can I offer you a hot drink? I think we might actually be out of milk.'

Emma sits on the edge of the couch.

'Oh no, you're all right, thanks. Do you know how long Mrs Rawlinson will be?'

'She should be here soon,' I say.

'And how are you holding up, Mr Rawlinson? It must be very hard for you, too.'

I look down at her and she's smiling again. She gives a gentle nod of the head. It's nice to be asked.

'Oh, you know. It's tough,' I say, sitting on an armchair opposite her and crossing my legs tight. 'I don't know if you remember, but it was a long journey just getting pregnant and—'

'I do remember, yes. Have you both considered seeing a counsellor?'

'I've been going to a group, but it's not really Victoria's style.'

Emma nods.

'Did they not offer any kind of service at the hospital?'

What?

'Which hospital?' I ask.

What has Victoria told her?

'The hospital up north – where the baby was born.'

I pause. Why has Victoria veered from the narrative? This is not what we agreed. I try to look relaxed and soften the muscles in my face.

'There wasn't a hospital. It was a home birth. It all happened very quickly in the guest house where we were staying.'

She leans forwards, her head cocked to the side to show she's really listening.

'It was awful,' I continue. 'Victoria was so incredibly brave, but luckily, the owner was a midwife. She was in good hands, all things considered.'

The leaflet from the guest house that came in the big brown envelope is still on the coffee table, right in front of Emma. She looks at it, then back at me, and then picks it up.

'This one?' she asks. 'Choristers' Lodge, is it?'

I find myself nodding and then quickly change the subject.

'Are you sure you don't want a drink? I could do a black coffee, or just some water?'

Emma looks at me, says nothing and reaches into her bag. She takes out a file, opening it up and flicking through the pages.

'Mrs Rawlinson told me on the phone that it all happened

at a small local hospital. She mentioned that you stayed in a guest house but said she was taken to a local hospital. She said you would know the name because she couldn't remember where it was.'

A hospital? Why has Victoria told her that? We went through this and decided that if we named a hospital, it would quickly lead to a dead paper trail that would raise an alarm. Is Victoria going behind my back? Is she trying to blow our cover?

Emma takes a pen from inside her uniform, looks at me and the leaflet and starts noting something down. What is she writing? I bow my head and place both thumbs over my eyes.

'Oh, sorry, I'm getting confused. We did end up going somewhere, just to get her checked out and stuff.'

'Do you remember the name of the hospital? I'll need to see the Certificate of Death.'

She's frowning at me and I don't know what to say next. I'm rocking on the sofa, back and forth. There's a tightness in my chest and I can feel a sweep of nausea pass over me.

'Mr Rawlinson, are you OK? Shall I fetch you a glass of water?'

I stand up, too quickly, and my vision is blurred. I can hear that my voice is raised as I stumble towards her.

'Just leave, will you? Just leave us alone. We lost the baby. We want to grieve privately. J-just . . . get out of the flat, please.'

She doesn't even try to object. She gathers her things under her arm, stands from the sofa, hurries to the door, opens it and leaves without speaking again. She seemed afraid. I glance down and see that my fists are clenched.

Chapter 23

Jamie

Monday, 8 March, 2.37 a.m.

I'm jammed into a cupboard under the stairs, surrounded by anoraks, duffel coats and tartan scarves, and I mustn't make a sound. I had to climb over piles of old clothes to find a space in here and even though I'm on the short side, I'm having to crouch, my neck crooked, to fit under the eaves.

The smell reminds me of my grandparents' old house, a combination of mildew and unwashed clothes, and I'm boiling hot. I'm making an effort not to breathe too loudly, but the very fact of having to be aware of the volume of my breath is making me anxious and causing me to take bigger intakes to prevent hyperventilation.

Victoria's big plan to get us out of the guest house, with Danny, is precarious at best, but I've promised to remain positive and I know that I need to stay focused if we are to have a chance of pulling this off.

Victoria first told me a basic version of her plan, in a whisper, when we woke up this morning. Then after breakfast, with Danny downstairs with Fiona and Barry, we were given permission to head upstairs and have a shower. We went into the bathroom together and Victoria ran the bath, putting both taps on full blast, talking me through it, step by step, still whispering even though there was no way they could have heard us over the water. And then I spent the rest of today in a daze, avoiding all interaction with Barry and Fiona for fear that I might blurt something out.

In the afternoon I found myself alone in the bedroom while Victoria sat downstairs with them, feeding Danny and engaging in pleasantries to continue the illusion that we'd accepted our fate.

I can hear Victoria's voice across the hallway in the kitchen. She's deliberately taken the seat nearest to the door and is speaking up a bit, so that I can keep track of their conversation, to give me some warning as to when it might be time for me to emerge from my hiding place. The plan depends on a predictable chain of events, on an assumption that everything will run similarly to how it did last night. I told her that the likelihood of everything happening in just the right sequence, as expected, was too small to assume that this might work. But we agreed that it was the only viable shot we had and that we'd try this, night after night, until we succeed.

'It's really not hurting as much tonight, you know. I think we're getting into a rhythm.'

And then murmurs from Fiona that I can't hear, followed by an extended period of silence.

She'd never intended to breastfeed. It felt like whenever she told someone this, during the pregnancy, they'd be passive-aggressive about her decision, as if we'd confessed to choosing to be inferior parents from the outset. It wasn't just nurses and midwifes, but also strangers at the antenatal class, asking ever so politely why she'd made that choice and being affronted when she didn't want to talk about it. I know that she must be finding it hard and I want to be there to help her.

Fiona's voice is still too soft and I strain to try to work out what's happening. I reassure myself that the important thing is that I can hear Victoria, just in case things progress as we want them to, so I'm ready for the cue.

'I thought I'd dressed a bit warmer tonight, but I really am chilly again. Do you have a spare blanket or something that I could put over my shoulders?'

A hushed response and then Victoria again.

'No, that jumper's dirty now and I didn't pack anything else. Can I borrow something of yours?'

This is Victoria's attempt to get Fiona to go upstairs, to send her on a mission to fetch something to allow us to be alone downstairs. It wouldn't work to have her go fetch the same jumper, because she'd go into our bedroom and find me not there. I came down once they were in the kitchen and Victoria delayed feeding Danny for a minute so his cries would cover any creaks from the stairs. Fiona had left our door unlocked last night after opening it to get Victoria and she did the same tonight.

'Oh no, your dressing gown won't fit me,' Victoria says. 'You're far too slim. I just need something thicker to go over my shoulders. A blanket would be ideal.'

And then I hear the squeak of a chair and footsteps as Fiona approaches the hallway. What if she looks in this cupboard for a blanket or a coat? We hadn't anticipated that. I tense up and hold my breath, rehearsing in my head what I might say if she opens the cupboard and finds me lurking inside.

I left something in here and was just looking for it?

Doesn't work.

I thought I heard a noise coming from in here so I thought I'd investigate.

Absolutely not.

What would they do to me if they found me here? Barry has already shown his violent side – would I be tied to the oven again? Or worse – would he take it out on Danny? But the footsteps fade and I relax, for a moment, and then I hear Victoria singing – the signal.

'You are my sunshine, my only sunshine.'

And then she repeats the same line.

'You are my sunshine, my only sunshine.'

It's all happening so quickly. I didn't expect it to be this straightforward, for us to be able to try at the first attempt, and I hesitate for a moment, scared that she's pulled the trigger too soon. What if Fiona hears me as I open the door? Victoria sings the tune one more time and I know I just have to go for it. So I stumble forwards and grab the handle to the door as gently as I can.

I try my best to open the door slowly, without making a sound, but it's stiff and the friction of the wood causes a creak as I hoist it open. Every sound is amplified – I can hear the squeak of my trainers as I step out into the hallway and then find myself ducking, as if by lowering my head I might be less visible if Fiona were to turn round and come back down the stairs.

I creep over to the kitchen, where Victoria is sat at the table, Danny cradled in her right arm and a large bunch of keys in her left fist that she's successfully retrieved from the pocket of Fiona's dressing gown. She throws me the keys and I almost catch them, the sharp edge of one of them scraping me on the finger, but I've never been good at this kind of thing and they rattle loudly as they hit the wooden floor and then echo.

'Sorry, sorry,' I whisper, and Victoria puts a finger to her mouth.

Both Victoria and I look up, suddenly, as we hear a click coming from above us. Is that Fiona turning off a light? Has she heard me? Has she checked our bedroom and seen that I'm not in bed? Neither of us moves and Victoria keeps a finger over her lips.

After a few seconds, we relax and I edge with the keys towards the front door. I gesture to Victoria and she moves to the edge of her seat at the table, ready to make a quick dart.

The front door has two locks and the bottom one is obvious – it's a Chubb lock and there's only one key that can fit in it. I slot it in and turn it slowly, and Victoria carries on singing to Danny to try to cover up the noise.

'You make me happy, when skies are grey. You'll never know, dear, how much I love you.'

The other lock is a much more standard shape and there are five or six keys that might fit. I'm afraid to turn on the hallway light, so I'm relying on the light shining in from the kitchen, but it's not enough for me to see what I'm doing clearly. I'm trying to be methodical about it, taking one key at a time, working by process of elimination, but my mind is racing and my hands are buzzing with adrenaline. I'm petrified of being caught – that at any moment Fiona or Barry will come down and it'll all be over.

As each key doesn't work, I get increasingly frustrated, aware of the itch of my jumper's cuff on my wrist, conscious that Victoria is waiting, on the edge of her seat, for the door to open. My hand is numb and I'm finding it hard to get each key into the slot. As each key fails, I feel increasingly emotional, like I'm going to burst into tears or start screaming and kicking and capitulate.

I turn back to Victoria, raising my hands in a panic. I told her that it wouldn't work. Why would Fiona be so lax as to leave the key to the front door for us to pick up so easily?

And then on my last attempt, a rose gold key slides in smoothly, crunching as it turns, without a fight, and I hear the clink and release of the lock. I push down on the gold handle and the door opens. I look back to Victoria and beckon her over, waving my right hand back and forth in the darkness, mouthing *now, come, now.*

Has she seen me?

She takes a second to react, but then she stands up, the chair squeaking slightly as she slides it back. Danny lets out a little yelp, so she places one hand over his mouth and edges her way out of the kitchen.

I rush out into the night and it's pouring with rain, so hard that the din of the downpour drowns out the sound of my feet on the gravel. I rush past our silver Ford Fiesta and towards their red van, pointing the remote key fob in its direction. Two orange lights flash on the side and as I open the door, I look back.

Where are they? Why is it taking her so long to get out?

The van is facing the front door, but it's so dark and with the only light downstairs coming from the kitchen, I can't see if they're out yet, so I edge up, looking over the open van door, and then I see them: Victoria and Danny. And Barry, too. He's blocking their way.

'What the hell do you think you're doing in my van? Where did you get the keys?' he yells through the rain.

I panic, get in the car and slam the door. It's suddenly silent and I try to force the keys into the ignition, but my hands are shaking too much. I drop the keys on the floor and bend down, scrabbling around to find them in between my legs.

What do I do? If I drive off, will they kill Danny? Would they actually do it? Could they kill them both?

Victoria must be able to get to me with Danny. I've just got to make sure I keep hold of their van and grab him from her. I've got the power now.

I find the slot and turn the key. The engine roars and I remove the handbrake. It's automatic! Thankfully, it's automatic. I can drive this.

The car is facing the house and I can see Barry is still shouting, but with the window closed, I can't hear him. I press down on the pedal and turn the wheel towards the house, but I see Barry again and this time he's holding Danny above his head. Danny is soaking, his neck too far back, and Barry is shaking him back and forth, back and forth. I slam down with my right foot on the brake, rip up the handbrake and push open the door. The cry coming from Danny is like nothing I've ever heard before, piercing rhythmically high above the constant patter of rain hitting the gravel. Victoria is shouting, too, trying to overpower Barry, her arms flailing up and down in desperation.

'Get off him! Get off him! What are you doing? Get off him!'

I jump down from the van and rush back towards the house. Fiona's there too, now, joining the struggle, grabbing at Barry and Danny and pleading with him to hand her the baby.

'Barry, stop it! Stop it! His head is too fragile. What are you doing?'

Victoria lunges towards him from behind, her fist in the air, and in the struggle, Fiona manages to take Danny off him, retreating back into the doorway, holding him close to her chest, kissing him repeatedly on the forehead. And I rush towards Danny, too, wiping rain from my eyes as I crunch on the gravel with my trainers and then step into the warmth of the house. I'm distraught that we're still here, but thankful to Fiona that she's saved Danny from her husband.

I hear it first. A strained, extended moan and then a thud on the wall. I turn and watch as Barry staggers back into the house, past Victoria, and then slumps forwards onto the welcome mat by the front door, his white nightshirt wet and stained red, the green handle of a kitchen knife in his back.

Chapter 24

Jamie

'Jamie, are you even listening?'

'Sorry, yeah, of course. Sorry, what were you saying?'

I asked Andy if we could meet for a drink because I needed to see a friendly face. We're at a table at the Lord Palmerston, a pub a few doors down from the church where my bereavement group meets. Andy is sitting on a bench with his back to the wall of the pub and I'm on a chair opposite. He knew instinctively to take the bench as I would have struggled to manoeuvre myself through. He laughs and takes a big swig of his beer.

'I was just saying that you and Victoria are solid,' Andy continues, stuffing dry roasted peanuts in his mouth. 'Obviously, you've had your ups and downs over the years, but ultimately you're solid. You're so obviously meant to be together. She's even said that to me, that there's no doubt in her mind you'll be together forever. I really don't think you need to worry about your marriage.'

'Yeah, thanks,' I reply, having to raise my voice slightly

to reach over the voices of other drinkers and the dance music playing from a speaker behind Andy's head. 'I think you're right. I just wish she'd let me in a bit. I'm worried about her. Oh, and I'm sorry for the way she acted at your place.'

Andy lets out an exaggerated laugh. It's fake.

'It was funny, really.'

We both know that isn't the case.

'Let's not indulge this, seriously. You're always worrying about Victoria and you know you don't need to. Trust me, she's madly in love with you.'

I change the subject. Andy has been trying to get a new job, so I ask about that.

'It's not going great, to be honest. There's just not that much coming up. Might sign up for the temp agency again. Got to help pay the mortgage, you know?'

And I know he doesn't like this, but I have to ask.

'Will you let me lend you some money to tide you over? Or I could see if we have any space for you to fill in. There's someone on maternity leave and we could probably do with the help.'

Andy shakes his head, downs the rest of his drink and grimaces as it goes down.

'You can get the next round in, though, if you like. I'll come with – help you carry them over.'

The pub has got a lot busier since we arrived a couple of hours ago and I have to force my way through drinkers talking in huddles to make my way to the bar. I step on a woman's foot as I brush past her and she gives me a dirty look, so I give her one back. I can see the security guard out of the corner of my eye, by the front door, watching me as I stumble forwards. I've been chucked out of pubs and clubs before for seeming too drunk because of the way I walk.

It takes a while to get the barman's attention and Andy and I keep missing our chance because we're doing impressions of Lauren's sister and laughing. I'm holding a round Guinness beer coaster in the air and shouting 'Oh yaahhh, it's actually recycled from elephant dung. Amaaazing stuff, so ecological,' when the barman finally gestures to me and I get the order in.

As I pay for the beers, I can feel my phone buzzing in my pocket – an email coming in – and I feel a short prick of anxiety. The compulsion to check it immediately is intense, but I don't have any hands free. I pick up the drinks, hand one to Andy, who is standing just behind me, and make my way back to our table, focusing on my steps so I don't spill it and feeling the weight of my phone in my jeans pocket.

Andy puts his pint down and then turns and walks back towards the bar, shouting over the din of the crowd as he goes.

'Toilet! Broken the seal!'

I take my seat, have a sip of my pint and get my phone out. I open my work email first, out of habit. I'm usually obsessed with all the details and find it hard to disconnect, but for the first time I really couldn't care less about the weekly finance report. And then, in my personal email, I see two words in the 'from' field that send a sharp incision right through me: Choristers' Lodge.

My finger hovers over the screen for a second and then I can't resist. I open the email and see the photo first: Danny, in a navy blue babygrow, lying on a bed with that ghastly green floral bed linen from the guest house. I feel totally shaken, freezing cold all over. His hair is the same, wispy and dark, and his eyes are open, still deep blue. He's looking right at me, alert, a person in his own right.

I swallow hard and try to regulate my breathing, but it's hard to focus, impossible to take it all in. I scroll down and read the message, rereading each line to be sure, then go back up to the photo to look at it closer. It gives me such a shock that I drop my phone on the floor.

'Are you OK, mate?'

Andy's back and he's bent down to help me pick up my phone. It's still on and working but the screen is a web of small cracks, making it almost impossible to see the display.

'I'm fine, I'm fine. Just . . . I am capable of picking it up myself.'

I don't mean to lose it with Andy – he only means well – but I'm so pumped with adrenaline, so desperate to take another look at that email, that I can't censor myself. I need to get out of here, home, to my computer.

'Sorry, Andy, something's come up. I need to get home. You can have my beer. I'll call you, OK?'

I pull my chair back, stand and hear a slam as the chair lands backwards on the floor. Everyone in our corner of the pub stops talking and Andy calls after me.

'Mate! What's going on? Come back.'

'I'll explain soon. I'm sorry, it's important,' I shout back.

But I'm out now and I'm going fast. Outside is quieter and the change is disorientating. I do my best to focus on my feet, concentrating on staying steady, because the last thing I need now is to fall. My vision is blurred by the concoction of alcohol and panic, but thankfully, the flat is close. I continue to focus on my feet and each step, the cracks and the pavement.

I look up to cross the road when it's clear and then look down again, counting the last steps to the front door. It takes me a few seconds to get the key in the lock because my hand is trembling so much. My ears are still buzzing with the background noise from the pub. Once I'm inside, I go straight to my computer so I can open my email again.

I get my password wrong, twice, typing too fast, and then the email is up there, on the screen. I focus this time, reading it thoroughly, not allowing myself to look at the photo again until I've processed every word.

Dear J and V,

I trust you are well. Have you received my letters? I just wanted to make sure you remembered what is at stake. Did you know how severe the sentences would be for your crimes? I was surprised by some of them. Life imprisonment even for manslaughter – and that's the most lenient charge you could possibly be facing. Many more, in reality.

Harrison is doing well. He's taken very well to the formula and is getting better at sleeping for longer stretches. I know just how to soothe him when he's grumpy – just a little tickle on the cheek usually sends him back off again.

I received a phone call from a midwife on Wednesday. She was asking questions about Harrison, about you, about the birth. What have you told her? How did she know to call me?

I made it plain what the terms of the arrangement are. You are to speak to no one. This isn't an idle threat. I don't want to hurt Harrison, but if you make me, I will.

After I put down the phone, I went straight to Harrison – to confirm that I am capable of doing what I must do if you betray us. Looking down at his face, I saw in his expression your betrayal. I found myself putting on a rubber glove and putting the kitchen knife against his throat. That knife that Victoria knows so well. I tried the same with the hunting knife – Jamie's knife, I call it, because of the prints – and got so close to cutting him, then and there, but decided to give you one last chance.

Soon, we'll be going away. Somewhere you'll never find us. But in the meantime, if the midwife calls again, or there's even the slightest suggestion of investigation from anyone else, know this: I will go through with it. I'm a woman of my word.

Going away? Where?

I look again at the photograph. On my computer monitor it's larger and clearer. Danny seems startled, his eyes wide open, looking straight at me. Then I see it, next to him, no longer camouflaged by the bed sheets. It's the green handle of the kitchen knife, the silver blade angled towards Danny. On the other side of him is the hunting knife, the curve of the tip of the blade millimetres away from his neck.

Chapter 25

Victoria

Monday, 8 March, 2.50 a.m.

Jamie falls to his knees, pulls the knife from Barry's back and lets it drop onto the wooden floor. He presses the wound hard with both hands, to stem the bleeding, but blood oozes through the spaces between his fingers. I'm at the bottom of the stairs, sitting and watching, calling Jamie's name, but I can't hear myself over the ringing filling my ears. My skin burns with adrenaline, my scalp is on fire. I can't see Danny, I can't hear him. I need my baby, I need to run and scream, but I can't move.

'We need an ambulance!' Jamie shouts. 'I don't know what I'm doing.'

I try to look around for Danny, left and right, and then see her, Fiona, wearing yellow kitchen gloves, rocking him wildly just inside the kitchen. As her thin arms swing him forwards I see the black of his hair and then she swings back and he's gone. Hair and then gone, hair and then gone.

'It was a mistake,' Jamie shouts again. 'He must have slipped. Call an ambulance – I can't stop the bleeding.'

Fiona screams back, her voice loud between wails. Are they Danny's wails? I hadn't heard them, but now they're incessant.

'What are you talking about? Your wife's a maniac. Turn him! You need to pump his heart! You need to pump his heart!'

She looks at me, her eyes bulging.

'She stabbed him! She stabbed him! She had a knife.'

Jamie growls as he tries to turn Barry onto his front, gripping his wide arms with both hands and howling as he pulls and pulls until Barry's body arches and falls in a dull thud.

'Pump! Don't you dare stop! Barry – can you hear me?' Fiona screams from the kitchen doorway.

Jamie tries to apply pressure to Barry with both hands but keeps losing his balance on his knees.

'Use both hands! Barry!' Jamie increases the pace of his pumping, his hands now a deep red.

'Please, Fiona. Please call. Don't you want to save your husband? I don't know what I'm doing,' Jamie begs.

But Barry's limbs are floppy, his head arched back, and we all know it's too late. It was so easy, the blade slipping into his flesh. It must have taken force, surely, I think, but it felt so effortless.

'He's dead,' Fiona says, quieter, looking at Danny, now silent in her arms. 'You murdered him,' she says, meaning me but still looking down.

'Fiona,' Jamie pleads, wiping his hands on the floor but no longer pumping, pulling himself away from Barry, trying to keep his hands away, heaving, breathless. 'It might not be too late. Please. Give me a phone. Let's call for help.'

He tries to steady himself, but everything he touches is stained with bloodied fingerprints, little patches of red on the wooden floor, the white walls, the skirting board, his clothes.

'Where are the mobile phones? Please, Fiona. Please!'

I will my limbs to move, try to force my legs to spring into action, but I can't feel them. I'm frozen. I look for Danny. Fiona is kneeling, balancing him as she squats, close to Jamie and then turns away, walking back to the kitchen, to the worktop. I have to get to my son. I have to take him.

I let myself roll forwards to the floor, to Barry's body, and Jamie springs to me, staining me with blood as he helps me up and to my feet, supporting my weight with his right side.

'We need Danny,' I say to him. 'Get Danny.'

He moves forwards and I'm amazed that I don't fall. I should turn myself in to the police and explain what I've done. I didn't know what I was doing. They'll understand, won't they? How is this happening to us? I feel a wave of nausea sweep up through my stomach and vomit onto the floor, inches from Barry's body, bile mixing with blood.

I hear a scream from the kitchen, Jamie begging Fiona to stop. I manage to run forwards and see her, and Danny, a flash of yellow from the gloves she's still wearing, and the glimmer of steel.

'It's your choice, Jamie,' she's shouting, her eyes wide and alive. 'Don't come closer! I'll kill him! I have nothing left, nothing. You've taken everything from me.'

I run towards her, but the knife is up and I yell 'No!' and stop a few feet away. 'Don't hurt him! Don't hurt him! Please, don't hurt him.'

Jamie is beside me, his palms open in front of him in surrender.

'We'll do anything,' he says.

Fiona is still facing us but starts walking backwards, slowly, step by step. She's no longer soothing Danny and his cries are now quieter, hoarser.

'The knife has your DNA on it, not mine,' she says. 'If you go near me, I will kill him. My life has been ruined, all because of you. Push me and I'll do it – I'll stab him with the knife and you'll have killed Harrison and Barry. Then I'll call the police.'

And then she screams, her eyes wide and protruding again.

'Stay back or I'll do it.'

'Fiona,' Jamie says, his voice strong and calm. 'Please stop. We'll stand back, won't we, Victoria? We won't come close. Please.'

Fiona stops and brings Danny close to her. She shifts the knife to the hand under his body, too close, before reaching with the other for a dummy inside the Moses basket on the table. He takes it and starts to quieten. Jamie uses his right arm as a barrier in front of me, making clear that we won't move.

Fiona quickly puts the knife down, places Danny inside the basket and drags it back to the other side of the table. She leans forwards and picks up the knife again, then sits on a chair next to the basket, holding the knife above Danny as he sleeps.

'The last thing I want is for anything to happen to Harrison,' she says. Her hands are shaking and the blade is vibrating in the air. 'The only way he'll be safe is if he stays with me.'

My legs are juddering and I'm freezing cold. I ask to sit and she agrees. Jamie pulls up two chairs at our side of the table. I lower myself, hold my hands in front of my mouth and blow to warm them. I'm desperate to keep looking at the Moses basket, to make sure Danny is still alive, but I have to let my head fall between my legs, to feel the blood returning.

I shut my eyes and float above my body. I leave my mind. I hover above the Moses basket, above her, above Danny. I can be close to him if I hover.

'We can come to an agreement,' Fiona continues. 'You've killed my husband, Victoria. You stabbed him. The evidence is all here. If we call the police, you'll be charged with murder, or manslaughter if you're lucky. Either way, you had a knife on you and you killed him. You'll spend many years in prison. Whatever happens, you can't be with the baby.'

I lift my head and feel tears staining my face and stinging my eyes. I have done this, I think, to me, to Jamie, to Danny. This is my fault.

Jamie grabs my hand and squeezes. He feels stronger than usual.

'It was self-defence,' he says. 'She was defending herself. And our baby.'

Fiona cocks her head back and lets out a laugh.

'She stole a knife from the kitchen and stabbed him in the back. It was planned. Premeditated. Yes, maybe she could say she was mad as she'd just given birth. But Barry and the baby would be stabbed to death with a knife with her prints all over it. Juries don't sympathise with baby killers.'

I feel sick. The knife has stopped shaking in Fiona's hand. She looks like she's enjoying this. Why is she not showing more regret for the loss of her husband? He's just a few yards away, decomposing by the front door. Would the police really take this madwoman's word over mine? Would a jury really see me as a child killer?

Fiona continues, leaning forwards over the Moses basket, over Danny.

'If we hide Barry's body, if I keep my baby, no one need ever know. I can start again. Somewhere far away where no one will bother us. Help me to hide his body. I'll never say a word. Victoria, you'll walk free and Harrison will live. We can all move on. You've taken my husband from me – now leave me with my son.'

I stand up and push my chair back. It screeches against the wooden floor. I'm too exhausted to shout.

'He's not your son and we will never leave here without him. I'd rather . . . we'd rather . . . Whatever you say, we'll be going to the police. You won't get away with this.'

Fiona reaches into the Moses basket and lifts one of Danny's arms up. She holds the knife to his wrist, tiny against the long blade, pale against the brown stains of Barry's blood. His little fingers. The tiny lines on his palm. It's too much.

Jamie screams. I beg her to stop.

'Call the police,' she whispers, still holding the knife to Danny's arm.

He's starting to squirm, to bleat. Fiona remains calm.

'I'm not stopping you. Try to grab him. I'm not stopping you.'

Fiona lowers Danny's hand and soothes him again, still holding the knife.

'Jamie, the choice is simple,' she says. 'You can save your wife, if you leave the baby with me. Victoria, you're still young. There will be more children for you both, I'm sure. I'm offering you a way out. If you agree, if you don't go to the police and you don't force me to kill him, then you could even see Harrison in the future, if you want. If I know I can trust you, I can let you hold him again one day.'

Everything is a blur. Jamie's face is so pale it's almost translucent, and the crimson of the blood on his hands and T-shirt are a deep maroon, close to brown.

'It's not your fault,' Jamie says to me. 'You haven't done anything wrong.'

I don't look at him and I don't look at her. I look towards Danny.

'I didn't mean to kill him,' I say. 'It was a mistake.'

I look back to Barry's body, heavy on the floor by the front door. I didn't wear gloves because I never meant to use the knife. It wasn't planned. I'm not a violent person. I've never been in a physical fight in my life. And now, the consequences will be severe. But despite this, if there's one thing I know for sure, it's that I'm glad I had the knife. Yes, when all is said and done, I'm glad I killed Barry.

Chapter 26

Jamie

'Hello?'

I hate that her voice is so familiar. Just one word from her and I'm there again, and I see her standing in her house, cradling our son, living our lives. I'm sitting at my desk in the living room, my phone in my hand and my desktop computer in front of me. My heart is pounding, the tip of my tongue stinging as I put on my most convincing Welsh accent.

'Hiya, my name's Richard and I'm calling from BT, British Telecom. Am I speaking to Fiona Johnson?'

I went to university in Cardiff, so this accent comes easily to me.

'Yes, speaking.'

Why can't I hear Danny in the background?

'Good morning, Mrs Johnson. How are you today?' I ask, moving my mouse right to left to keep the screen on.

I feel sick. I have no idea if this will work or if she'll put the phone straight down.

225

'Yes, fine, thank you, although rather busy. What's this about?'

I pause, look at my phone and almost end the call.

'Hello?'

I put the phone to my ear again.

'Sorry, yes, hello. I'm calling from British Telecom. We're receiving some error notifications from your router to our BT main tower with regards to your internet connection. Are you finding that your internet has got very slow recently?'

People trust a Welsh accent. My company partnered with Citizens Advice on a study two years ago that concluded that Welsh and Yorkshire accents are the most 'reassuring' so are most likely to be successful on scam calls. The point then was to prevent the fraud.

'Oh, it's got so much worse recently, actually,' Fiona responds.

She's engaging and the tightness at the top of my chest descends into my belly.

'Yes, I'm afraid it is, madam. Thank you for letting me know your internet connection is slower than you'd like it to be. I'd like to try to diagnose the problem for you today and check that you've got everything optimised on your devices to make sure it's connected to our BT main tower.'

I'm getting into the swing of it now.

'The thing is, though, we're just about to move away from the area. I doubt there will be any internet signal at all where we're going.'

I shut my eyes and breathe out gently, clenching my teeth before I continue.

'Oh, congratulations. When are you moving? Whereabouts are you headed?'

Silence, and then I hear her sniff. I need to carry on before I lose her.

'Well, if anything, it's all the more important that we get the router fixed for you, if you're going somewhere even more remote. You can take the router with you and then with the changes, you'll be all set to go irrespective of location.'

I'm talking too fast. I need to stay calm.

'Well, how long is this all going to take?'

She's falling for it.

'Five minutes. Not even that.'

I hear her exhale. My ear is burning.

'Go on, then. What do you need?'

I ask her to confirm the first line of her address and postcode and her date of birth.

'I'll just need to access one of your devices, but now that you've passed all the security questions, I can do that from here,' I reassure her.

This is always a key red flag that we tell people to look out for at our seminars. Any reference to remote access should start ringing alarm bells.

'Where did you say you were calling from again?'

She's on to me. Did I let the accent slip?

'British Telecom, madam. Can you tell me what kind of device you use to access the internet? A desktop computer, laptop, tablet, phone?'

People underestimate me. They think, because I walk with a limp, that I'm weak. That my physical restrictions mean I'm intellectually slow. That they can just walk all over me.

'OK, I think I can see what the problem is,' I say. 'I'm getting a lot of administrative events showing up. Lots of blocked gateways. They need to be open for you to access fast internet. I can sort that out for you today.'

Fiona follows my instructions willingly, step by step. As we go, I reassure her, I make her laugh, make her feel comfortable with me. So comfortable that when I get her to download software that allows me to control her computer remotely, she thanks me for being so helpful. So at ease that when I ask her to type in the password to her email, and her Amazon account, and her social media pages so that I can test the broadband speed, she doesn't question me.

'Make sure you don't tell me the passwords. Just type them in yourself. You should never tell anyone your passwords,' I say.

I imagine her nodding, rolling her eyes at all the other old ladies whom she imagines aren't as clued up as her on modern technology. She doesn't know it, but as she's typing each password, every character is appearing on my monitor, too. I have no need to look at her bank accounts – I don't need to steal from her – but the opportunity to have the upper hand in every way is too tempting to resist. She's chirpy now, relaxed even, and I feel calmer.

'Oh, I know about passwords, dear,' she says. 'People think anyone over forty is totally clueless when it comes to the internet. I've always been quite savvy when it comes to these things.'

I can't help but smile.

'That's good then, Mrs Johnson. So important.'

I have a pad of paper next to my keyboard to write

down each of the usernames and numbers and each of the corresponding passwords. Her email is the most important. She's not very imaginative when it comes to passwords – Harrison with a capital H followed by her year of birth. Every time.

'That's all sorted for you now then, Mrs Johnson. It can take up to seven days for you to see the full changes, so don't worry if nothing happens immediately. What we do recommend is that you leave the computer on for the next day or so, just so that the changes can take effect. There's no need for you to do anything.'

I'm talking more quickly, gabbling my way through the script now. I've got what I need now. I just need to end the call without making her suspicious.

'Oh yeah, that's fine,' she says. 'To let it all configure, I imagine. I've got to go and see to my son now, anyway.'

Her son. I'm on the verge of letting go, of tearing into her. I bite my bottom lip, hard, and release. I feel the pressure of tears forming in my eyes and try to hold my voice steady.

'Absolutely,' I say, remembering the accent. 'And congratulations again, by the way. It must be a very special time.'

'Thank you very much. Yes, we're very lucky indeed. Goodbye now.'

The line goes dead and I stand up and wipe my face with the back of my hand. No more tears. No more moping or worrying about what the consequences might be for me or Victoria. In the guest house, with the knife so close to Danny, Barry's body in the hallway and Victoria facing years in prison, the decision seemed so clear. Leaving and keeping quiet was the only way to keep Danny alive and save Victoria. But something has shifted.

We sacrificed our son – left him with her to protect ourselves. I feel disgusted. As long as he's with her, Danny's life is in danger and, no matter what it means for us, I will save him.

I get in the shower and make myself something to eat then head back to my computer. The more I know, the more prepared I can be. I log in to her email account.

Chapter 27

Jamie

Monday, 8 March, 4.45 a.m.

The night is so still that I can hear the tinkle of moving water. It looks deep enough here, but what do I know? As I step out of the car, my forehead is instantly numbed by the cold. The faintest breeze tickles an icy breath around my neck and down inside my clothes onto my back. I can see the outlines of hills on the other side of the lake and, at the top, a few patches of snow, the white just about visible in the dark.

I place the key in the lock of the red boot and look round before turning it, to check that there's no one else in sight. The door to the boot pings open and an orange light reveals a pile of tat: gardening tools, a bag of gold golf clubs, a jerrycan, towels, empty plastic bags. The smell of mildew.

Victoria and I stare at the large tartan suitcase lying on the top of the pile. I grab it with gloved hands. Victoria does the same and we drag it onto the ground. It lands with a dense thud. Victoria darts back. Which part of his body hit the road?

'It's fine, it's fine,' I whisper. 'Will you close the boot?'

Victoria speaks, the first time since we've got out of the car.

'Don't you think we ought to find something to weigh it down a bit?'

She seems more alert, perky even, having had the car journey to adjust to the plan.

'What do you mean?'

The orange light from the boot shines on the top half of her face. Her eyes flutter in a repeated blink.

'The heavier the suitcase is, the less likely it is to rise to the top of the lake.'

And so we open the suitcase and there he is, limp, his right arm flopping out over the side. I don't want to look, but curiosity gets the better of me. I shine the torch on his face and he doesn't look any different at all. His lips aren't blue, his skin no paler than it was before. From the neck up, he looks as though he's asleep. I find myself sniffing in his direction, curious to know if the decomposition process has yet begun, but there's nothing.

'What are you doing, Jamie? We need to get a move on – it's going to be light soon.'

She passes me a handful of towels and I stuff them into the suitcase, tucking them around Barry's legs.

'I'm not sure that's going to make much of a difference,' I say, and she throws her head back and scowls at me.

She picks up the golf bag and manages to get a few clubs in, slotting them right at the edges, one by one.

'You just stand there and watch, then, why don't you? I'm not an expert at this either, you know, just doing my best.'

That stings, because I don't want Victoria to think that I'm not pulling my weight. I'm the one who came up with the plan. I try to lift the jerrycan, but it's full and heavy, and it's wedged in a corner. She has to help me to maneouvre it out and in. She bends down, zips up the suitcase and together we hoist it up on its wheels.

'Come on, let's go,' I say, shutting the boot. 'Let's both keep looking up to check there are no cars.'

Together, we wheel the body across the road. Between us and the lake there is a low stone wall and then a short, sloping grassy field, a few trees and another stone wall. We take either side of the suitcase by the first wall and lift, managing to haul it up and then almost rolling it over. There's a muted thud when it hits the wet grass and then Victoria rolls herself over the wall, clutching her stomach. I try to scale it too, but my left leg won't go high enough, so I lunge over it, head first, and land on my right side, next to the suitcase and now sodden with dew.

If we were on a walk here, I'd have given up, refused to try to get over it. It's amazing what my body can overcome when it needs to.

I get up and try to drag the suitcase by myself, but it sticks to the grass. It's just too heavy for me to take on my own.

Victoria shakes her head and comes to join me. This must be one of those moments when she wishes her husband was strong like everyone else's.

'I'll do it,' she says.

But she can't manage it on her own either, so we pull together and it budges.

Together we can move at a faster pace, but the grass incline is steep and I struggle. I feel like I'm falling with every step, dragging and jolting. I'm breathless, panting, and my left knee aches and my ankle bends, the Achilles tendon pulling, but I need to power through.

Twigs and leaves crackle and crunch as we pass over them, flattening them with Barry's suitcase, and in the distance there's a cacophony of animal sounds that make me dart forwards and back. Having always lived in cities, the mysteries of the animal world at night have always put me on edge. I imagine cows, sheep, toads fighting, the bleats of two owls in conversation, the unbearable yelps of a pair of foxes in their pained lovemaking. It's so dark that I can only make out Victoria's silhouette as she strides and pulls beside me.

We pass the trees and then the lake fully reveals itself behind the last wall, perfectly flat, an immense shard of black glass. The beginning of tomorrow's light casts a shimmer of silver-blue around its edges, but it lies there otherwise unperturbed, totally oblivious to what it's about to receive.

'Wait, wait, Victoria. I want to do it. I want to be the one to drop the suitcase in. So it's not all on you.'

We stand on the edge and she lifts and rolls the case up the wall with me until it's perched at the top. I steady myself, breathe in and push.

I do it with all the strength I have left in my arms and in my chest. The weight of the thing yields a terrific reverberating crash, and I place my hands to my ears and apply pressure, willing the sound to subside. I watch as the suitcase becomes gradually engulfed by the black of the water until there's nothing left but ripples, large bubbles, small bubbles, then nothing. I hadn't noticed, but Victoria has put her arm round my waist and I now shuffle closer to her, leaning my head against hers.

'It's not going to be easy, Victoria, but it's the only way we can save him and save you.'

Victoria lets go of my waist and turns away from me. I watch her breath cloud in the air.

'How did this happen? What did we do wrong?'

I bring her back in, close, her hair making my nose itch.

'Let's go back to the guest house now. One last time. She'll have to let us say goodbye.'

I think again about going to the police. What if we drove to a station now? I imagine the solace in telling the truth. But then there's the blood at the scene, the body in the lake. The knife, the prints. Who would believe us?

We head back up the grassy verge, step by laboured step. Victoria shines the torch on the ground at our feet and in places I can see the tracks from the wheels of the suitcase. I do my best to stamp over the tracks, shuffling leaves with my foot. And then we go back over the stone wall to the road. Victoria helps me over this time, finding a large rock for me to step onto and holding my hand as I scale it, sit on the top and slide down. We get back to the van and I put the key in the ignition, remove the handbrake and drive away from the crime scene. Victoria sobs and there's little I can say to comfort her.

Chapter 28

Victoria

Saturday, 1 May, 12.08 p.m.

There's no answer when I buzz. He can't still be asleep.

I sit down on the low brick wall outside the front door of our building, take my phone out and call him. It rings and it rings, and eventually his voicemail kicks in. I wait just a few seconds and then call again, so he knows it's urgent. If he doesn't pick up, I'm really going to start to worry. Has he done something rash? Does he think she's harmed Danny? Is he ignoring me? I know I've behaved pretty badly – is he screening my calls? Has something happened to him?

'Hey, Jamie, it's me. Where are you? I'm outside the flat. Are you still asleep? I want to chat. I'm worried. I assume you've also seen the email from Fiona. Call me back as soon as you get this, OK?'

I fish in my handbag for the key to let me into the main door and hesitate. What are the rules here? If we've agreed to live apart for the time being, should I be giving him privacy?

I find myself opening the door to the building and then quietly open our flat's front door, as if trespassing into a building where I'm not welcome, creeping through the hallway and straight into the kitchen for a glass of water.

The stench is the first thing to hit me. It's a stale, sweet smell of leftover food – a whiff of sweet-and-sour sauce and spring rolls diffused through the air by central heating, which is on full blast. The smell clashes with my wine and sleeping tablet hangover. I've never seen the flat in such a state and it's disconcerting.

In the first few weeks after we returned from Cumbria, Jamie cleaned the flat meticulously. He took total control of things at home, rinsing plates as soon as I put them in the sink, sponging surfaces, scrubbing the inside of the oven and putting fresh loads of laundry on every other day. It drove me mad. I'd make myself a mug of coffee, have a few sips and as soon as I'd turned my back, he'd have cleared it away.

Today, it's an utter tip. In the living room there are piles of half-empty plastic takeaway dishes on the mango wood coffee table, with deep red-and-brown stains underneath, and a massive bottle of Coke Zero, half drunk but with the top off. Cushions have been left on the carpet and the remote control for the TV is also on the floor rather than in its designated cradle. The lid to my piano is up, the keys exposed and gathering dust.

What does this mean? Why has Jamie allowed things to slip so quickly? I feel a pang in my chest. Out of nowhere, I imagine him hanging in the bedroom cupboard, or submerged in water in the bathroom, with a bloodied arm draped over the side of the bath.

I walk across the hallway and feel a sting of foreboding, convincing myself that he's in the bath, lifeless, broken, waiting to be found in a pool of his own blood. I peer round the corner and feel relief to find the bath empty but for a cluster of suds gathered towards the plug hole, the smell of lavender doing something to mask the lingering of the Chinese food in my nostrils. He must have had a bath or shower this morning.

I pull down my jeans and underwear and sit on the toilet. Reaching across to the cabinet under the sink, I open it to find a half-empty packet of tampons. I take one and hold it in front of my eyes – a reminder of my fertility. My body will recover. When will my next period come? It should be soon. If my body can regenerate, can my mind? I put it back in the cabinet, feeling pleased that some of my possessions persist in this flat that has transformed so quickly. I flush, wash my hands and go back into the main room.

The computer monitor is on standby and I go over and sit at the desk, typing in the password. I've never wanted to be the wife who snoops on her husband's internet browsing history, but here we are.

There are lots of tabs open, but the first is the email from Fiona. He's read it. I bet that he's read it a hundred times, like I have, agonising over every word. The next tab is a Facebook page with an image of a hand with its thumb up and bandaged. Above it is the message: 'This page isn't available. The link you followed may be broken, or the page may have been removed'. But I look closer and the web address bar at the top is www.facebook.com/ ChoristersLodge, showing that he's been searching for the guest house. Another tab shows a Google search for the guest house, at the top of which is a notice that says 'permanently closed' in red.

What is Jamie doing? He's the one who is always reminding me that every search is tracked, that every time you click on an article, or search for a name, there's a record. We promised that we'd never utter their names again and hoped that in time we'd forget them, forget what they did to us and what we became complicit in.

My hands are shaking and I reach into my pocket for my phone again. As I unlock it, it rings. It's Jamie.

'Jamie, where are you? Where are you going?'

'Sorry I missed your calls. I've been driving and I don't have the Bluetooth thing. I'm on the hard shoulder on the motorway.'

I look at the computer monitor.

'Why are you on the motorway? Are you going back? Without me? What's going on?'

'I can't talk – I need to get up there. Did you see the email from Fiona? I've done some digging and she's going to take him away. We need to stop her.'

How does he know she's going away? The phone is hot against my ear and almost out of battery. I can hear the buzz of the motorway.

'What are you talking about? And what did you say to the midwife? Why did you tell her where we stayed? You'll push Fiona, you will, and then she really will do something to him.'

He shouts back and it's unusual for me to hear his voice like this, so aggressive.

'Look, our son is in real danger now. She's literally got the knives at his throat. We can't just stand back and let it happen.'

'Jamie, just think it through properly, OK? Can you just . . . Where are you now? Wait for me – I'll meet you somewhere and we can chat it all through properly. Don't go there without me.'

'Don't lecture me about thinking things through. Look, I really can't talk here like this. I need to get to them before it's too late.'

I need to be there, too.

'I'll get a train,' I say. 'I'll meet you. She's so volatile, Jamie. You'll make her angry and she'll kill him. I really think she will.'

The sound of passing cars on the motorway goes right through me. His voice is muffled now.

'Carlisle. Get to Carlisle and text me what time you get in. I won't do anything without you.'

He hangs up abruptly.

I search for train times and book a four-hour journey from London Euston to Carlisle leaving in just over an hour. I text him the arrival time: 5.46 p.m.

Whatever he's got planned, I need to stop him.

Chapter 29

Victoria

Monday, 8 March, 6.54 a.m.

The whole drive back to the guest house, we don't exchange a word. I feel shivery and sick, hot and cold, like I've just woken up after an anaesthetic. Jamie keeps his focus straight ahead, on the road. The sat nav we used on the way to the lake is gone – I smashed it with my foot in the car and then chucked it out of the window – so I have the map out. Even though I have no energy left, no fight, I find the route and stick to it with my finger.

When we pass a sign for Garrigill, a few miles from Choristers' Lodge, I wince at the familiarity of the roads and wonder if I'll ever shake off the memory of this horrible place. The sun is rising over the guest house as we approach and to another pair of eyes, the reds and oranges might be beautiful, but I see rust and glare. A spotlight directly on us, on our son, threatening to expose our secrets.

The front door is ajar and we step in to see our bags by the bottom of the stairs, a couple of feet away from where Barry died. We tried to clean up the blood but the wood is stained with a cloud of darker brown. The scent of bleach hits the insides of my nose and the back of my throat. Our car keys are also there, on the first step, and beside them are both of our phones, but we rush past them into the kitchen to find Fiona sitting at the table, Danny sleeping in one of her arms, still alive, sucking the dummy. She's still wearing the gloves. The kitchen knife is in her other hand.

'Stand back. Don't come any closer,' she shouts at us. 'I assume everything has happened as we discussed?'

The sight of the knife, so close to my baby's helpless body, is too much to bear and I break down, losing control of my legs, until I'm slumped against the wooden kitchen door frame.

Jamie shuffles beside me, his left hand grazing the back of my head, and then he takes charge.

'It's done, Fiona. He's at the bottom of the lake. Please put the knife down. Please don't hurt Danny. This only works if we can trust you – know for certain that you'll care for him.'

She gives a quick smirk and then the coldest glare. Her eyes seem suddenly darker, veiled, like she's looking right through us.

'His name is Harrison. And I'll put the knife down when you leave. I've taken the liberty of packing your bags. You'll find your keys and phones on the stairs too. Harrison is more loved than you'll ever know. Please, just leave us in peace now and I won't have to do anything.'

Leave. Without Danny.

I've lost it now. I'm crying and Jamie is stroking the back of my head, soothing me.

Fiona continues, her voice now softer.

'Come on, we've been through this enough now. Think of yourself as someone who has given me – given us – the greatest gift possible. Each other.'

I look back at Jamie for an answer, for a way out, but he's already decided what we're doing. He has already negotiated our way out.

Jamie leads me, taking my hand, guiding me into the hallway. He picks up our phones and keys, puts them in the pockets of his jeans, and then flings both small bags over his right shoulder.

At the threshold to the door, he turns back and says softly, 'Take care of him. Please, we're begging you, take care of him.'

As I'm led out, my feet drag across the gravel and I feel myself whimper. Before I've had a chance to turn back for a final glimpse, to say any last words to my son, I hear the door to the guest house slam shut.

Chapter 30

Victoria

Saturday, 1 May, 3.50 p.m.

The policewoman gets on at Crewe and we lock eyes. She's coming towards me, staring right at me. The train is still in the station – are they waiting for me to be removed before setting off? She's older, maybe in her fifties, and has a blonde-highlighted floppy side parting like the lead singer in a boy band.

'Is anyone sitting here?'

I'm at a table and she's pointing to the seat opposite me. I'm too stunned to say anything, so just nod my head and slide my feet back, to allow her to come through.

'Thanks, love.'

She pauses. Is this when I get caught?

'Is everything OK?' she asks, looking me up and down.

'Yes, I'm absolutely fine, thank you. Sorry, can I help you?'

She looks puzzled as she takes off her jacket and places it on the seat next to her.

'No, just taking my seat. Can I you help *you* with anything? Are you all right?'

I nod and I can feel my face burning. She's just on the train, a passenger, and I'm drawing attention to myself. I pick up my phone and start furiously scrolling, as if in the middle of some very important work, and she gets a bottle of Coke out of her bag and starts drinking it. Should I move seats? That'll just cause suspicion.

I've got a few unread emails and most of them are probably spam, but I'm going to read every word of each of them to give myself something to distract me. She's still watching me and I need to give the impression of being occupied. There's an email from the Mamas & Papas baby store about a sale and excruciating though it is, I spend a few minutes looking at different play mats, reading the customer reviews and determining which one I'd order were I to have the need.

There's also an email from Mum – she's forwarded an article on the importance of vitamin K for bone strength, with just the words 'Worth looking at for Jamie? Xx' at the top. And then an email from Malcolm Casey, personal injury claims consultant, which looks like spam. Do these people really get any business from these emails?

Dear Mrs Rawlinson,

Your mother passed on your details. I understand that you lost a child in unfortunate circumstances recently and I'd like to talk to you about your right to claim for compensation in the case of medical negligence.

Please do give me a ring on the office number below and I'd be delighted to help you get the compensation you deserve.

Kind regards,

Malcom Casey

I delete the email immediately and text Mum.

> Did you get in touch with some kind of rogue lawyer? Please
> don't do stuff like that on my behalf. There wouldn't be a claim
> anyway. Please just leave it.

I've also got an unread text message from Andy. I start reading it and delete it before I get to the end. The midwife, my mum, now Andy. I feel like closing all of my online accounts, changing my phone number, changing my name and running off somewhere where nobody can find me. Could I draw a line under my current life? Accept that Danny is gone, that all of this is part of a life that I have to leave behind?

I look up at the policewoman and she's staring at me again. She's looking at me with a frown of recognition, as if our paths have crossed before, but I know they haven't.

'Off anywhere nice?' she asks, smiling.

'Just visiting my sister and nephew in Preston. It's his birthday.'

Is it a crime to lie to the police? It's a stupid thing for me to have said in any case, because unless she's getting off before or at Preston, I'm going to have to get off the train early or at least move carriages not to raise suspicion. I'm getting so used to making up stories, to creating alternative realities for myself, that I'm finding myself doing it even when it's not necessary.

'What about you? It looks like you're on duty, which is no fun for a Saturday.'

She laughs, screwing the top back on her bottle of Coke.

'I can't remember the last time I didn't work a weekend. Nature of the beast.'

I laugh and then go back to my phone, refreshing my inbox to see if any more emails have come through. There's a gentleness to this police officer. She's the kind of person I could confide in.

'Do you have any kids?' I ask.

She looks taken aback but gives a warm smile.

'Well, they're not kids any more. Jessica's twenty-eight. She was a police officer for a bit as well, but it wasn't for her. She's retraining now, to become a chiropodist, of all things. And Danny has just turned twenty-five. Soon to become a father himself and has no idea what's about to hit him.'

My chest tightens at the coincidence and it just comes out. I can't help myself.

'I have a son called Danny.'

'Oh, do you? How old is he?'

I tense up and lunge forwards, my mouth half-open. What would happen if I just told her the truth? As a mother herself, maybe she'd understand . . .

Chapter 31

Jamie

When I see Victoria emerge from the station, she looks dishevelled, like she's just rolled out of bed, reached for the first clothes she could find and bundled herself out of the flat. I'd usually recognise her in a crowd in an instant – her auburn hair is usually so easy to spot, phosphorescent – but the colour has been darkened, more of a dark brown, and she blends into the crowd.

She's staring aggressively at a group of students in college jumpers who have barged past her as she searched in her handbag for her phone before walking through the electronic gate. She approaches and I pick up my own bag and head towards her, unsure how to greet her. My instinct is a quick kiss on the lips, but are we in that place right now? Should I offer her a hug? Take her bag?

When she gets through the ticket barrier and reaches me, she pulls me into a tight hug. Her smell is like home.

'Jamie, what's going on? Whatever you've got planned, it won't help.'

How do I tell her that I want her to give herself in?

'Let's go to the hotel. I've booked one – it's down the road. Have you eaten? There's a restaurant in the hotel, I think. We can talk everything through.'

Restaurant is a strong word for this establishment. It's one of those depressing little places that serves Heinz tomato soup and has certain items crossed out on the menu. We sit in a booth and Victoria reaches for a pile of napkins, trying to mop a puddle of spilled Coke from a previous customer but just spreading it across the plastic table and onto the floor. We both order a burger and there's a moment of silence after the waitress walks away from us. Where do we begin?

'How have you been?' I ask, keeping my hands in my lap. 'I've missed you.'

She exhales, puffing out her cheeks. She's avoiding eye contact with me.

'Yeah, you know. Up and down.'

I slide a hand over in her direction, feeling the sticky liquid from the table on my arms. I take her hand in mine and I'm relieved when she doesn't resist.

'What's going on then, Jamie? What are you planning?'

I look around and see that the waitress is headed in our direction. I stall, waiting for her to give us our cutlery before answering Victoria's question.

'Sorry, forgot to ask if you guys wanted a drink. What can I get you?'

'No, we're good, thank you,' I interject before Victoria has a chance to respond.

I wait for the server to go back behind the counter before continuing and check nearby tables for anyone who looks like they might be listening in – any sole diners who might be pining for a bit of gossip, some distraction from their solitary meal. The place is virtually empty but for a family of four, who seem far too consumed by their own conversations to be bothered about ours. Still, I speak softly.

'Remember the night we arrived at the guest house? Fiona said she wanted to move to the Hebrides. It's happening. She's going there tomorrow. She's taking him away.'

Victoria puts her head in her hands and then looks up at me. Her eyes look smaller, less brilliant, contracted by the puff of the surrounding skin.

'How do you know this? And what difference does it make, anyway? Please don't do anything rash.'

'She's booked a ferry tomorrow at 1 p.m. To this remote island. Islay, it's called. It leaves from a place called Kennacraig, about 200 miles from here. We have to leave tomorrow before 8 a.m.'

I haven't raised my voice any higher than hers, but Victoria puts a finger to her lips, shushing me like a disobedient child.

'Keep your voice down, will you?'

She looks down and picks up a stained white paper napkin in front of her. She folds it until it's scrunched into a small fanned cube.

'How do you know that? And how will that help us, anyway?'

Why can't she look me in the eye?

'Let's just say I put my professional experience to good use. We'll drive up there tomorrow morning and confront her in public. With other people around, she can't do anything to him. We can call the police as soon as we see her, when we're all together. Tell them the truth about everything.'

Victoria unfolds the napkin and flings it down in front of her.

'Everything? And what about me? Are you about to send me to prison?'

Now she's the one raising her voice and I signal with my hand for her to calm down.

'We made the wrong decision, back in the guest house. We have to put our son first.'

I can see the server coming, a plate in each hand. Victoria notices her and snaps.

'Can you just leave us alone, please? We don't want the burgers. Where's your bathroom, please?'

The waitress darts back, waving an arm towards the back of the restaurant.

'Sorry,' I mutter to her. 'Leave them here. I'll have mine.'

Victoria grabs her bag and shuffles out of the booth before heading to the bathroom.

'Did you want any sauces? Ketchup? Mayo?'

I smile at the server, shake my head and she leaves.

I hear my phone ping and take it straight out of my pocket. An email from Victoria. Why is she emailing me from the toilet? But then I see it. The email isn't meant for me.

Before leaving London, I added Fiona's email account to my phone. To keep an eye on any developments, any last-minute changes of plan. I look up and see my wife coming out of the toilet, stuffing her phone into the pocket of her trousers. With my phone under the table and my heart beating fast, I read.

From: Victoria Rawlinson
To: Choristers' Lodge
Subject: Jamie
Message: Turn back. Don't go to the ferry port. He's got a plan.

Chapter 32

Jamie

'Goodnight. I've set the alarm for 6.30 a.m. The ferry leaves at 1 p.m., but I'd like to get there in plenty of time.'

I check Fiona's email account one more time – the inbox and sent items – tilting my phone away from Victoria, and then place my phone on the hotel's bedside table. I deleted the email from Victoria to Fiona and can only hope that I did so in time, before Fiona had the chance to read it herself. Victoria is next to me in bed, facing away. And it's for the best. I can't look at her. I'm sleeping with a stranger.

'I still don't understand how you know about the ferry,' she says. 'Why won't you tell me?'

She rolls over and strokes my chest under my T-shirt. Her hand is cold and coarse, her alien fingers enveloping themselves round the wisps of my chest hair, and for the first time in my life, I find her repulsive. We haven't been intimate in months. Why is she trying to seduce me now? Her smell is familiar, that night-time mix of faded shampoo and musk. Tonight, rather than being comforting, it's sickly and sickening.

'Look, I'm not really in the mood for talking. Or anything else. Just . . . I'm going to sleep now.'

I remove her hand from my body and turn over to face the wall. I'm desperate to confront her, to tell her that I saw the email and ask her why she's communicating secretly with the woman who stole our baby.

How long have they been in touch? What kind of agreement have they come to behind my back? It's not the first time she's betrayed me. Betrayal in a marriage is hard enough when you know the details, when you know why and when and who and how. It's frightening when the betrayal is impossible to explain. But I know that if I want any chance of saving Danny, I need to keep quiet. I need to postpone my anger, let it simmer quietly, until I have him back.

I hear her get out of bed. She crashes around, huffing to herself, tutting, sighing, closing the bathroom door a bit too violently. She wants me to react, to ask her what's wrong, but I don't take the bait. I put my fingers in my ears to block out the sound of her pissing – it's an intimacy that I don't want to share.

When she gets back into bed, she tries to spoon me, her right hand hovering just over the band of my boxer shorts, and I shuffle further towards the wall. She sighs and turns the other way. A double bed has never felt so small. Our bodies aren't touching, but she's too close. I feel claustro-phobic, hemmed in, like I don't know where to hold my limbs. The thin sheets scratch my back and sand my legs. Is this the last night we'll ever spend together in the same bed?

My heart is beating fast as flashes of tomorrow appear, an anxious kaleidoscope. I won't sleep well tonight. I start breathing more heavily and then pretending to snore, I think of Danny, of everything we'll do together, just me and him.

I can hear Victoria sobbing, gently, next to me and I'm glad. I don't know what she's done, or why she's done it. But if everything goes to plan, and Fiona arrives at the ferry port with Danny in the back seat, at least soon it'll all be over.

She thinks I'm asleep, but I can hear her mumbling, ever so softly, right next to my ear.

'I'm sorry, Jamie. Please forgive me.'

Chapter 33

Victoria

Sunday, 2 May

The windows are open and gusts from the shore are pulsing into the car. I can't hear each vehicle approaching the port, but I see them through the rear-view mirror in the distance on the long, straight road behind us. First just a colour and then the details: a windscreen, a number plate, the faces inside.

Every time another colour emerges, I feel a lump at the back of my throat and Jamie bites the nail on his left thumb. We both look, watching for red. For him, it's hope that it'll be her van. For me, it's a relief every time when it's not. Each time a vehicle comes towards us and it's a blue hatchback, a white four-by-four or a massive mobile home, I allow myself a little respite, let myself believe that she's received my email in time and aborted the plan. She hasn't replied and I've got no way of knowing if she read it or not before setting off from the guest house. Throughout our correspondence, she hasn't been as quick to respond as I'd like.

I've always wanted to do a road trip along the Scottish coast – the views are spectacular. And yet, there's been something jarring about the serenity of the surroundings, the warmth of the granite peaks and the soft green glens.

Inside the car, Jamie and I have been stalagmites, frozen in silence, more distant from each other than ever before. I still don't understand how he knows about the ferry and even less how he's aware of the specific day and time that she's planned to leave. He loves doing impressions. Could he have called her, somehow convinced her to tell him? Could he have pretended to be from an estate agency or a travel company – tricked her into booking a trip and allowing him to pick the dates? He says he won't tell me so I'm protected, so I'm not complicit.

He's barely said a word to me all morning, his responses to my questions monosyllabic. I've tried to convince him to turn back, to remind him of Fiona's threat, but he won't engage. He's being cagey, guarded, as if he realises that he can't trust me. Is there any chance he's seen our emails?

I keep wondering if I've been careless, if I've left my phone within his reach, or if he's known the whole time. But it doesn't make any sense – Fiona and I only message by email and we agreed to delete each one as soon as it was read, to delete any trace of our conversations. All that Jamie has taught me about internet privacy over the years has made me vigilant.

Now, sitting here, parked by the large rocks protecting the shore as cars fill the lines to the ferry in front of us, I try one more time to eke something out of him.

'Have you got something you need to tell me, Jamie? I don't understand how you know that they're coming. Please – talk to me.'

But he just looks ahead, his face unmoving, as if he hasn't heard me, as if I'm not here at all. He leans over and turns on the radio. The reception is patchy, the occasional hint of a melody between hisses, and he turns the dial up and down, eventually settling on a station because it has the clearest signal.

'When we're children, we're told that the number of spots on a ladybird corresponds to its age. In actual fact, that's a myth. What the spots can tell us, both their number and their colour, is which species they belong to. And when we have that information, we can have a better understanding of the kind of habitats in which they thrive.'

I tune out and focus on all the activity outside the car window. It's getting busier now, departure time edging ever closer. A couple of security guards have appeared, standing in front of the lanes leading from the jetty onto the ferry. It's just another day for them and they're bored, blank, going through the motions, the same checks as yesterday and the day before.

Vehicles are lined in rows to drive onto the ferry, but there are also some people on foot: a couple of keen pensioners in coats flapping around passports that they don't even need, grasping freezer bags of sandwiches; a woman with a toddler on a leash, desperately trying to lure him away from the water; a young female couple holding hands and looking so gleefully, naïvely in love as they throw their heads back, laughing. And then suddenly, a dot of red in the rear-view mirror.

It grows. It looks larger than a car. The windscreen is wide, the visors are down. Fiona is arriving.

Chapter 34

Jamie

Sunday, 2 May

'I'm calling the police.'

My hands are shaking as I reach into my pocket for my phone, take it out and start dialling. Victoria knocks the phone out of my hand and it slips down the side of the driver's seat.

'What are you talking about? You know we can't do that. Do you want me to go to jail? That's what you want, isn't it?'

She starts to open the door and I lean across to pull it shut.

'What do you think you're doing?' I shout while leaning back to my seat.

Victoria starts hitting her head with her fist, rhythmic bangs to her forehead on top of a low moan from her mouth, and I grab her arms to pull her away from herself.

'What is wrong with you, Victoria? I saw your email to her. Tell me what's going on.'

She opens the door without looking back at me, climbs out and runs across the lanes of cars towards where Fiona has pulled up, to our right. I open my door and the wind whips my face as I climb out of the driver's seat and bend down to find my phone. I can see it but I can't quite reach with my weaker arm, so I lean over, turning my hand at just the right angle, and scoop it up against the fabric of the inside car wall.

I grab it and run, as quickly as I can. Victoria knows that I haven't got a chance of catching up with her, but I follow in an uneven gallop, going faster on my feet than I ever have before. While I'm going, I dial 999 and they pick up. They ask me what the emergency is and I don't know.

I hesitate and then shout 'Police, police, please come!' as loud as I can over the wind beating between my ear and the phone. 'I'm at Kennacraig! Where the ferries are. It's my baby son.'

They ask me another question, but I'm too breathless to respond in detail and have to focus on running.

'Just come!' I shout into the screen, tilting it to my mouth, keeping the call going but unable to hold the phone to my ear as I go. I gesticulate wildly in the direction of the two security guards in the distance, but they don't react.

I look back and I see that I've left the car door open. The people on foot are watching as Victoria reaches the red van, screaming to get Fiona's attention and banging at the passenger door. A girl has got her phone out to film and it's a moment – it's becoming an incident. There will be a record of this and that's exactly what I want.

What is Victoria doing?

As I get closer, I see the window is down and Victoria is gesticulating, shouting, looking back at me and into the back of the van. And then suddenly, the van is reversing and pulling forwards to turn towards the exit.

I turn in front of the van, yelling 'Stop! My baby!' as loud as I can so people are watching, waving my arms, willing her to brake.

I look over and a woman next to the girl filming is warning me, waving her arms in the air as if I haven't seen the van.

'She's got my baby! That woman has kidnapped my baby!' I shout, bracing myself to be hit.

The screech of the brakes is deafening and sweet burning rubber shoots right up my nose and out through my mouth. The van stops in time, but I lose my balance and use my hands to break my fall. There's an immediate throbbing pain in both knees and little stones swimming in blood on my palms. I hear Victoria's voice. She seems close.

'Jamie, what the hell are you doing? Do you want to get yourself killed?'

But I can't talk to her, I can't engage. She's betrayed me and I need to get to Danny. I get up, my hands numb, and throw my body towards the passenger door on the driver's side – and he's there, in a car seat.

He's in a green babygrow, an elephant on his tummy, a little red dummy in his mouth, and he's staring at me, his eyes wide open. I feel no more pain. I don't hear the wind. He's here. I pull at the door but it's locked, so I bang on the window as if expecting Danny to open it.

'Don't worry, Danny,' I mouth through the window. 'Daddy's here now. Daddy's here.'

But then his bottom lip starts to quiver and I hear him wail through the window. I see the driver's door open and hear Fiona before seeing her.

'Get away! Get that man away from my baby!'

She steps out and comes towards me. She's wearing a paisley scarf round her head and is so close to my face that I can feel her breath.

'He doesn't know who you are, Jamie. You're scaring him.'

How dare she! I raise a hand, but Victoria jumps in between us, pushing us apart like two warring teenagers in a playground.

'Please! Not here!' She looks at me, pleading. 'Not like this. Jamie, calm down, will you?'

I look around and see that a crowd is gathering. People are out of their cars, whispering. A few are now filming on their phones.

Fiona looks to them and starts yelling again.

'Help! Get that man away from my baby. He's mad. He's trying to hurt my baby.'

A short grey-haired man in jeans and a T-shirt, rubbing his arms in the cold, shouts at me.

'Mate, get away from that baby! Leave her alone.'

'I don't care who sees this or who hears it,' I shout back, looking into the car, making sure Danny is still there. He's crying. He's alive. 'The police will be here any minute. It's time to come clean. We're going to be honest with them. Tell them everything, from the very beginning.'

Fiona turns to Victoria, spitting her words.

'From the very beginning? Really, Victoria? Are we going to tell them *everything*?'

Victoria is crying now, crouched over the bonnet of the van, her head bowed.

'Please don't,' she says, her voice muffled by the wind.

'He doesn't know. I haven't told him.'

'Told me what?' I ask, spinning to her.

She stands straight and turns to me, her eyes red raw.

'She's mad – I've no idea what she's talking about. Let's just get Danny. Now! Let's go!'

We hear a thick Scottish accent, gruff, authoritative.

'Can everyone mind out of the way, please? Clear the scene, please. Please stand back, madam.'

Two police officers appear from among the crowd, one much taller than the other, and I feel immediate, overwhelming relief. The black and white of their uniforms, the radios, the caps. Behind, the two security guards from the ferry port are speaking to the bystanders, trying to give the impression that they're in control. The shorter of the two police officers addresses me.

'Can you step away from the ladies, please, sir? Come this way. Raise your hands and come towards me.'

I do as I'm told and plead with the officer as I approach him. I should feel terrified – I'll probably be arrested. But I don't care – Danny is safe.

'She's stolen our baby, our son, Danny. There's a baby in the back of the car and she's stolen him. She's passing him off as her own. She's about to get on a ferry and take him away from us.'

The taller police officer turns to the two security guards.

'Can I ask you both to watch the baby in the back of the car while we get backup? Keep him in his car seat – make sure he's safe. Who owns this vehicle? Please open all the doors.'

Fiona looks over, talking quietly.

'There's a child lock on. You'll have to open it from the inside. Take good care, will you? He's not used to other people.'

They open the doors and I hear Danny crying, bleating over and over, high above the low wind. The officer in charge turns to Victoria, who is lingering by the passenger door.

'I assume you're the mother of the little one, madam?'

'*I'm* the child's mother,' insists Fiona, bounding over. 'You need to arrest both of these people. They killed my husband, Barry Johnson, and buried his body in Ullswater Lake. And now they're trying to take my baby.'

The crowd that's still watching is now loud, talking and gasping. The taller officer speaks into his radio.

'We're going to need backup, please, at Kennacraig Port. And we need to alert child protection and have someone come down, please, ASAP.'

Child protection? I won't have my son taken away from us by another stranger. I struggle forwards, trying to make my way past the officer who is blocking my way.

'It's true, there was a struggle. They tried to steal our son and her husband threatened him. Her husband tried to kill our baby and we had to act in defence.'

The officer picks up his radio again, placing his mouth right up against it.

'And we'll need to alert the force local to Ullswater Lake. It's down in the Lake District. They'll need to send a search team.'

I look over to Victoria and she's on her knees now in front of the van, sobbing and shaking her head. I can't touch her from where I am.

'Danny is safe,' I say, trying to get her attention. 'That's all that matters. Our baby is safe.'

Fiona throws her head back and starts cackling. It's an evil howl, from the depths of her.

'Our baby? You pathetic cuckold,' she says, staring at me while trying to move the security guard away from Danny so she can reach him. 'Do you really have no idea? He's not your baby, Jamie. You're not even his biological father. Victoria planned this, the whole thing. She never wanted to keep the baby because he's not yours.'

I look over to Victoria and she's still now, her head on the pavement and her hands covering her ears. I hear myself screaming. It's instinctive. Everything becomes distorted, the voices muffled, my vision blurred. There are sirens, more police officers. I'm in handcuffs. An officer tells me I'm arrested on suspicion of murder.

As I'm bundled into a police car, I watch as a woman and an officer approach the van and take Danny, trying to soothe him. A couple of other officers have arrested Victoria and Fiona and they lead them to another police car, together.

Chapter 35

Jamie

Sunday, 2 May

I watch the streaks of greens and yellows through the window of the police car and the enormity of Fiona's words begins to sink in. My instinct is to disregard what she said, because how could she know something about my son, about our marriage, that I don't? If Danny isn't my son, if Victoria has betrayed me, what do I have left?

When we reach the station, I'm led straight into a cell and a female officer invites me to sit down on the bed.

'Don't I have to sign in or something? Why have you just brought me in here? Where's my wife? I need to talk to her urgently. Where's my son?'

In fact, I've got no idea what my rights are, what should be happening and when. The police officer is kind and offers me a gentle smile.

'It's a small station and your wife is just being signed in at the custody desk. Once the team has finished with her, we'll be able to take you through. The custody officer will talk you through everything and arrange a phone call with the duty solicitor. In the meantime, I'll wait with you in here. But

I'm afraid it's not going to be possible for you to speak with your wife at the moment – she'll be questioned separately.'

After about ten minutes, a voice comes through on the officer's radio.

'OK, ready at booking-in desk two now. Please bring him over. Has he been searched yet?'

I follow the officer across a dingy corridor and can hear the squeak of my shoes on the floor. She turns round and looks at my left leg.

'What have you done to your leg? Does that need to be seen to?'

There's never any let-up.

'No, it's OK, it's a chronic thing. It's cerebral . . . never mind. I'm OK, honestly.'

When we get to the check-in desk, I'm transfixed by the CCTV camera pointing right at me, watching my every move. I picture a man in a little back room, watching grainy footage of me as the custody sergeant confirms my name and the arrest.

They ask me if there's anyone I'd like to call – a family member – and I ask again if I can have a quick word with Victoria, just in case that's possible. It's not. I ask where Danny has been taken and who is looking after him, but they don't respond. I'm ordered to empty my pockets and they place my phone, wallet and keys in a plastic bag and into a locker behind them. They guide me into a side room, where two burly men are waiting for me, their hands in gloves.

They aren't rough, or particularly aggressive, but exposing myself to two strangers and waiting while they examine my body, on the assumption that I may be hiding something illegal, is the most demeaning experience of my life. It's quick enough, but my disability feels more exposed than ever.

I find it very difficult to maintain my balance when standing on one foot and I have to take a breathalyser test because I'm stumbling while they inspect the soles of my feet. 'Come on, lift your foot a bit higher, please,' is a reasonable demand for most people, but not for me.

They don't find anything incriminating on me, of course. My fingerprints are taken. I'm photographed. I have to ask for a chair too so I can put my trainers back on and they look at me like I'm a leper, as if they've never come across anyone with a disability before.

I have a quick phone call with a duty solicitor and she advises me of my rights, reminding me that they can't keep me in the station for more than twenty-four hours without charging me. She seems to be in such a rush to get off the phone that I don't get the chance to ask her very much more. What happens after that?

In the interview room there are two new officers, one male and one female. I tell them that I don't need a solicitor here and that I'm going to tell the truth about everything. I tell them exactly what happened, from the evening we arrived at the guest house to the day we left and throughout the weeks after. I recount the agony of having to keep up a pretence, of having to lie to our friends and family about what really happened, and I think they sympathise. I ask them if they have children and they both do. They seem to understand that losing them, having to give them up, might cause them to do things that they regretted.

They have lots of questions about Victoria, about her influence over me, and I'm conscious of not painting her as a demon because she's not that – she's just a mother dealing with extraordinary circumstances. They ask me whether I think she might be suffering from postnatal depression and about how she behaved when she was pregnant. It's the first time I've thought about it in those terms, but I say that I think that she is, or at least she was, and that I wonder whether I might be too, and they laugh at that.

They ask me what I knew about my wife's infidelity and I say that it was just hearsay, that Fiona is angry and confused, trying to tear us apart. They look at each other and the female officer writes something down. They ask if I know anything about Victoria's relationship to Fiona and I ask them to repeat the question.

There's a recording device capturing every word that I say and I keep glancing over at it, at the black machine, knowing that everything I'm saying will live on, definitively, indefinitely, and that there's no turning back now.

They say that they need me to stay overnight, with a possibility of further questioning tomorrow. I remind them that any further questioning will have to be in the morning before we reach the 24-hour threshold. They laugh. A custody sergeant leads me up the stairs and across a corridor of cells, and as I pass each one, I wonder if Victoria might be in there. Has she been interviewed yet? Is it still going on? What's she told them?

The sergeant stops at the last door on the right. He opens the door and gives me the guided tour, pointing at each object with a lacklustre gesture.

'Bed, sink, toilet, flannel. Did you want an evening meal?'

'Oh, I'm not so hungry, but . . . yes, I'll have something, please.'

'Gives you something to do if nothing else.'

The officer leaves and I cower at the din as the thick door closes behind him. I hear the jangle of his keys, the click of a clock, and I'm a prisoner. There are two low beds on either side of the room and I sit on the one on the right, just because that's the side I'm used to sleeping on when sharing a bed with Victoria. Is there a chance that another accused person will join me at some point in the night?

I don't know if I'm going to be able to sleep, knowing that at any moment I may be joined by someone, a drug addict or a thief or someone accused of bottling someone in the face. If they're violent, I won't be able to protect myself.

There's a small sink in the top left corner and a tiny flannel hanging on a hook underneath. I wash my face and inspect my left hand, where a bruise is forming across the second and third knuckles. There's also a graze on my arm and both knees from when I was out in front of Fiona's van.

After just a few minutes lying down, the plastic mattress on the bed is sticking to me, fused by the sweat on the back of my neck. I get a shock and jump up when the small enclave in the cell door opens and they push a tray through. It's some kind of curry and I take a few bites, but the rice is so soft it's virtually liquid and the meat has the consistency of rubber. I put my blunt plastic knife and fork neatly across the plate and slide it back through the slot, virtually untouched.

And then I just lie there on the bed, staring at a patch of damp on the ceiling, with nothing to occupy me but images of Danny, wrapped in a blanket, in a stranger's home, once again displaced, not where he should be.

How long have I suspected that I couldn't have been Danny's biological father? If I'm truly honest with myself? I'd been told by the fertility experts that natural conception was impossible. The embryo transfers had all failed. When we then celebrated a miracle happening, falling pregnant naturally the month after the last transfer, did I not once think, really, is this not a mistake? Why would a miracle happen to me?

The timings were wrong. After years of trying to get pregnant, tracking ovulation every month and going through cycles of egg retrieval, embryo creation and then transfers, I'd become obsessive about female fertility. My mum used to joke that I knew more about women's bodies than she or any of her girlfriends did. Our last transfer was June the twelfth. Victoria has a very regular 28-day cycle. Our due date was 26 March and I'd done the maths. The only possible window for her to have got pregnant was at some point in the days right at the end of June and the first week of July. But I knew we hadn't had sex then.

I remember clearly the first time we had sex after deciding to end the treatment. Our wedding anniversary is July the eighteenth and that evening was the first time we'd made love in months. I was stressed about it at the time, worried that months was too long to have gone without sex at our age, that it meant our marriage was failing. I was relieved when we finally had sex after a low-key night in with takeaway pizza and an expensive bottle of red wine that we'd been saving.

I didn't know at the time, but as we were eating and laughing and kissing in bed, reconnecting, the cells were already multiplying inside her. She was already pregnant. I knew it within minutes of her calling me at work a few weeks later to tell me she'd done a test and there were two lines. I worked out when her last period was, when we knew for sure the transfer hadn't worked. The dates didn't seem right. But then I buried it – the maths, the dates, the doubts – deep at the back of my mind. And I suffocated those thoughts with every toy that I bought online, every rush of adrenaline I felt when telling friends and family about the miracle, every heavy jolt of excitement of planning the twelve-week scan and buying clothes and a buggy and a cot.

But now that it's been said out loud, I can't bury it any longer. And I don't need to ask Victoria who the biological father is, either. If it's not me, I know it's Andy.

It's always been Andy.

Chapter 36

Fiona

Monday, 3 May

Victoria has always been single-minded, even when she was a little girl. Her mother, my sister, used to gloat about it, as if it were a good thing that her daughter refused to share toys. 'Oh, when she really wants something, there's no stopping her,' she'd say with a proud grin. 'She's a persistent little madam.' Spoilt is what she was, but I never said that out loud.

Glynis was born when I was four and one of my first memories is looking out of the window of the front room with Grandma Julie, waiting for Mum to come home with the baby. We lived in Wythenshawe, South Manchester, which I suppose was one of the most deprived areas in the North of England at the time. All of my friends on the estate had little brothers and sisters, and I'd been desperate for a sibling. And I don't know if I'd been given the wrong impression of what it would be like – if it had all been built up to something too big in my mind – but when she arrived, I remember feeling distinctly underwhelmed.

I was expecting a new dolly to play with. A little girl with long blonde hair to brush, not a feral little animal with pained, high-pitched squawks that occupied all of my mother's attention. So those first years kicked off what can only be described as a pretty dysfunctional sibling relationship.

At first, we fought. And then as we got older, we just kept out of each other's way. Even though we lived in the same home, we barely saw each other. She always did well at school, got into 'acting' and entered a competition to star in a radio drama, which she won – we never heard the end of that. I, on the other hand, missed a lot of school and spent most of the time roaming the streets of the estate, smoking cigarettes that I stole from Grandma Julie and drinking cheap cider that the owner of the local shop used to sell to me if I was wearing the right shirt. She was prettier than me, less gangly.

My one thing was the piano. It was a tattered old thing – the only object of any worth that we owned as a family. Hundreds of years old, apparently, and we had to keep it in a locked shed in the garden because there was no space for it elsewhere. I was self-taught and not particularly good, but there was something about being able to go out there, on my own, and just play. Be free. Create something.

Our mother died, suddenly, when I was sixteen and Glynis was twelve, and that brought us closer together for a time. Grandma Julie moved in, but she was getting pretty immobile by that stage with her emphysema, so I had to start looking out for Glynis. I'd met Barry by this point and he always had a soft spot for her, so we were suddenly spending more time together.

Barry and I got married in a rush on my twentieth birthday and it was barely a month after that that the bleeding happened. I can still see it now, Barry's face, after I walked out of the toilet and told him. I'd never been pregnant before, but I knew we'd lost the baby. We never talked about it – it just wasn't the done thing in those days. It was Glynis who was there for me at that point. I suppose she's always been attracted to drama.

The best way to get through the trauma of the miscarriage, I decided, was not to dwell on it but just to keep on trying, so we did. We didn't need any encouragement back then. After we lost the third baby, I said that I wanted to go and see a doctor, but Barry wouldn't have it. He said that in time it would work out, if it was meant to be. And the miscarriages stopped after that third time, which was a relief in a way, but only because from that point onwards, I wasn't falling pregnant at all.

It felt as if my body was forbidding the trauma, staging an intervention on my behalf, not allowing me to fall pregnant only to have the heartbreak a few weeks down the line. I took up midwifery as a consolation. If I can't have children myself, I thought, at least I could dedicate my life to helping it happen for other people.

Meanwhile, Glynis had taken the fast track, meeting Simon through her acting, getting married and moving to a house in Buckinghamshire owned by his rich family. She got pregnant the next year and when Victoria was born, I should have been happy for her, but all I felt was bitter resentment and jealousy.

That's when things started getting nasty between Barry and me as well. He was rising through the ranks at Greater

Manchester Police, doing really well at work, but he was drinking, too much, and he'd take it out on me. We'd row most nights and sometimes he'd go too far, lashing out, saying something really nasty. It's when he called me barren that it stung the most.

When I found out I was pregnant with Harrison, I was wildly anxious. I was elated, of course I was, and Barry was, too, but each day, each week, was filled with crippling nerves. An expectation that I'd wake up in the middle of the night and it would all be over, like every time before. It was hard to plan, to celebrate, because it felt like to do so would be to tempt fate.

When Harrison arrived, five weeks early, he was so small, so weak, that the doctors didn't expect him to live beyond a few days. But he was such a fighter and soon enough, he was out of hospital and growing stronger every day. You should have seen him on his formula milk – couldn't get enough of the stuff. He was all we'd dreamed of and more – a little boy with real spark, dark curls and striking hazel eyes. It was the best eleven months of our lives.

I don't remember there being a conscious decision, a specific conversation, but as soon as Harrison was with us, we spent so much more time with Glynis and her family. As parents, suddenly, for the first time, we had something in common. She invited us down to Buckinghamshire – the first time she'd done so in more than a decade since she'd moved.

I couldn't believe my eyes when we pulled up outside their house. She'd always had grand ambitions, our Glynis, and fair play to her, she'd bagged herself a husband with money, that's for sure. I can still picture it now from the outside: it was one of those houses that looked more like an embassy, with black iron gates on entry and fronted by four ivory pillars. It was all so over the top, in my opinion. But I have to admit – we did have the most wonderful afternoons there. The adults would stay downstairs in one of the four reception rooms and Glynis would put on the most amazing spreads: sandwiches, quiches, sausage rolls. All home-baked, as well. And we'd drink prosecco, which always sent me light-headed after a couple of glasses.

Meanwhile, Harrison would be in his element, too – upstairs in the playroom, being cooed over by his cousin, Victoria, who was seven at the time. He'd be rolling around on fancy play mats, bashing away at Victoria's toys, building towers out of Lego and knocking them down, pressing every button he could get his hands on. We'd take it in turns, Barry and I, going up there and checking everything was in order – and it always was. Victoria was at the perfect age: young enough to be interested in playing with her baby cousin still, old enough to be left in charge. Or so we thought.

The day it happened, we weren't even supposed to be there. We'd agreed that it was time for us to return the invitation, and Glynis, Simon and Victoria were due to get the train up to spend the day at our house. I was slightly daunted by the prospect, of course, feeling some pressure to perform. There was no way I could bake, I told Glynis, and she laughed and said that her expectations weren't high. That riled me, so I made a real effort, spending more than I usually would at the supermarket that week just to get in some nice pastries and the posh teabags.

But the day before, on the Saturday morning, Glynis called me to say that their train had been cancelled and would it be all right if we stuck to the normal plan and drove down to spend the day at their house. I didn't protest because I knew deep down that it wouldn't happen, that Glynis would feel too ashamed to bring her family back to the estate. We wasted all those pastries.

It's the sounds that persist most clearly, when I allow myself to think back to that moment. Over the previous few months, I'd grown accustomed to Victoria's whining – a persistent but relatively bearable siren that would induce either her mum or her dad to leap up and run to her side. We'd always be in the living room, directly under the play-room, so that if their little darling was in distress, they'd hear it immediately and be up like a shot, ready to soothe her. But this was different – it was a single piercing shriek that worked its way down the stairs, through the hallway and into the room where we were sat. And it was so shocking in tone and intensity that all four of us were on our feet immediately, heading towards the marble staircase.

I still see the flash of colour. Harrison in his little baby-grow, bundled at the bottom of the stairs. Reds and greens, I see, with a hint of yellow, and his dark curly hair, not moving. And then I hear Glynis screaming up to Victoria.

'I told you about the stair gate. You always have to make sure it's shut when Harrison is here. Why was it open? What have you done?!'

And Victoria yelling in protest, bawling that it wasn't on purpose, that she must have just forgotten.

There's nothing after that.

Part of me blames Glynis, of course. My sister, who I haven't seen in the twenty-seven years since, who raised Victoria to be so spoiled. She was always so careless with her possessions, yanking limbs off her dolls and then refusing to play with them, breaking her remote-control cars and losing things. I don't know if I ever saw her play with the same toy twice. I couldn't help but wonder whether she thought Harrison was just as dispensable as one of her toys – that because he was born on a council estate up north instead of in the Chilterns, his life somehow meant less.

Glynis tried to patch things up between us. She called, she wrote, she apologised on behalf of her daughter. But I couldn't engage. I didn't want to talk about what happened, about who did what or how it might have been prevented. I just felt this burning surge run through me every time I thought of them.

I'd picture Victoria leaving the stair gate open and running around Harrison on the landing by the first step, twirling her thick red hair and singing, showing off, not watching him, oblivious to the fact that Harrison was just there, crawling and trying to keep up, unaware of his limitations. I just couldn't bring myself to forgive them. Because an apology, however heartfelt, could never bring Harrison back.

And so, after that brief interlude when we were in each other's lives, my sister and I went back to our more comfortable state of being distant, and then distant morphed into estranged, and that felt like the way things were meant to be.

For the first few years after Harrison died, the idea of having another child felt like it would be a betrayal. I was so terrified at the prospect of getting pregnant that Barry and I barely had sex. I limited intercourse to the window in the month when I was almost certain it wouldn't be possible and even then, I didn't enjoy it. I just lay there and let it happen to me. Thankfully, he never lasted more than about five minutes.

It wasn't until I was in my early forties that I started thinking that we might replace Harrison. I was in the supermarket one Saturday afternoon, riffling through their selection of baby clothes, when I found myself picking out things for another child. Before I knew it, I was at the checkout, watching the girl on the till beeping through babygrows and little vests, smiling at the young mum at the adjacent station and then cooing over the twins in her buggy as I placed the items in my bag.

When I got home, I presented my purchases to Barry and declared that I was ready to start again, that I wanted another child. He laughed and then said a series of things that really stung: 'Not this again,' followed by 'That ship has sailed,' and 'Some women just aren't fit for the job.'

Then the dreams started. Detailed, vivid dreams, night after night. Images of myself pregnant, in a birthing pool, pushing, holding him, rocking him in my arms. The baby who came out of me was Harrison, but he wasn't. He'd be twisted or lifeless or, instead of crying, barking like a dog.

Grandma Julie had six children and she always used to say that one of the perks of being half-Irish was the unerring fertility. 'All I had to do was look at your grandfather and I'd be up the duff,' she'd say, and depending on my age, I'd either roll about in hysterics or cower behind the sofa.

But the thing is, when you're in your forties, even women with no underlying issues can find it hard to conceive and I knew my chances were small. I followed all the guidelines: I started tracking my ovulation meticulously, lost weight even though I've never been remotely overweight, cut out red meat and replaced it with lentils for B vitamins to boost my hormones. I ate more broccoli for the iron and beetroot for increased blood flow to my womb lining.

Barry started to be more supportive and as the months went on, he became more attached to the idea of having another son – a boy to take fishing, to introduce to his colleagues at the station. He started to become obsessed with the idea of having an 'heir', as if he were some kind of ailing monarch, and he talked about wanting to 'keep the family name alive'. I thought about making a joke about how common the name Johnson is, but I was glad to have him on board and always concerned that being critical of him might spark rage.

An added benefit of our plan to conceive was that it lit a spark in our relationship, not just in the bedroom, but in the sense that we had something to work on together, a shared goal. But it just wasn't happening. I did the home tests every month, but I knew every time what the result would be. And then my periods starting becoming irregular, for the first time in my life, and I knew that the odds of getting pregnant naturally were against us.

By this time we'd moved to the Pennines. I went to see a lady doctor in a surgery about an hour's drive from Choristers' Lodge, because I couldn't bear the idea of running into any acquaintances at our nearest practice and

I thought that a woman would be more sympathetic to our situation. And she was kind enough but advised that at my age, I'd struggle.

I then went to see a series of specialists and discovered that not only were my few remaining eggs of very poor quality, but I also had an almost zero chance of carrying a baby because of scarring in my womb. Irreparable damage to the very core of me. The last consultant, another lady doctor in London's Harley Street, told Barry and me that it would be unethical for any fertility clinic to take me on, even with donor eggs.

The 'take me on' bit made me want to launch myself over her grand oak desk and stab her in the eye with one of her fancy pens. Like I was some kind of naughty child being shunted between schools. I cried in her office, told her that she was a smug little cow, that I'd helped plenty of women to delivery over the years who were in much worse shape than me, and Barry had to escort me out.

We sat in the van outside and both cried. It was the first time since Harrison had died that I'd seen Barry like this. We weren't going to give up. One way or another, we'd become parents again.

I always thought that adoption would be an easy option. When Barry and I were first married and still living in South Manchester, there was a couple next door who had adopted three children through the local authority. It always seemed to me to be the worthiest way of becoming parents, providing a home for a child who had nowhere else to go. But even adoption, these days, is so much harder than it was twenty or thirty years ago.

Back in the day, when a young girl got pregnant out of wedlock, there was still so much stigma around abortion that it was rarely a viable option, so there'd often be a healthy newborn baby ready for a new family. These days, the number of newborn babies available is so small because women have more freedom to make a choice as regards to their pregnancy. And don't get me wrong, that's a good thing for them, just not for us. It means that for an older couple, living somewhere remote, it's slim pickings.

We went through a whole tortuous process with the council, where we were judged by social workers with clipboards and lanyards, for them to conclude that 'younger parents would be prioritised for babies'. I didn't want someone else's eight-year-old. I wanted a baby, someone to see through every milestone: first smile, first little giggle, first time trying pureed carrot. I needed to prove to myself that we could care for a baby again.

Victoria came back into my life during a night shift on the maternity ward. It was a quiet one – there was only one lady with a tattooed neck in established labour and I knew that as it was her first baby, we still had plenty of time before she'd be ready to push. Her partner was in there with her – a lovely lad who was doing his best to be supportive – and I couldn't bear the thought of sticking around more than absolutely necessary, stroking her hand and reassuring her that everything was going to be OK.

I was in one of those moods that night – a frame of mind that was becoming increasingly common at work, when I hoped something would go wrong. Part of me wanted that woman to lose the baby. When you're as desperate for a baby as I was back then, being a midwife isn't the ideal profession.

We're not supposed to go on email or anything personal from the ward computers, but all of the younger midwives do it and I needed something to distract myself from all the negative thinking. I sat myself down, looking over my shoulder to check that I wasn't being watched, and logged on to Facebook for the first time in a while.

I only have a handful of friends, but I'd recently set up a page to attract guests to stay in one of the rooms at our home – to use it as a guest house and bring in some extra cash – and every so often, enquiries would come through. No new messages, but I had a friend request from a Victoria Rawlinson and even though the last name was unfamiliar, as soon as I clicked and saw the auburn hair, I knew it was her. I accepted the request and spent the next few minutes looking through her photos and saw a woman in her prime: beautiful, married, a pianist.

Almost immediately, a message popped up from her. I could hear the tattooed lady in Ward 2 was in distress, but I had to read the message. I had to see what she had to say.

Hi Auntie Fiona,

I hope you're well. Sorry if this is a bit out of the blue. I know it's been a long time. I was hoping we could chat on the phone about something. I've got something I need to tell you, to talk through with you. It's a big thing, something pretty intense. A proposal. I guess you could say it's my way of saying sorry for what I did.

She left a phone number and I scribbled it on my hand, deleted the message and went to deliver the baby.

The first phone call was brief. I rang her on a break during a shift, perched on top of a toilet for privacy and also because that's where the phone signal is strongest. She said she couldn't talk, that we needed to arrange another time when her husband was at work. We agreed that we'd speak the next day, that she'd call me, so I spent the whole of the following morning staring at my phone, waiting for it to light up. What was it about Victoria that sparked such interest? Was it curiosity? Boredom? Or a mother's intuition – a feeling from that very first message that she was our route to having another child?

She opened up gradually. For the first few phone calls, it felt like she was skirting around the issue. But I knew that I couldn't push her. She told me about her marriage to Jamie, how they'd struggled to get pregnant. I could sympathise there, of course. She told me about the affair, with his best friend, and how shocked she was to find out she was pregnant.

She shared that she'd been to therapy, without her husband's knowledge, for the first time in years. She said that in the session, she'd been asked probing questions about her fear of being a mother and had found herself suddenly bringing up what she did to Harrison. She said the guilt that had been brushed under the carpet, all those years ago, when she was a child, had escaped and overwhelmed her. And then an idea had formed, she said. An opportunity for her to get rid of the baby that she didn't want, this symbol of her infidelity, and give me the child that I'd been longing for. Reparations, she said. Her baby, to make up for what she did to mine.

Every night before I go to sleep, I say a prayer for Barry, and even though I'm lying here in a cold cell, tonight will be no exception. I haven't really had the time to process what happened to him properly. I've been so consumed with Harrison and making sure I was doing everything right by him. A mourning, morose mother can do a baby no good. But I say a prayer for him, just a short one, to ask that he finds some peace and salvation, wherever he is.

I don't know how they expect me to sleep with all that light coming through from the corridor and even though I know it must be late, it's far from silent. I can hear people talking, the echo of loud male voices, laughing, coughing, the clicks of their shoes on the hard floors, and I'm freezing cold. I sit up, slide myself off the bed, if you can call it that, and request another blanket. A female officer passes it through the opening in the cell door and I wrap it around myself, shut my eyes, and will the night and tomorrow – full of more questioning, no doubt – to come and go.

Chapter 37

Victoria

Monday, 3 May

'Just to make sure you're aware, this interview is being filmed and at your request, your solicitor, Marsha Wade, is present with you and you're happy for anything to be discussed in front of her.'

I think it's Newcastle, his accent, or maybe Sunderland. He says 'filmed' as if it has two syllables: *filumed*.

'Yes, that's right.'

'And can you confirm your identity for us, please?'

'Victoria Cher Rawlinson.'

He looks up at Cher.

'As in the singer?'

His eyebrows are raised. I nod.

'Thank you. I am going to ask you some questions. You do not have to say anything, but it may harm your defence if you do not mention, when questioned, something which you later rely on in court. Anything you do say may be given in evidence.'

I smile and nod again. I feel delirious. Maybe I should

be shouting and screaming, protesting my innocence, but I feel so defeated, so exhausted, that there's relief in the thought that everything is coming to a head. I can't fight it any more. I've lost.

'For the benefit of the tape, Mrs Rawlinson nodded her head. Now, let's start with the basics. What is the nature of your relationship with Fiona and Barry Johnson?'

'No comment.'

I'm under strict instruction from my solicitor not to give anything away. I asked her if there was anything else I could say other than 'no comment', because it felt like such a cliché, as if I'd been watching too much low-rent late-night TV, but she told me that it was indeed standard practice and the most appropriate response. 'Wait to see what evidence they have,' was her advice, and I'm not in a position to contradict her. And in this case, if I were to give a full answer to that question, wouldn't they just laugh?

When I first started feeling a bit queasy, I put it down to the hormones I'd been taking for the IVF. We'd had a transfer, just over a month previously, and had gone through the same old disappointment of seeing just one line on the pregnancy test. In the past, I've felt sick for a few weeks after a cycle, the extreme levels of oestrogen in my body giving me vertigo, so it didn't seem out of the ordinary. But then the nausea didn't subside, like it usually did, and my boobs started feeling tender, so I bought another test and peed on a stick in the toilet of a Starbucks.

I called Jamie straight away, without a second thought, and then it was immediate celebration. An assumption that we'd finally done it. I took another test – one that estimated that I was two weeks pregnant – and went to my GP to have my bloods taken. It was confirmed – I was, indeed, pregnant. I must have got pregnant the month after the transfer and I knew it couldn't have been Jamie's.

Andy and I have such a complicated history. Obviously, we were together all those years ago. That's how Jamie and I met in the first place. But it was so brief, and meaningless back then. Then when Jamie and I first got together, I found Andy physically repulsive and would wince every time Jamie tried to tease me about the fact that we once slept together. Three years into my relationship with Jamie we had a break because I said I wasn't quite ready to settle down. Andy texted me to see how I was. He came to the flat in Deptford and we drank home-made margaritas. His jeans were riding low, so I grabbed him from behind and pulled them up. I don't know why, but I allowed my hands to linger. And then he turned and kissed me and before I knew it, we were having sex.

It was funny and messy and I wanted it. I expected to regret it as soon as it was over, but I didn't. He left and I took a shower and I felt energised. I could be uninhibited with him.

Clearly, it wasn't the kindest thing for Andy to have done to his best friend. When Jamie and I got back together, there was a period where things were icy between them – I could have kept it quiet, but Andy insisted on confessing – and there was awkwardness when we all hung out together. But over the years, it became something that we'd laugh about – that awful time when I was so desperate that I slept with Andy. And when Andy and Lauren got together, we used to joke that it would only be a matter of time before Lauren and Jamie got off with each other, to create a bit of symmetry.

Having fertility treatment can really take the fun out of sex. To have to go to a clinic and sit in a waiting room avoiding eye contact with the receptionist while your husband masturbates into a cup is hardly an aphrodisiac. And then to have to look at a sheet of paper, a list of numbers, and be told that the sperm morphology is low – and console a husband who sees that as an affront to his ego, a dent to his masculinity – makes it difficult to then go home and feel particularly in the mood for a night of passion.

Andy and I started seeing each other secretly again during the third round of IVF. It filled a void, again, for a while. He provided a distraction from conversations at home that were all so serious, so earnest, so grown-up. It started with a bit of flirty texting and then before either of us knew what was happening, he was coming over to the flat pretty regularly during the day while Jamie was at work. We'd sit and watch terrible daytime TV and open a bottle of wine. That quickly turned into sex and we'd pretend it was the wine's fault. We did it once over the piano and I had to wipe sweat off the keys before Jamie got home.

When I found out I was pregnant, I suddenly went cold on Andy. I knew the baby was his. He was the only other person I'd been with and because I was so used to trying with Jamie and it not working, we didn't bother with contraception. And so I stopped replying to Andy's texts and cancelled his calls. I knew that if I saw him, I'd have to tell him – and then my marriage would end and so would his. To betray Jamie through adultery was bad enough, but to have to tell him that his best friend, the man he's always trusted most in the world, had inadvertently created the baby that he couldn't provide would have been too much for him to bear.

Jamie immediately assumed that we'd got pregnant on the night of our anniversary – indulging in the way everything had aligned so perfectly – but I knew I couldn't have been ovulating then and we hadn't had sex for a while previously. I didn't correct him and it was just so easy to get caught up in the elation of it all. We celebrated, we told our families. Jamie became obsessed with planning, researching, reading baby books, practising putting nappies on using Isla's dolls, buying buggies and cribs and dummies and babygrows, and the further along we got, the more I shoved my secret further into the depths of my memory. For the first time in ages, things were going well with Jamie. We weren't at each other's throats. We had something positive to share, to look forward to.

It was when the baby started to kick that my mind started to change. I was fine when it was just the odd flutter here and there – a change of position or a twist that I could dismiss as wind. But from about twenty-eight weeks, the movements ramped up in intensity and I could see the outline of his limbs as he kicked and pushed up against me. He was angry – he knew my secret. He was warning me that I'd never live it down – that he'd always be there, looking up at me, judging me, willing me to come clean.

I'd wake up in the middle of the night and take myself into the bathroom, pull my nightie up and stare at the bump, looking at it with such disdain, this manifestation of my infidelity. What if he came out looking exactly like Andy? I started to think of various scenarios – ways in which the baby would just disappear. Abortion through official medical routes at that late stage wasn't an option and how on earth would I even entertain that conversation with our GP, who had been with us, supporting us, helping us to get state funding, all through our IVF journeys?

One night, after hours lying awake, listening to the gentle rhythm of Jamie's snoring, I climbed out of bed and headed out of our room and to the computer at the back of the flat. I knew that historically, there were places, makeshift clinics run by sympathising matronly spinsters, who would help young women found unwittingly 'in the family way'. But Google searches only yielded horrific stories told through news reports, of women arrested, of women dying of septicaemia as a result of botched attempts in religious communities, and I closed the windows and deleted the search history.

The next night I found myself at the computer again, trawling through forums of women discussing various DIY methodologies. Food supplements seemed to be a common one: an overdose of vitamin C, cinnamon (raw, not in cooking), parsley, pomegranate and papaya – a trio of p's – all easily picked up at the supermarket to stimulate uterine contraction. Others suggested a much more extreme method: a bottle of vodka downed in a boiling hot bath. I felt so traumatised, horrified at the prospect of burning my unborn child out of me, that I switched the computer off at the mains and curled up on the sofa, holding him and begging for his forgiveness.

A few hours later, Jamie came down to find me there and I told him that I was struggling to get comfortable in bed, so he went on his phone and ordered me a pregnancy pillow that arrived the next day. I took a break from my research for a few days at that point, resigned to the idea of having the baby, of living the lie, because I could see no viable alternative that wasn't utterly barbaric.

Then the dreams started. At first just at night, but then also in bursts during the day, when my mind wandered. Being ripped in two by a baby with Andy's face. Me at a hospital, throwing babies on the cold, hard floor. Blood and bones and tides of water. And Harrison, all those years ago at our house. The stair gate. The baby crawling towards it. The hard marble floor. The baby dead at the bottom of the stairs.

That's when I booked myself in for therapy. I did it without telling Jamie, because I didn't want to alarm him. What was I going to say? That I was having nightmares about our unborn son? That the pregnancy was causing me trauma because it was a constant reminder of how I'd betrayed him with his best friend? That I didn't trust myself? That I was worried that I might harm the baby because my baby cousin died in a horrific accident when I was seven and it was all my fault?

I didn't love the idea of opening up about my problems with a man. As soon as he started talking, I realised that I should have specified that I'd rather speak with a female therapist. How could he possibly understand my anxieties? He was so soft-spoken that at times it was no more than a whisper and his extreme calm had the adverse effect of putting me on edge. I wanted to reach over to his side of the desk and shake him into action. I didn't want questions – I wanted him to help me figure out what to do.

'What is it about being pregnant that makes you anxious, do you think?'

'You say you're worried about harming your child. Can you tell me more about that?'

'What specifically do you think might happen? Has anything like that ever happened to you before?'

'When you have these thoughts, is there anything else that you think about that you haven't mentioned? Any people or scenarios that keep coming back to your mind?'

'Is there anything in particular that you think might be sparking these feelings?'

And I don't know why, but my mind kept going back to that staircase. In a way, it felt like a more comfortable thing to talk about – easier to discuss than my infidelity because it was so long ago. And so I told him about Harrison. About how the memory was vague but I felt some responsibility for not looking after my cousin properly. He pressed me, asking me for details, and I just didn't have them. So I started crying and he passed me a box of tissues – just sat there nodding, with a slight frown – before telling me that the hour was up.

The next day, Jamie and I went for lunch at my mum's and Mary Walters was there with her two Dalmatians. Mary has lived next door since Mum and Dad moved into their house after getting married, and even though they're so different, they've always got on really well. When Dad died, Mary was a real crutch for Mum, in part because she'd lost her own husband to the same kind of cancer just a couple of years previously. She's one of those people who is just a really good egg. First to volunteer at the village fete, in charge of flower arrangements at the local church, sends birthday cards to everyone she knows – and their children – and always on time.

Mum had obviously told her that we were expecting, because she turned up at the lunch with a bag of baby clothes – hand-me-downs from her grandson, who had just turned two.

'There's some expensive things in there, dear. It's worth a rummage. If they're not for you, just pop them down to the local Oxfam.'

It was seeing Mrs Walters that day at my mum's that sparked the idea. As we were eating brownies in the garden, I remembered something that she used to do when I was younger. We used to call her the 'family fairy'. It was all done unofficially, via the Church, I think. She'd hear of a young unmarried woman who was looking to give up a baby and match her with a married couple who were having fertility issues and were in desperate want of a child. To all intents and purposes, she was arranging unofficial adoptions and perhaps she was breaking the law in some way – it definitely wouldn't be legal now – but the intention was there. Her heart was in the right place and it seemed to be legitimate because the Church was aware.

When Mrs Walters left, I asked Mum if she was still in touch with Fiona, her sister, and she looked so aghast that I quickly changed the subject. But that night at home, when Jamie was in a deep sleep, I went on the computer and searched for her. I remembered that Barry was a police officer. He used to pretend to arrest me when I was cheeky to him as a kid. They weren't hard to find.

I continue to answer 'No comment' to every question, but the officer is undeterred. You'd think that, after a while, he'd spot the pattern and cut his losses. As far as I can see it, there's literally no point in this interaction. They're asking me questions, I'm not answering.

'Have you ever given birth to a child and if so, can you confirm where and when this took place?'

'No comment.'

The drug we used was called Misoprostol. At the antenatal class that Jamie and I attended, they dedicated a whole session to different methods of induction and this wasn't one of the drugs mentioned. I trusted Fiona but also did my research and read academic trials showing how using this drug could significantly speed up induction compared to other drugs, but it could also cause complications. One of the possibilities was overstimulating my uterus, making the contractions last more than two minutes at a time and, potentially, causing Danny to lose oxygen.

When I brought this up with Fiona during one of our phone chats, she was reassuring and knowledgeable. She had no doubt that she'd get the dose right, to make sure that things would start happening relatively quickly without harming me or the baby. I trusted her. If the whole point was for her to have a son, I knew she wouldn't risk his health.

The night we arrived, she followed me to the bathroom and we did it there while Jamie was sat in the kitchen with Barry. It was uncomfortable – an insert in my vagina

– and I stared at the white toilet ceiling, speckled in the old-fashioned way with little protruding bubbles of white, while she made sure it was positioned correctly. I already knew it was working when we went to sleep that night. I could feel my body reacting, my womb twitching, the skin either side of my belly tightening. I had another one of those dreams that night. The baby ripped me apart again, but this time his face was Fiona's.

The officer takes a sip of water and then reaches into a drawer, taking out an evidence bag containing the knife with the green handle. It's not been cleaned and I can still see the brown stains streaked up to its tip.

'Do you recognise this knife, Victoria? You know we've taken your fingerprints and are doing a DNA check on it, so it's very important that you're honest here.'

I didn't have any interaction with Barry at all before we arrived at the guest house. I knew he was on board, he had to be, but it was Fiona who was driving it. I also knew about his position in the police and we worked out a way to incorporate that – to help Jamie to understand that we had to leave Danny with them.

Fiona said it was Barry's idea to threaten to kill Danny – to make sure Jamie had no choice but to comply. In the end, what happened in the guest house is so far from what any of us planned and I never meant for anyone to get hurt. Was something happening in my body and my mind when I was pregnant that meant I made decisions that I already can't understand? Of course. I felt so guilty at the time that it was impossible to tell Jamie what I'd done – that his longed-for son wasn't really his, that I'd betrayed him again. And I knew he'd never have just agreed to give our baby away. We had to force him.

Would I make any of those same decisions again? Of course not. I changed my mind as soon as I held Danny and saw him with Jamie, but it was far too late.

I still don't know if I'm thinking rationally now, but one thing is completely clear: Jamie cannot take the blame for any of this. His intentions have always been pure and any hand that he did play in any of this – in helping me to get rid of the body – was because he had no choice. It was only ever to protect Danny and me. I'll do anything, I'll take the blame for all of this, swallow the sentence, admit to it all, if it means that I can spare Jamie any further anguish.

'Mrs Rawlinson, I'll repeat the question, as you haven't responded. Do you recognise this knife?'

I nod and then put in my request.

'Can we take a break, please? I'd like to consult with my solicitor.'

Chapter 38

Jamie

'Daddy, can we go swimming today? You said yesterday that if the weather was good, we could go.'

I'll definitely take him swimming one day. I'm not the most confident in a pool myself, but as long as we stick to the shallow end and there's a lifeguard on duty, it'll be fine. What's the worst that could happen? People don't drown in public swimming pools. Maybe he'll be into football, which would be fine, too. I could get into it for him. I wouldn't be able to play, of course, but I could plonk myself in goal, or drive him to a Saturday morning five-a-side and be there on the sideline, cheering him on. We could go to a proper match together, at Tottenham or Arsenal. I could buy him a little kit.

I stop daydreaming, and I'm back in the cell. Considering how secure these doors are, presumably, they aren't as soundproofed as you'd expect. Last night I drifted off a bit, but I'm a light sleeper at the best of times and every time I fell asleep, I was then jolted awake by the slam of another cell door, or shouting from one of my neighbours.

I had to give them my watch when I was checked in, so haven't been able to keep track of the time, but I judged that it was close to morning when a guy was brought in utterly trashed, shouting at a female officer to join him for a cuddle in his cell. It must have been the end of quite a rough night. Then he turned his attention to a male officer.

'You're never even President Obama! You're not even fucking Obama!' he was shouting, and I'm sure in his head this made perfect sense.

I've never been the jealous type. Ever since I was a kid, I've been sensitive and insecure about lots of different things: my limp, my grades at school, my professional accomplishments in comparison to people I've never even met. But my relationship with Victoria has, for years now, felt like one area of my life that was safe and predictable.

We had a bit of a stumble, a few years in, and split up briefly, but I think that was just because we were so young when we first got together that we both felt like we needed the opportunity to see what else was out there. I think I felt like that at the time, although now I'm not so sure. I told myself that I agreed with Victoria when she said that was how she felt.

I know about Andy and Victoria's past, but I've been naïve, or in denial, to believe that it had stopped. Andy was the one who told me that they'd slept together when we were on that break all those years ago. It would be untrue to say I was shocked, in tears, distraught. Somewhere deep inside me, a voice just said 'of course'.

I could never really understand why Victoria wanted to be with me when there are so many other men she could have had. Ones who were as strong as her, as fast as her, who didn't need help walking down a hill or sitting down on a low bench in a pub garden. Who could go jogging with her, on adventure holidays, who could use both feet properly and drive manual cars. Why wouldn't she want to see what else is out there? It stung that she chose Andy for her bit on the side, but in some odd way, I took it as a sign that she didn't want a total break from me. She stayed close. She must have been thinking about me, feeling guilty. Maybe she'd come back.

I wasn't with Victoria at the time, so I agreed that it was more Andy's responsibility to tell me than hers. He called me and I let him speak, then I put the phone down, without saying a word. I didn't respond to any of his follow-up calls or texts. I cut him out of my life.

I enjoyed wallowing in the sadness of it all – the excuse not to go out, to spend weekends in bed with my laptop on the covers, streaming full series in a day. I didn't bother trying to sleep with anyone else. I just wanted Victoria. And then one day, I was bored and the point had been made. I texted Andy and asked if he wanted to go to the Regent's Park open air theatre with me, something we did together every year.

We arrived early and wandered around outside trying to spot celebrities. There were usually one or two. This time it was Pierce Brosnan – 'Look at that massive white beard he has now!' – and Anjelica Huston, and we spent most of the afternoon flailing our arms about, doing impressions of the Grand High Witch. It was silly and fun and we didn't once mention Victoria.

And then a few months later, she came round to the flat I'd started renting. Andy gave her the address. I tried to have a furious argument with her, but she didn't put up a fight, just kept saying sorry, so we watched a film and we kissed when she left. We didn't mention it again until much later on in our relationship and then it was just a joke: remember that time you two slept together – how ridiculous!

But then there was the time more recently when I came home from work early because I had a headache and his car was parked outside our flat. I went inside and they were sat together on the bed, our bed, watching *Ally McBeal* on her laptop. Andy had been going through a hard time, having just been laid off at work, and Victoria was going through a dry spell when it came to gigs, so it made sense that they should hang out together during the day, but it felt like a betrayal because they hadn't told me about it.

They weren't being intimate in any way, but it felt like I'd stumbled on a secret. When I asked Victoria whether or not it was a regular thing, she couldn't look me in the eye and I suspected that she had something to hide. Would other men have dug further, caused a scene, maybe even rummaged through the bin in the bathroom looking for an empty condom packet or demanded to check messages on her phone? I didn't want to be that kind of husband and it felt like too much of an accusation, on too little evidence, so I pushed it to the back of my mind.

But then it was always there, gnawing away at me every time I saw Andy and when we were all together. Their renewed connection may have been going on for a while, but once I'd spotted it, I couldn't unsee it: all the little looks, the smirks, the times when Lauren and I were left alone in the dining room for just that little too long while they were washing up in the kitchen.

Despite this, Victoria and I have been good. She makes me wildly happy when we're alone together. And I've always felt that ultimately, we have each other's backs, that we trust each other and that she'd never do anything intentionally to hurt me.

When we got the positive pregnancy test, it was instant elation. With those two blue lines, the whole landscape of our existence changed. Somehow, against all the doctors' predictions, we'd done it. Personally, it was a triumph, wasn't it? I'd overcome another part of my body that was trying to stunt me. Yes, I knew the dates didn't match my memory, but it was easier to convince myself I must have been wrong about when we'd had sex – I must have forgotten one time – rather than consider the alternative explanation.

Footsteps in the corridor, the clump of a man's shoes, a heavy rubber heel and then the jangle of keys and the door to my cell opens. It's an officer, broad with a ginger beard and a low voice.

'Good afternoon, Jamie. Good news for you. You're free to go. We're not going to be questioning you any more. We may need to bring you back in in the future, but it'd be as a witness.'

What?

'I . . . um . . . that's great,' I say, sitting up. 'What happened? Where's my wife?'

The officer is still standing by the door but won't look me in the eye.

'I'm afraid I can't give you any information on that, sir. The duty solicitor may know more and can talk to you after you've collected your things. Follow me.'

I hadn't anticipated that I'd be let out without any further questioning and without a charge. I helped to bury the body. I told them – don't they care? Have they found the body in Ullswater Lake? I was the one to push it into the lake.

I follow the officer to the booking-in desk, where I'm given the see-through bag with my belongings.

'Did you want to see the duty solicitor? I can ask her to come down if you like.'

'Yes, please.'

Why are they not questioning me any further? It's amazing – they've taken our side, they believed me when Barry said they wouldn't. Will I see Danny? Maybe today? But what about Victoria? Is she out, too? What's Victoria said? Have they charged her?

The duty solicitor meets me in one of the side rooms, just by the exit to the station. She has huge puffs under her eyes and the foundation on her skin is too orange, badly masking some acne on her chin. She's wearing what looks to be a blue linen suit and it's got a shimmer to it that seems unintentional, like it could do with a good dry-clean. I put out a hand to shake hers and her skin is coarse – it itches against mine.

'I didn't have to do very much, to be honest,' she says, skipping a greeting. 'Sounds like your wife has come to an arrangement.'

'What do you mean? Where is she? What's she said?' I ask, leaning on the back of a plastic chair.

'Listen, strictly speaking, I shouldn't be telling you this, but they've found the body at Ullswater Lake. Didn't take the search team long at all, apparently. I understand your wife has been charged with two separate offences but that she's negotiated some kind of plea in exchange for information about Fiona Johnson. She's said that you had nothing to do with the plan and that's obvious from all of the online messages between Victoria and Fiona. They've accepted that you were forced to dispose of the body against your will. They've got no evidence against you, so you're free to go home.'

'What were the charges against her?'

She looks in her notebook.

'Conspiracy to kidnap and manslaughter. But you should be celebrating! You're off the hook.'

How can she say this? I'm not some teenage delinquent, in and out of the police station, being let off for shoplifting. What does she think I'm going to do? Go back to my friends and brag about getting off without even getting a caution? And what does she mean about me having nothing to do with the plan? What was the plan?

'What about Danny?'

She looks at me, puzzled.

'Danny?'

'The baby. Our baby. When they took us from the ferry port, someone took him away. If I'm free to go, I need to be with him. I need to look after him. He can't go into care.'

She shrugs her shoulders and exhales deeply, like she's bored of me already.

'I'm not sure it's as simple as that. But give me a second – let me go and find out. He's your son, is he?'

And my answer is quick, without a second thought. 'Yes.'

Because the genetics don't matter, do they? We're beyond that now. Danny is my son.

Chapter 39

Victoria

Thursday, 15 July

I've always dreamed of having my picture in the papers. I had a mention once before, in the local gazette, when I won a piano competition at the Royal Festival Hall as a child, but there was no photo. Given the prominence of my two front teeth at the time, that was probably for the best. My parents were so proud that they bought ten copies and I've got one somewhere, in the flat, with all of my diplomas and exam certificates. I'd say Mum is less likely to buy ten copies of this one, although she has picked one up this morning from her local shop.

'Are they even allowed to run a story like this?' she asks, throwing the paper down on the kitchen table next to the empty cereal bowls.

'Yes, Mum, because I pleaded guilty. Marsha said there might be some more media coverage in the days before the sentencing. What's the headline?'

I'm still represented by the same solicitor, Marsha, who came to the station that first night after I was arrested, and she's fierce. Her rates are usually extortionate, but she was a good friend of Dad's at university and agreed to take me on for a fraction of what she usually charges. Mum points towards the newspaper and reads out the headline.

'Callous mum's plot to have her baby kidnapped,' she says. 'It's ridiculous sensationalist nonsense. They've interviewed a midwife, an Emma something, who says she always suspected something strange was going on, like this is an episode of a telenovela. The things people make up for a moment in the limelight! Thankfully, it's not on the front of the paper and I daresay we don't have too many friends who buy *The Mirror*, but what about the internet? You can't get rid of this.'

If my mother genuinely believes that this whole thing might have gone unnoticed by the other members of her bridge circle, she's even more deluded than I previously thought. It's just about the most exciting thing that's happened to anyone in her friendship group, surely beating the previously top-billed scandal of Angie's son going to prison for his part in a dodgy tax evasion scheme.

'Actually, Mum, it's not sensationalist, is it? That's exactly what happened. I'm going upstairs for a lie-down. I don't want to see the article – it won't do me any good.'

'Oh, poor Jamie,' she says to my back as I walk past her. I stop and turn round, and she continues, 'I can't even bear to think about what you've put him through. What time is your train up there tomorrow? Have you packed everything you need? And are you *sure* you don't want me to come up with you?'

I leave the table and slam the kitchen door harder than I intend to. Suddenly, I'm very aware of how much this whole situation has made me regress to a teenage version of myself. After we'd agreed the plea bargain, I was told that there'd be a wait before sentencing and I was released on bail. Marsha told me that I was lucky that they agreed to bail at all in my case, and it came with a few strict conditions that included providing one address and agreeing to stick to a curfew.

I ended up moving into Mum's house in Buckinghamshire, back to my childhood home. Of course, I couldn't go back to living with Jamie and the prospect of knocking about by myself in the studio was too depressing. I'm finding that I need company, even if that company is my mother, even if I don't really want to talk about what happened, or what's likely to happen to me next.

I need to remember to count my blessings. What Marsha has managed to negotiate, given the charges, is nothing short of remarkable. Of course, it's helped that I've been upfront since that very first day in the police station and I've shown regret for what I've done. But I've ended someone's life. I secretly tried to give my baby away and trick my husband into thinking his life was in danger. It's hard to imagine that any other crimes could be worse.

When Marsha first suggested a defence of postnatal depression, it seemed like a suitable ruse, a smart way to secure a more lenient sentence, but now I'm not sure it is a ruse at all. For lots of women, pregnancy can be one of the happiest times of their lives. I'm not one of them. People talk almost flippantly about the baby blues after birth. I didn't feel blue, I felt utterly conquered. All I knew of myself had been erased because of what I'd done. Every inch my body swelled was a reminder of how the lie was growing, out of my control. My body changed, new hormones twisted my brain, my thoughts and nerves morphed in ways I couldn't understand.

I take responsibility for my awful decisions, starting of course with my infidelity. And then at each opportunity, I chose to tell another lie rather than brave the reality of my situation. But I also accept what the doctors say: that by the time I was in the late stages of pregnancy – and then at the guest house, giving birth on their bed, being forced to breastfeed the baby I was to give away – I was showing signs of mania, even psychosis.

The Crown Prosecution Service decided to drop charges relating to Barry's death, given my mental state and that I was clearly acting on impulse to protect Danny. But they're still pursuing me for what I did to Danny.

I don't regret coming clean. In telling them the full story, of how I reconnected with Fiona and Barry and the plan we forged. I've implicated Fiona and provided all the evidence needed for them to charge her for her crimes. But at the same time, I've implicated myself, allowing them to proceed with charges against me for conspiracy to kidnap. I know my mind wasn't working like it usually does. At the time, I truly believed that finding other parents for Danny was in his best interests. But in doing so, I put his life in danger, I put my own life in danger and I expected my husband, whom I love more than anyone, to have to live with this awful lie.

It's difficult to know what to pack for prison. Last Tuesday, Marsha's associate sent me a PDF by email entitled 'Doing Time: A Guide to Prison and Probation'. And when I opened it, there was a picture of a stick man behind bars at the top, so I closed it immediately and deleted it. But I'm sitting here now, with an empty holdall, and I need some inspiration.

I go into the trash folder on my email and open the document, scanning down the list. A lot of it seems pretty futile: I don't own a pair of flip-flops, so I'll just have to take the risk of a verruca or two in the communal showers. Earplugs are recommended, because 'almost all men snore and many women, too', but I'm pretty sure that after years of sleeping next to Jamie, I'm immune from being bothered about that. I've packed a few tracksuits, some trainers, a couple of books and a pen, in case I fancy writing any letters while I'm in there. 'And finally,' it says, 'make sure you pack a few photos of your loved ones, even if it's just a pet.' I don't have a dog. I'll be OK without photos.

Could I ask for a photograph of Danny? Surely that wouldn't be allowed and I'm not sure I could cope seeing his face every day – the continual reminder of the harm I caused to the one person I should have protected more than anyone.

I don't think I've written a proper letter since I was a child. I used to write love letters to a boy in my class, Rob Mahon, and on reflection was completely undeterred by the fact that he never wrote back to me. I've taken some paper and an envelope from Dad's old study and it's all very formal, with the address at the top alongside a little embossed emblem. He'd have insisted on writing with a fountain pen, but the best I can find in the drawer in my bedroom is a red biro with the lid dented and chewed.

According to the bail conditions, there's to be no contact between Jamie and me, and that hasn't been easy. I miss him – touching his arm on the sofa while watching TV, feeling his leg against mine in bed – and I worry about him, although I also acknowledge that I haven't earned the right to do so. I know, through Marsha, that he was released without charge and that's a huge relief, because the idea of him taking any blame for this would be the worst punishment. It just feels funny not to know how he's doing. We've been together for a decade and even when we've been through rocky times, we've always been in contact. How is he coping without me?

I know it's against the rules, but now, the night before my sentencing, what have I got to lose? I want him to read, from me, why I behaved the way I did.

Mum comes upstairs to go to bed just after eleven thirty and gently knocks on my door.

'Victoria, are you there?'

I stay silent, hoping that she'll think I'm already asleep. I'm feeling quite delicate this evening and run the risk of breaking down in her arms if I let her come too close.

'I'm going to bed now, sweetheart. I'll put some breakfast on for you in the morning. Eggy soldiers?'

She lets out a heavy sigh and I picture her face, downturned, aghast at what her daughter has become.

I hear her shuffle across the landing and the door to her bedroom open and shut. I wait a few minutes and then fling on a jumper and some trousers and creep downstairs, down the marble stairs. We never changed them in the end. She's left the light on in the kitchen, as she always does, and I know where to look for the cash. She keeps it in a little red tin at the back of the drawer under the sink and was either completely oblivious to how much was in there at any one time, or chose over the years to pretend not noticing that the odd note here or there went missing. I grab my house keys from the kitchen worktop and let myself out into the night.

As I take each step down the residential road towards the high street, I look down at my right foot and know that I'm being tracked. Will a police car sweep round the corner and stop me? Will there be a helicopter in the sky? I don't care – it's worth the risk.

I reach the little taxi office on the main road and there's one free now. I get in.

'Can you take me to North London and back?'

'Sure.'

'Dartmouth Park Hill, please. Near Tufnell Park tube.'

I don't want a confrontation. I'm sure Jamie wouldn't get aggressive, it's just not in his nature, but I do feel exposed – nervous that he might try to stop me. He's such a stickler for rules, what would he do if he saw me breaking my curfew, approaching the flat?

The taxi driver asks me a question and I pretend not to hear, sticking my head out of the window, opening my mouth, sucking in the cool breeze as we head towards the M25. Soon, we're on the M1 to London and within half an hour, we're off at Hendon and on the Great North Way towards Archway.

It's a Thursday night in summer and there are still a fair number of revellers, staggering between pubs in Highgate, queueing for an ATM, running in clumps across the street just in time to avoid an oncoming car. How uncomplicated their evening is, how average. For everyone else, nothing has changed. The beat of life goes on, the walks, the meals, the arguments, the sleep. The world is oblivious.

We pull up outside the flat and I ask the driver to wait, giving him half the fare. I walk up to the communal front door and open it with my key, then walk through to the front door of the flat. I take the letter out of my pocket and slip it under the door. Then I turn back and walk outside. It's mild and I feel the breeze on the back of my neck. I lift my arms in the air and feel the tickle on my palms.

Chapter 40

Victoria

Friday, 16 July

'Will the defendant please rise.'

I stand and look up and behind me towards the public gallery. Who are all these people and do they have nothing better to do with their day? They're all looking at me – some with a sympathetic smile, but mostly with disdain. They don't know the circumstances – they're just here for the dramatic bit, the grand finale.

We were crowded by journalists and their photographers as we walked into the courthouse, which Marsha had warned me about when we first met at a nearby café this morning. The reporters were much younger than I expected – blondes with Dictaphones and microphones and scruffy boys with notepads. The older photographers are like monkeys, darting around, smashing away at their toys.

'There's no need to duck or cower or cover your face or anything like that,' she said. 'But I'd advise you not to say anything if they start firing questions at you.'

They did bark at me, but it was all so quick that I didn't

catch any question clearly enough to answer anyway. Just flashes of 'baby', 'Fiona' and 'Dad'. I know that they all want to paint me as a demon, as the adulterous wife who tried to give away her baby.

'Victoria Rawlinson, you have pleaded guilty to conspiracy to kidnap your son, who is known by the name of Danny and who is currently in foster care under the jurisdiction of Cumbria County Council Children's Services,' the judge begins, and I look down at my feet.

I'm in a new pair of Sketchers and am wearing a simple black jumper with stretchy jeans that are actually more like tracksuit bottoms. I thought I might as well be comfortable. I keep looking down.

'You sought out a casual adoption scenario for your son by communicating with Fiona and Barry Johnson, arranging a complex and unusual plan to deliver him and hold him captive in their guest house, Choristers' Lodge. Your defence team has presented a compelling case for mitigating circumstances relating to your mental health and I have taken both this, and your early guilty plea, into account when considering your sentence.

'However, as a mother myself, I cannot let it go unsaid that your behaviour was callous and calculated. In choosing this path for your unborn child, you not only circumvented important public services, but also put your baby in a significant amount of physical danger. You are hereby sentenced to eight years in jail, with the possibility of parole review after four years.

'I know there has been some public interest in this case and there are some members of the press present in court today, so I would like to remind everyone of the various resources available from your local council should you find yourself in a situation where you are unable to look after a child. Thank you and good morning.'

I hear a buzz in my ears and my vision is blurry. I want to sit, but I don't know if that's allowed. I see the outline of two officers approaching me and I look over to Marsha, but she's looking down, gathering documents in her little folder.

I don't struggle as they take me down from the dock and I decide to hold my head high, so that everyone can get a good look. Take a look at the woman who kidnapped her own son. Take a look at the woman who doesn't even deserve to be considered a mother.

As I take my first steps down, I look up at the public gallery. Amid a wall of strangers, I see Mum, stony-faced, her hair newly dyed. There's Emma, the midwife. And Jamie.

We lock eyes. There's still love there, still a connection, but then he closes his eyes and rubs them with his right fist. He bows his head as I'm taken to my cell.

Chapter 41

Jamie

Monday, 22 November

'Oh, you're so good! Doing the supermarket run and looking after the little one as well. My husband's never done a shop in his life and he freaks out if I leave my son with him while I go for a wee!'

It's not easy being a single dad. People just assume that you're babysitting, that Mum is having a day off, that you're doing her a favour and stretching the limits of your masculinity by begrudgingly taking your own child out solo. I'm pretty new at this, but I think I'm doing a good job.

I've got nappy changing down to a tee now – I had worried that I'd find it hard because of the weakness in my left hand, but I've found a way round it by entertaining Danny with my left hand, or using it to stop him from rolling around while holding the nappy in place and doing most of the folding and sticking, the hard stuff, with my stronger right hand. It's fine. I think it's a bit of a talent, actually.

I also worried about taking the buggy out alone, but it's not been a problem at all. I avoid having to fold it up and down too much, and I manoeuvre it pretty fluidly in and out of shops, up and down edges of pavements and between crowds by Tufnell Park station.

Danny is with me at the supermarket in his buggy, facing me, playing with a teething toy shaped like a red hippo, and I'm filling a basket balanced by his feet. The storage bit at the bottom of the buggy actually makes carrying shopping home much easier for me than it's ever been before.

'Oh, it's just me and him at home, actually. His mum is . . . well, she's not around.'

I used to ignore people when they assumed I was just on a rare daddy day-care morning. But I've gained the confidence to call people out on it – not in an aggressive way, but just to demonstrate that it is possible for a man to look after a baby on his own.

Obviously, people who know us know the truth about where Victoria is, about why I'm bringing him up on my own, but I haven't quite plucked up the courage to come out with that bit to a stranger. It's complicated, disarming, and not something you can just spring on someone as they're beeping your sandwiches through the scanner at a supermarket.

We're just picking up a few things for the journey. Danny's still on formula milk a couple of times a day, but he's also eating purees, porridge and some finger foods. He's pretty easy-going as far as food is concerned, with the exception of mushrooms. Even if I try to sneak just a bit of mushroom into a mix of other vegetables, he spits it out and flaps his arms in panic. I feel neutral about mushrooms, so leaving them off our weekly shop is an easy sacrifice.

I carry on round the aisles, adding a few baby food pouches and little carrot puff snacks to the basket.

'We've got to hit the road, Dan. We've got a long drive ahead of us, and I want to get there and back before it gets dark. You can have some of these treats when we stop.'

He looks up at me and squeezes his face into a little giggle, waving his toy at me and kicking his legs at the basket. Who knows if he understands any of what I'm saying? At eight months old, he can't yet speak, but he sits up really well and has just started to crawl after weeks of teasing me, pushing himself up into an arch with his arms and legs, and then falling back down and laughing.

He has dark hair, short and naturally spiky, and his eyes, which were blue when he was born, have now turned bright green, just like Victoria's. The smile he gives me when I go to get him from his cot in the morning, or after one of his daytime naps – the excitement he feels at just seeing me – are things I never imagined before and will never forget. He loves music so much that I can't play any before bedtime – it makes him too excited – and he's always been like that, since he was a few months old.

I first got the chance to have a phone call with one of the sets of foster parents with whom he was placed when everything was being sorted out. Lovely people – a retired couple from Kendal near the Lakes – and they said that for the first few weeks after he arrived, his eyes would brighten and he'd flap his arms when they played an old recording of Pachelbel's Canon. I wish I could have seen that with Victoria. She'd have been so happy.

Victoria is in Foston Hall, a women's prison near Derby.

It houses some of Britain's most notorious female criminals and there's something ironic about the fact that she's ended up there, when we used to spend so much of our time watching low-rent true-crime documentaries about criminals serving their sentences in that very prison.

Fiona is still awaiting trial, for conspiracy to kidnap, and my solicitor advised that she'll likely face ten years or more. In my opinion, her sentence should exceed Victoria's. She was the mastermind behind all of this. She took control as soon as Victoria got in touch with her. Victoria is in some ways another one of her victims, manipulated when she was most vulnerable.

Victoria has been writing to me regularly and I know that it's in Danny's interests for us to remain amicable, so I reply, without exposing myself too much. The first letter I got from her appeared quite mysteriously under the door of our flat, waiting for me when I got back from the sentencing in Carlisle. I knew it was her immediately, because I used to tease her about insisting on writing on envelopes in all caps. There was no stamp on it, so it must have been hand-delivered by someone who could get into our apartment block. Could she have come the night before the court date, without telling me? There wasn't any post for me when I left for Carlisle the previous day, so I'm not sure exactly when she did it.

My solicitor had advised that it would be likely that she'd be prevented from contacting me before the sentencing as a condition of her bail, which explained why her phone went straight to voicemail and she didn't answer any of the messages that I sent her after I got back to London.

Opening her letter felt dangerous, like I was once again complicit in her crimes. I lay back on our bed, rolling to her side, and unfolded the paper. I had to read what she had to say.

Dear Jamie,

It feels funny writing you a letter. Old-fashioned, quaint, like I'm a character out of a Jane Austen novel and we're courting. Perhaps I should be calling you Mr Rawlinson.

If you were to screw this piece of paper up without reading it, I wouldn't blame you. If you are reading this, then let me start by thanking you – thanking you for giving me a chance to apologise and give you my point of view. I don't expect you to accept my apology, or write back, but I need to get it all down.

It's been hard not being able to have a conversation in person since that day at the port. I know you've tried to call me, and I've read your texts, but officially, I'm banned from contacting you. I shouldn't even be sending you this letter, so keep it between us, if that's OK.

It all happened so quickly that day and things were said in the heat of the moment that weren't supposed to come out the way that they did. I should have found the courage to tell you myself.

I think you already had your suspicions about Andy and me. I promise you there wasn't anything romantic there, no feelings – it was purely a physical thing. It was convenient. Does that make it any better? I don't know.

When I found out I was pregnant, I so wanted the baby to be yours. There's nothing I'd want more in the world than to have a child with you, Jamie – a child that was half you and half me. But when I found out and I did the maths, I knew that it must have been Andy's.

We were stupid. We should have been more careful. We shouldn't have done it at all, but after years of not using condoms, the possibility of me falling pregnant naturally felt so remote.

I'm a terrible person. I know that all this is a massive betrayal of trust and that you'd never do anything like this to me. I guess I'm getting my comeuppance now. I lied to you and to everyone and by the time I became convinced that I couldn't keep the baby, that having him would make life unbearable, it was too late to have an abortion.

I wish I'd told you years ago about Harrison. I can't even remember what you know and what you don't know. Did I ever mention that I had an aunt? The truth is, I spent my whole childhood trying to forget about her and about what happened. It was just too painful to think about it.

Harrison died at my parents' house when he was a baby and I was seven. I went upstairs with him to play and left the stair gate open. He was crawling and I must have looked away for a moment. He fell and died. It was horrific and I know I was also just a child, but I've never fully dealt with the guilt. Ultimately, his death was my fault. They cut off all contact with us after it happened.

I genuinely thought that Fiona and Barry were deserving parents and that I was doing the right thing by getting in touch with them again. I thought that Danny would have a good life with them – an older couple with so much more life experience than us, with so much love to give. They lived

*through so much trauma, Jamie, with the death of their own
son, and all because of me.*

*Getting in touch with them, offering them this baby who
I knew I couldn't keep, felt like the right thing to do. Like
I was turning something terrible — my betrayal of you — into
something good. That by offering them the chance to have
Danny, I was somehow making up for what I did to them.*

*I knew you wouldn't agree to it, and there was no way I
could somehow pretend to you that I'd gone into labour and
had a miscarriage without you finding out, so we came up
with our own plan. I know it was insane and every day, I
wish everything had gone differently.*

*What would you have done, in my shoes? I thought about
trying to terminate it myself. Would you have preferred that?
Should I have just come clean from the very start and asked
you what you wanted to do?*

*I've got a feeling now, with the benefit of hindsight,
that if I'd just been honest from the outset, you might have
wanted to go ahead with the pregnancy anyway. I know how
desperate you were for a child. I don't know if that would
have made it better or worse.*

*I heard via my solicitor that you've been enquiring about
parental rights for Danny and I want you to know that
whatever you want to do from here, I'm fully supportive.
I hope you've seen, since Danny has been alive, that I've
developed compassion for him, too. That in spite of my
behaviour in the lead-up to his birth, since holding him in my
arms, since looking into his eyes, since seeing you with him,
I've shown nothing but love for him.*

There's nothing I'd want more than for him to be with you,

Jamie, and all I can do is thank you. Most other men would run a mile. Most other men would look at this boy, the product of his wife's betrayal, and turn away. But when it really comes down to it, Danny is your son. Genetically, he may be related to someone else, but Danny is the child who you've longed for, who you sang to when he was in my womb, who you've fought for and, ultimately, who you saved.

I think we both know what the outcome of the sentencing will be. Maybe it'll be two years, four years, or maybe even longer, but I'm going to prison for what I've done, and I deserve it. I know Andy and Lauren won't want to bring Danny up and I won't have him shifted around from one foster home to the next. So, whatever needs to be done, whatever permission you need from me, I'll immediately grant it.

And maybe write back to me if you feel like it? I have no expectations and won't be surprised if I never hear from you again, but I hope that you can hear my apology and find the strength to let me in, in some way. Because despite everything, I love you, I love Danny and I always will.

Victoria

xxx

As can only be expected, there's a very strict set of rules about visiting and we need to be there by midday. Danny is fast asleep in his car seat by the time we hit the M1 (it's a fancy spinning car seat on a fixed base to make it much easier for me to get him in and out). He seems to love being in the car. It's a new one, a small green SUV on a lease deal, and something about the rhythm of the engine sends him off. He always wakes up briefly when we hit traffic and groans a bit, but I've got this trick of leaning back and rubbing his temple gently, and that soon sends him off again.

We pass a signpost just after 11 a.m. and the hairs go up on the back of my neck as we come off the motorway and head down an A road towards our destination.

As far as possible, I plan to be honest with Danny when he's older. I think it's easy to patronise children, to speak to them in baby language and assume that their understanding of the world is more limited than it actually is. It's been really important to me, since he first came to live with me, that he should be aware of his mother. While she did some bad things, he should also know all the wonderful things about her, the things that make her special.

So I play him a YouTube video of her playing the piano at Wigmore Hall and tell him that it's his mummy while he sits on his mat, holding on to his feet and making funny sounds along to the music. I sit him on my lap at the piano and tell him this is where Mummy would play.

I'm sure there are other people who, in this scenario, would shy away from the truth, dodge the conversation or, worse still, poison the child against the other parent, but the last thing I want is for her to become a demon in his eyes. It's only a few years until she'll be out of prison. I don't know exactly what the arrangements will be after that. I'm Danny's legal father and have sole custody of him, following a short legal procedure that involved social services and Victoria's consent. They gave Andy the chance to contest it, but he declined.

There's little doubt from my perspective now that my marriage with Victoria is over. There are some challenges that a couple can overcome, but this level of betrayal makes our marriage beyond salvageable. But that doesn't mean that I don't want her to have a relationship with Danny. I'm not going to be vindictive – she's serving her sentence and who am I to impose further sanctions upon her?

I'm excited for Danny to meet his grandparents finally, too. My parents are coming back from South Africa for a fortnight over Christmas, so I've said that Danny and I'll go and stay at the small house they still own in Finchley so they can spend some quality time together. I'm also open to their suggestion of us spending a few weeks next summer with them. It'll be Danny's first trip abroad – his first holiday, really – and they have a swimming pool at their house in Cape Town, which he'll just love.

The other thing I'm really set on is making sure that Danny has a relationship with Isla. I don't see Andy any more, but Lauren has full custody of Isla since they got divorced and it's important to both of us, despite the rather unusual circumstances, that Danny and Isla have each other in their lives. Genetically, they're half-siblings, after all.

When I get out of the car, there's an eerie stillness in the air. It's a relatively mild morning – I can get away without a coat – and the sound is dominated by cars zipping past on the dual carriageway behind us. I put on my baby sling and open the back door by Danny, swivel his seat to face me and unbuckle him. He starts to stir and tries to squirm his way out, but I gently lift him through and into the sling, face forwards.

'We're going to meet Mummy,' I say, and I can feel his legs kicking in front of me.

Epilogue

My darling son,

I'm sorry that this is the first time I've written to you. It doesn't mean that I haven't thought about you, every day, since I've been here. I lie awake after the lights go off and I picture you out there in the world, getting on with your life, reaching milestones, making new friends, overcoming challenges, and it hurts. It hurts to know that I'm not there with you, celebrating your achievements, consoling you when you're down, helping you to fight your battles. Because we all have battles to fight, don't we? I want you to know that I love you and that one day soon, we won't have to fight any more. All the barriers that have been keeping us apart will disappear and we'll be happy.

Against all the odds, I've made some good friends in here. I get on particularly well with someone called Catherine. She's the one who got me into embroidery and to be honest with you, I'd have said that embroidery was for old ladies, but she's actually younger than me and is so passionate about it. She talks about it day and night. Obviously, the attention to detail is important, but it's also about having a 'creative vision', she

337

says, being able to dream something up from scratch and picture what it's going to look like as a finished product.

She wants to set up a little online business for it and says I can be her associate. But I've got a long way to go before being good enough for that. I'm just making small things for now — you know, little bits and bobs. I'd love to make something for you. What about a nice pair of gloves for the winter?

Then there's Debbie, who helps out in the library. She was a primary school teacher on the outside, very fond of kids. I'm sure she'd like you. I like to pick up the children's books. I read them out loud and pretend I'm reading them to you.

I like that we don't really talk about what brought us in here. There are rumours, obviously — people talking in hushed tones in their cells about the new inmate and what her sentence might be, what it says online — but there seems to be an unspoken agreement. An understanding that once we're in here, we're on a level playing field, not to be judged for what we might or might not have done before. If someone asks me directly, I don't lie. I know what I did and I'm upfront about it.

Catherine doesn't have any children, but Debbie has three girls, so she understands what it's like. She does see them from time to time, but it's not the same, sitting in a cold room on either side of a table, flanked by guards, on edge that you'll get too close or say something incriminating. I can't wait to be alone with you, to have the intimacy of a conversation that's not being monitored, to be able to hold hands, hug whenever we want to, be a shoulder for you to cry on.

I've had a lot of time to reflect on what I did and I'm not proud of it. I want you to know that I'm sorry for everything that happened. It wasn't how we intended it and if we'd *known that this might be the outcome, maybe everything would have been different from the outset. I'll make it up to you, though. We've got so much lost time to make up for and I'll cherish every moment. Not long to wait now, my darling. As soon as I'm out, I'll make sure we're together again.*

For years, I would lie awake at night, thinking about what happened all those years ago. I've never admitted it before, but I know that it was me that left that stair gate open. How different things would have been, had I just closed it, like I had every time before.

But lately I've started seeing it all from a new perspective. Since being locked up here, I've come to realise that it doesn't matter who did what and why and when If there's one thing I've learned, it's that things always work out as they are meant to. Yes, tragic though all that was, it's what led me to you, and for that I'll be eternally grateful.

Sending you hugs, kisses, and all the love in the world.

Your mother,

Fiona

Acknowledgements

All the rumours are true: writing a second book is *hard*. But the big advantage, when compared to the utter gamble of writing a debut, is that often for a second book there are lots of people nearby to offer advice, expertise and moral support along the way. I'd like to thank a few of these people in particular:

My agent, Madeleine Milburn, who has championed this book right from the very first time I pitched it in her office at the end of 2018. Maddy, your kindness and encouragement every step of the way is more than I could ever have hoped for in an agent – you have helped me learn to believe in myself as a writer. Thanks also to Maddy's peerless team and, in particular, Rachel Yeoh, whose diligence and great editorial eye has been a huge help on this book.

The team of editors at Orion, past and present, who have helped shaped *The Guest House*: Phoebe Morgan, Katie Ellis-Brown, Rachel Neely, Karen Ball, Francesca Pathak, Sarah Fortune and, most of all, Sam Eades who helped me work through some tricky plot points and challenged me to go bigger, darker and bolder.

My fellow crime writers and the amazing community of book bloggers that I've got to know over the last few years – you know who you are! Writing would be a lonely business, I think, without such a strong network of support, encouragement and celebration. The friendliness of the community has been one of the most pleasant surprises of the whole writing experience.

Leah Hazard, midwife extraordinaire: you were so generous with your time, and patient as I asked difficult questions about how a midwife might abuse her power. I've really enjoyed getting to know you, and gaining an insight into your wonderful profession.

Nazir Afzal, for your advice regarding the legal and judicial system.

My two grandmothers, Grandma Eva and Booba Beryl, who both died while I was writing and editing this book. You were both voracious readers, and I'm grateful for the example you set with this and so many other things.

My husband Pauly, who has been with me, as always, every step of the way on this novel. This book just wouldn't have been written were it not for your support, encouragement and ability to spot and delete clichés. Thanks for being a sounding board on every plot point, my first reader, my geography expert and my biggest champion.

Solly, our son who arrived as I was finishing the first edit of this book. Working on a story with these themes while welcoming you into the world has been challenging, but also fortuitous in that I've been able to understand how strong a parental bond can be. Read this when you're older, if you fancy, and know that you are loved more than anything or anyone.

Mum and Dad, for showing me that despite some medical and physical setbacks early in life, I could have the same aspirations and dreams as anyone else. Many characteristics of Jamie's physical disability are drawn from my own experience of cerebral palsy. I wrote Jamie because I've never read a thriller featuring a protagonist living with a disability similar to mine before. He has physical limitations that may not always be immediately visible, but nonetheless affect him every day. I hope that in the future we'll meet more protagonists with disabilities, and that we'll be able to turn to fiction to see disability represented with all its nuance and in its full glory.

And a final thanks to you, for reading until the very end. I love hearing from readers: do send me an email at hello@robinmorganbentley.com and I'll do my best to write back!

If you loved *The Guest House*, don't miss Robin Morgan-Bentley's gripping first novel . . .